DEEP SHIFT

KILHAVEN POLICE 4

BROCK BLOODWORTH

H. CLAIRE TAYLOR

CONTENTS

"You keep that perverted bloodsucker away from my kids!" The porcupine-shifter's eyes were wide, the short-cropped hair on her head standing on end, poking out in all directions.

Sr. Officer Norman Green sidestepped quickly to remain between the suspect and her children. "Ma'am, Officer Ridley is not a threat to your children. I'll ask you again, do you currently have any drugs on you or in your vehicle?"

But the woman wasn't deterred. "Just 'cause you give one of 'em a badge doesn't mean they ain't still bloodthirsty!"

Despite exhibiting every sign Green knew of being high on methamphetamines, including the erratic driving that had precipitated this stop, this bristling woman raised a solid point. It was one Green had been considering during the last month of field-training this particular rookie.

Ridley wasn't the first Green had supervised, but he could very well be the last. Because, beneath the fresh academy training and vows to protect and serve, Jeremiah

Ridley *was* bloodthirsty. All vampires were. Green had seen that more than ever in the nearly four years since the raid on the wolfenvamp laboratory.

In the nearly four years since the Treaty of Hornstooth was blown to shit.

It was a different world now. One where murders were up by seven hundred percent, desperation was up even higher, and screening requirements for the Kilhaven Police Academy were down a solid tenfold. Who would want to be a cop now? He definitely understood the appeal of it for vampiric psychos like Ridley, but for anyone else?

"Mrs. Verona, Officer Ridley—"

"He'll suck their blood! He'll suck it right through their eyes. I seen it happen!"

That was definitely the meth speaking, but Green spared a glance at his trainee anyway. Jeremiah Ridley had the sickly, pale skin of every vampire Green had ever met. It paired with a perpetually smug expression on his frightfully red lips, the particular shade of which seemed handpicked as a reminder of what substance was intended to flow between them. Not every vampire's lips were so vivid—Detective Jason Felps's certainly weren't, which was a point in his favor—but Ridley's were. It was as if the rookie's very biology (if such a thing existed for the undead) was built to be as obnoxious and unsettling as possible.

However, at the moment, the vampire wasn't doing anything that could be construed as a genuine threat toward Mrs. Verona's children. Instead, Ridley did a whole lot of nothing as the three kids sat on the curb next to where he stood with his arms folded. He showed no sign of compassion, just stared ahead into the darkness, not sparing a single glance for the distraught children at his ankles.

But in the limited light from the gas station, Green could make out a thick cord of muscle in the vampire's lean jaw and hear a *tick tick tick* as he clicked his teeth.

Oh yeah, the guy definitely wanted to suck the kids dry. Green bet the fangs were even extended behind the tight line of those blood-red lips.

Green turned back to the frantic mother. "Listen, Mrs. Verona, your children are fine, and if you were so worried about them, maybe you shouldn't have been driving them around in the middle of the night high as a kite. Now, are there more drugs in the vehicle?"

Thirty minutes later, once a family friend had picked up the kids, and Mrs. Verona was occupying herself by yelling hysterically in the back of the cruiser, Green supervised while Ridley did a full search of the Veronas' vehicle.

Or at least it was a full search in name. To actually qualify, the rookie would have needed to fully search rather than giving a smattering of locations inside the vehicle a quick visual inspection.

It would have been nice if Ridley's smugness came with a dose of competence, but the former always seemed to supplant the latter.

Green inhaled and bowed his head, asking the powers that be for patience. On the exhale, he said, "Were you planning on going back to the center console later, or…?"

"Yeah, I'm getting to it," snapped Ridley. But the rookie had already moved on to the back seat. No one searched a vehicle like that—front seat then back seat then center console.

Add it to the daily report.

At first, Green had felt bad about his low marks and long responses in the "other concerns" section of the FTO daily report forms. But after a week of it, the guilt had disintegrated into resentment. He was tired of it. Ridley wasn't even trying. The other rookies had at least tried, some so much that it became to their detriment. They keyed in on a single fact regarding a suspect or a single bit of evidence so myopically that they missed the crucial details. But at least they'd tried. And he'd simply given them average ratings across the board, knowing that his honesty wouldn't result in any sort of negative consequences for their careers in a department this starved for new hires.

But not this time. Yesterday's "other concerns" section had taken Green forty-five minutes to type out as he detailed Ridley's obvious indifference to the feelings of a stabbing victim's wife, opting instead to give the freshly widowed woman his cell phone number.

While Green hadn't specifically stated his suspicion that Ridley would turn the woman into his personal blood donor, he didn't have to. The act would have been inappropriate no matter who did it, vampire or not.

Today's report would be all about incompetence, though. Green began composing the first line of it in his head as Ridley failed to push up one of the armrests to check the space between the back seats.

It was baffling how someone could be so confident and so ineffective in a single moment. Fucking astounding.

I wasn't like that, was I?

He dismissed the thought immediately. Confidence wasn't something he'd come on this job with much of, and rightfully so. He couldn't attest to how effective he'd been in that first month, but at least he didn't *believe* he'd been so. It had taken so much before he'd come to the conclusion that he could handle himself in high-pressure situations.

Shooting that human only eight weeks in had answered some of his questions about himself while only raising more. Managing the bust on the warehouse and taking on all those goddamn shillelagh-wielding leprechauns with only a little curse as a result had also been a boost. Bonus: he'd survived the curse. And not only that, he'd used it to great effect against even more shillelagh-wielding leprechauns, plus a crew of vampires. And he'd saved some missing children in the process.

We didn't save anyone.

That wasn't Green's voice speaking, though. That voice had a gruff feminine tone to it, and he knew exactly whose it was.

He'd been thinking about Heather Valance a lot more this last month, which was truly unfortunate. Before Ridley graduated and joined their shift, Green had gone entire days without thinking about the psychotic werewolf who had been *his* field training officer.

He tried to imagine Valance training a vampire, but the image just wouldn't surface. She never would. And only an imbecile would assign one to her.

Her days of field training were long behind her, though. After their long administration leave following the laboratory raid, Valance had decided not to return to the Fang 900s. She's said she couldn't stand that shithole anymore and requested a transfer to the Alpha 300s.

How can she stand it? Alpha was easily the dullest sector in all of Kilhaven, even during the unofficial war between vampires and werewolves. Exorbitant amounts of wealth could apparently shield people from violence, and the residents of Alpha were nothing if not stinking rich on the whole. Nearly four years of responding to fruitless suspicious-persons calls sounded to him like her personal hell. But if it'd driven her to a breaking point, he hadn't heard about it. He hadn't heard much of anything about her, let alone from her, in the time since her transfer.

"Here we go!"

Green snapped to and saw Ridley holding up a small plastic baggie.

"I think it's meth!"

"Yeah, looks like it." Green tried to muster enthusiasm, but a little bit of meth wasn't much to cheer about. Any Shankwright County judge would dismiss that amount.

Growing tired of this, Green sighed, leaned in over the front passenger seat, and popped open the center console.

For fuck's sake.

He snapped a picture of the lode where it was then held up the gallon bag for Ridley to see. "This is also meth."

"I told you I was getting to the center console!"

"I got tired of waiting." Ridley scowled, and Green fought the urge to roll his eyes. "Here. Take some pictures, and you can start on the report on the way to jail."

And as Green called for a tow, Ridley did neither of those things, opting instead to hold the bag up in front of the suspect to taunt her with it. "You're going away for a long time, shifter!"

No, Green had never acted like this prick when he was on field training. Valance had had it easy with him, which was more than that crazy bitch deserved.

We didn't save anyone. Her words, the last ones she'd spoken to him at the hospital after they'd gone through the rigmarole of blood tests and before they had been separated for their initial interview—those words were like a blood clot in Green's brain. *We didn't save anyone. All those kids are already lost. And we don't have a fucking clue why.*

No one saved. More deaths. More questions. Why wolfenvamps? To what end? What were they for?

Her crusade had only accomplished one thing: the world as they knew it was now a complete shitshow.

"Give me that." Green snatched the bag out of Ridley's hands, feeling a deeply suppressed rage balloon in his chest. "Taunting the suspect? Really? Get in the fucking car, and do yourself a favor by shutting the hell up for the rest of the night."

"He's gonna eat someone," Green said, stuffed into a boxy chair with narrow armrests that didn't agree with the bulk of his vest and duty belt. The sergeant's cubicle at the substation was cramped and uninviting, and Green suspected that was half the point.

Bruce Bannockburn, now sergeant of the Fang 900s, had listened patiently as the senior officer voiced his concerns, not for the first time, about the rookie. While it was just the two of them, Green could hear the click-clack of typing on an ancient keyboard a few cubicles over, so he knew whatever he said was likely to make its way around the various gossip channels. He didn't care. Not about this. Not anymore.

Sergeant Bannockburn shook his head. "You don't know he's going to eat someone."

"Fair enough, sir. They don't really eat people anyway. But he's definitely going to *drink* somebody."

"You don't know that."

"Come on. Can we drop the bullshit? This is the third

time I've had to talk with you about him *this* week. Ridley is a liability. You know it."

The werewolf sighed, deflating as he leaned back in his creaky rolling chair. "We're doing all we can."

"He shouldn't be out on the streets. I'm not joking; I saw him lick blood off his hand just last night at that shooting. He was definitely eyeing that sucking chest wound the same way I look at a pepperoni pizza."

"Green. We're doing all we can." The sergeant's voice was firmer now. "What do you think I should do, fire him? You think your eyewitness accounts of him licking blood off his hands a few times are enough to go up against that wrongful termination suit? Because I can tell you the City doesn't feel that way."

Bannockburn had a point. But still. "How in the fuck did he even make it through the academy?"

"He applied. Come on, Green, you know as well as I do that no one wants to be a cop right now. After the deaths and the recent retirements—we were already stretched skintight across this city. And now only psychos would want to join up. So, we get a lot of psychos. It's not a huge mystery." He leaned closer, lowering his voice. "And you know what? I don't want to hear you complain about it. I certainly won't. Because it's *our fault* things are like this now. Heather clearly thought the world would be better off without the Treaty of Hornstooth for the vampires to hide behind. But I guess even a myopic crusader with severe PTSD and the world's largest chip on her shoulder can get it wrong sometimes. And we helped her do it. So now we have bloodthirsty vampire rookies on the Force. And now our city is overrun with homicides that would be easy enough to solve were it not for the vast quantity of them." He leaned back, and only then did Green realize the typing a few cubicles over had stopped. It started again. "We live in a screwed-up numbers game now. If a vampire officer drains two people but saves a hundred in his career, that's considered *good* and *acceptable*."

Green struggled to unclench his jaw so he could speak. "You know as well as I do that if we'd had any idea what her end game was, we never—"

Sergeant Bannockburn grimaced like he'd tasted something bitter and held up a hand. "You and I saw the same department therapist after the incident, don't forget. I know what you're about to say. She told me the same thing for all ten sessions before I could get the hell away with my job intact. Looks like you're still seeing her, though."

"No, I'm not," Green said. But only because he'd already blown through his insurance's allotted number of appointments for the year. Bannockburn didn't need to know that, though.

The sergeant sighed. "Okay, Norman. I'll level with you. Yes, Ridley seems to be a killer just below his eggshell-thin exterior. You should probably make a point of avoiding any calls that involve children for the time being because he's probably also a pedophile—I can't go into the details, but I've seen his file. Anyway, you signed up to be an FTO. You need to keep doing everything in your power to train him." He paused. "Or you could think about promoting."

Green arched an eyebrow incredulously. "Promoting?"

"Yeah, the test is coming up later this year, and you've finally got enough time under your duty belt to qualify. You thought about that at all?"

"Been a little busy with other stuff. Haven't stopped to think."

"You've proven yourself to be a real asset on the streets these last few years, Green. In fact, if I told Bruce from four years ago that you'd survive an unofficial turf war between werewolves and vampires for this long, he wouldn't believe me. But you're good. You'd make a good corporal on some shift."

"I dunno."

"Hell, if Lawrence can do it, you certainly can. Or you could go for detective. You'd be good at that, too. You certainly have experience sniffing out trouble."

Green only had to consider *that* option for a moment. Rising in ranks meant added political bullshit, and he felt the brunt of that enough just trying to do his job on patrol. "Maybe in a few years."

Bannockburn shrugged and sat up straight in his chair again. "Okay, then. Anything else you need?"

"Besides one of those stake launchers Valance had?"

"Which I've already said will *never* be allowed by the department."

"Then nothing."

Green made it to the edge of the flimsy cubicle when the sergeant added, "Don't write off the test yet. Think it over. You'd make a better detective than FTO."

CHAPTER THREE

Green tried not to let his amazement show as he watched his new shift mate shoot. One dead center of the heart, four in a row between the eyes, then, for good measure, one in either shoulder.

The report of the shots echoed in the enclosed space of the indoor gun range as Ivory Namises lowered his pistol.

Green removed his ear protection and cursed admiringly. "Shooting drills must be a hell of a lot more intensive up in the Pan City academy."

Namises grinned, checked the chamber of his pistol, then slid his ear coverings down to hang around his neck. "The academy there was shit. I've just had a lot of practice."

They'd been shooting for the last half-hour, and Green's shoulders were feeling it. Surely Namises's were, too. The man was stout, but more soft pudge than muscles. His skin was so dark that it made Green's own latte coloration, which had been a point of consternation in his human hometown, seem entirely unremarkable, even pale by comparison. Namises was new to the department, and whether those in charge thought it would be a fun prank to drop him right into the most dangerous shift in the deadliest sector, statistically speaking, or if it was just a matter of which team needed help the most, Namises was now a Fang 900.

And Green had hit it off with him immediately.

They left the firing range and entered the swank lobby of the private club.

Green nodded toward the door. "Want to grab some food? My treat."

"I *am* hungry. Guy like me needs to keep his carbs up, you know. They have some good grub upstairs."

Green followed Namises's gaze to the stairs, next to the sign indicating VIP members only beyond that point. "You're a member? Shit, no wonder you're a sharpshooter. Glad I didn't put money on it."

A few minutes later, Green found himself sitting in a leather armchair, holding a crystal tumbler of expensive bourbon poured over an artisanal block of ice. It felt refined, but he knew that he would be labeled soft in a different context, say, his local bar, if he were within arm's reach of artisanal ice cubes. But it was impossible to label anyone in such a way while they relaxed in the VIP lounge of a gun club.

It was a pleasant and unexpected turn to his day. He wasn't used to surprises being good.

"So why'd you make the move?" he asked.

"From Pan City PD?"

Green nodded.

"Ah, I needed a change. Also, if you think Kilhaven is a clusterfuck, you should go check out that place. The department was never what one might call organized, and now... Kilhaven has its problems, but the fact that it's mostly shifters means the problems are manageable."

"What do you mean? What do they have up in Pan City that's got bigger chaos energy than shifters?" He realized what he'd said too late. "I mean, not that *all* shifters are like that. You know."

Namises waved it off. "I forget I'm a shifter sometimes anyway. Don't feel like one."

Green decided to go for it. "I, uh, I did some scent training a while back, so I can tell the main variety, but you're...?"

"Elephant. Very few of us on this continent; I haven't met a single one since moving to Kilhaven. So, I don't blame you for not recognizing it. You know you can just ask shifters what animal they prefer, right? You don't have to be shy about it."

Green shrugged.

"Anyway, I'm glad I got assigned to Fang. Reminds me a little bit of the action I saw in Pan City. But more of a *neutral* chaos. Not malevolent. Just self-centered individual shifters trying to get their needs met."

"What about the vampires? You got as many of those up there?"

"Couldn't say. The ones we do have don't cause that much trouble, even now. Yeah, there's been an uptick in vampire–werewolf violence lately, but not nearly as much as there has been here."

"How come, you think?"

Namises sipped his drink, taking his time. "Nothing keeping the vampires in check here."

"But there is in Pan City?"

"Mm-hm." Namises stared thoughtfully at the surface of

his bourbon, where his large ice cube rotated slowly in the center. "You weren't in the war."

"No. Humans couldn't be. And I was too young by a couple years."

"Right. Don't let anyone shit on you for that. It wasn't a fun place to be. And with the draft... It wasn't like people were choosing to go. There was no honor in any of it. No honor to be had, really. Not in a war like that."

Green wasn't sure what to say. He worked alongside plenty of veterans, but he'd never heard one speak this way about the war effort on the whole. He tried to think of the last veteran he'd talked to who spoke favorably of it and realized he couldn't think of a single one. To most, it seemed to be just a thing that happened, a crucible they'd gone through, something they'd survived so they could keep living on the other side of it. Nothing positive to be said for it, but nothing negative either. Just a reality of the world.

Namises's sentiment felt verboten. But Green was in no position to argue. He hadn't been there. He'd only heard snippets, and none of them, now that he considered it, had sounded especially valiant.

"Where were you?" he asked.

"A few places."

"Ever in Guatemala?"

Namises inspected him silently for a moment. "We were never in Guatemala." Then a grin broke through, and he chuckled in a deep baritone.

"Is that where you learned to shoot like that?"

"Nah. Shooting like that is what kept me alive. Would've been too late to learn it in the middle of a war."

For all the wisdom and nostalgia he seemed to carry on his shoulders, Namises didn't appear to be older than forty.

Green was left to conclude the man had entered the war young, which meant he'd learned to shoot even younger. There had to be a good story there. But before Green could settle on whether or not to ask it, Namises spoke again.

"I get the impression from Sarge that the 900s used to be a lot different."

"No doubt. We used to have some long-timers on the team. All kinds of experience. Now I'm the most senior officer, and I only have four years. Well, I guess you have more from before you transferred."

"Was there a reason everyone split?"

Green eyed him, trying to get a read. Was this a pointed question, or had the shifter just stumbled upon this touchy subject by accident?

Namises seemed more focused on a wealthy woman in skintight clothing who'd just entered the lounge than the question he'd asked. So, Green was left to conclude it had been a casual, if not distracted inquiry. "I think everyone was tired of each other's shit. Some of them wanted to get off the street, too. Sarge promoted, went to the Alpha 300s for a while, then got transferred back. Brooks is on Robbery now, Lawrence is a corporal, Marrow transferred to a day shift to spend more time with her kid in the evenings, and Harmon finally retired."

And Valance is… What is she doing in Alpha?

"But you stayed here."

"What the hell else am I gonna do?"

Namises laughed. "Good point. That's how we all end up cops in the first place. You ask yourself, 'What the hell else am I gonna do?' enough times, then suddenly it's your first day of the academy, and you're getting your ass smoked and thinking of all the other jobs you could've done instead."

They both laughed and enjoyed their drinks in companionable silence. Green took in the movement around the rest of the VIP lounge. The occupancy was sparse, no more than a dozen in a space that could easily have fit ten times that amount on a busy night.

And not a vampire to be found in any of the clusters of leather furniture. He felt himself relax, even as a small voice told him this was prejudice, and maybe Valance had left more of a legacy behind than he'd care to admit.

Namises broke the silence a few minutes later. "You thinking of promoting?"

That called for the rest of the glass, and Green drank it down. "No."

"No?"

"No."

"Why not?"

"I got enough shit on my plate."

"That Ridley is something else."

"That's one term for him."

"You think he's gonna drink somebody?"

"Chug 'em. Yeah."

Namises laughed. "You may be right. Man, the world is some shit, ain't it? You want another drink? On me."

Green sighed, dreading the moment he would have to leave this vampire-free mini-oasis, this complete delusion of his identity and his importance in this world. "I'll take what I can get."

CHAPTER FOUR_

"Should we light him up?" Officer Ridley asked from his position behind the steering wheel. The two officers, fresh off a pit stop for coffee, had just pulled off Highway 7 onto the frontage road and landed behind a slow-rolling sedan with the taillight out.

From his position riding shotgun, Green had already keyed the license plate into the Human Accessible Monitor and was waiting for any possible hits via Kilhaven's mud-slow wireless by the time the rookie asked. "Not yet."

They remained behind the vehicle while it turned onto Fang's main thoroughfare, heading toward Alpha sector. *Ding!* Green checked the HAM. The plates came back clean. Registered to Lindale Cumberland, vampire.

"Yeah, just follow him for a few blocks, see if we get anything else. If not, we'll pull him over and let him know about his taillight as a courtesy."

There were vastly more important leads for cops to be pursuing in Fang on a Friday night, but all of them held a high likelihood of Ridley's tenuous self-control snapping and him finally just chugging someone.

They approached a red light, and the car ahead of them slowed but didn't completely stop before taking a legal right on red.

"He rolled through that one," said the rookie eagerly. "Light him up?"

Green tried not to let his annoyance show in his tone. "It's night; the intersection is obviously clear. We're not gonna get him on rolling through."

"He's driving twenty-five in a fifty," Ridley announced a moment later.

"He's realized we're behind him."

"It's suspicious."

"Sure. You gonna be able to articulate that in your report?" Green had had enough of this, though. The driver knew they were there, so they weren't going to catch him on any real violations now. Might as well wrap this up and move on. "All right, let's tell him about his taillight."

When the whirling blue and red made their fancy entrance, the sedan pulled over onto a dark side street leading into a sleepy neighborhood. It was one Green almost never had occasion to visit. "You got lead on this," he said, and he prayed he didn't regret that decision ten minutes from now.

Ridley jabbed the seatbelt release like he was going for a pressure point and stepped out of the driver's seat in a single decisive movement.

For fuck's sake.

Green got out as well and followed a few yards behind the rookie. The driver's window was already down by the time Ridley approached. Even bathed in the colored lights swirling over the scene, the driver's skin appeared milky white.

Green hadn't given the rookie a heads-up on who the vehicle was registered to, mostly because Ridley should have known to ask. But also because he wanted to see how the interaction shifted.

Sure enough, the rookie's demeanor changed the moment he identified the driver as one of his own, and the overdone command presence withered away. "Evening, sir."

And so, the typical exchange started. Green felt himself relax. A vampire was unlikely to do anything violent to a fellow vampire, or so the argument went. This courtesy call could very well be the chance to eat up some time in the shift. Only a few more weeks with Ridley, then the walking liability would be someone else's problem. Or, you know, *everyone* else's problem, as tended to be the case when talking about public servants.

The vampires chuckled amiably over something relating to the driver's ID. As they did, movement in the back seat, obscured through the tinted windows, caught Green's attention.

There was someone back there.

He nudged Ridley aside to shine his beam on it through the driver's window. A girl, likely no older than sixteen, squinted against the sudden light. She didn't share the driver's pearlescent complexion. Or his scent.

She was a werewolf.

Nope. This was *not* right.

"Sir, can you step out of the vehicle?"

No one appeared more shocked or insulted by this abrupt order than Ridley. But the driver complied, which was all Green could ask for. The man didn't have to be happy about it, but he *did* need to get the fuck out of the car.

Ridley watched with arms folded tightly across his chest, and Green took the lead. "Can you verify your name?"

"Lindale Cumberland. Is something wrong? I just found out about the taillight. It wasn't like that last time I checked."

Green rejected the impulse to shine his flashlight directly into the suspect's eyes. "What are you doing out this late?"

"Heading home."

"Who's the kid?"

"That's just Cherie."

"What's your relationship with her?"

"I'm a friend of her parents."

Every muscle in Green's body was on high alert. He felt the adrenaline pulse into his legs. "So if I call her parents and tell them she's driving around with you just before midnight on a Friday, they won't be shocked to hear that?"

"Not at all. I'm happy to give you their number."

Green muttered, "Keep a close eye on him," to Ridley, then instructed Cherie to please step out of the vehicle. She didn't speak, just looked frightened, but of what, he couldn't be sure. He led her a good distance away from the others so their conversation could be private. Still, she appeared scared.

Ah, she was afraid of him. Right.

He did his best to open up his body, relax his posture, appear as unthreatening as someone could while toting that many weapons at his waist.

Meanwhile, Cherie hugged herself tightly. She was a scrawny thing and fit awkwardly in her clothing, as most girls her age did. The scent of werewolf was unmistakable on her, but had she even experienced her first shift? Now that she was out of the car, she looked even younger than he'd guessed. Thirteen, fourteen tops? His mind jumped to the most recent picture he'd seen of his baby sister. Kim would be about the same age now.

Looking into Cherie's scared, vulnerable face, Green felt guilt for not keeping up with Kim stab him in the ribs.

You couldn't have if you'd tried. Mom and Dad wouldn't let you.

His last conversation with them, almost three years ago now, hadn't ended on a pleasant note. They'd all but disowned him for the role he'd played in dismantling Hornstooth. Any chance of reaching his sister under their watchful eye all but disappeared. She was on her own now to deal not only with their folks but his worthless older brother Keller, too.

You can't save them all.

It was true. But he would have liked to save that one. His sister.

Maybe he could save this one, then. He dropped into a crouch to seem less intimidating to the young girl. "My name's Norman. You're not in any kind of trouble. It's just that when I see a man his age in a car with a girl your age this late at night, and it's clear there's no family relationship, I have to ask a few questions. I'm not mad at you, and there's no reason *you* should feel ashamed about it. I just want to make sure everything's okay. Then I can let you head out."

She nodded.

"What's your full name, Cherie?"

"Cherie Nicole King."

The last name caught his attention. One of the old

families, along with the Silvertons, Valances, and Bannockburns. He didn't need to ask the next question, but he did anyway: "Werewolf, correct?"

"Yes, sir. Timberwolf."

His desire to ask her if she'd had her first shift was nixed by the inappropriateness of asking a girl her age that question. If there were more obvious signs of illegal activity, he could justify the intrusion into her personal life. But he didn't have those. Yet.

"And who is this man you're riding around with?"

"Lin. He's a family friend."

"Your parents know you're out with him?"

"Yes, sir."

"They trust him?"

"Yes, sir. He goes to our church."

Green had to suck on the inside of his cheeks to keep from making a face. "Draculan, I presume?"

She nodded.

He caught himself wondering what Valance would have to say if she found out a King family was attending Draculan services.

Who gives a shit what she would think?

"And what were you and Lin doing out this late?"

"We were bowling. He was taking me home."

That was not the answer he'd expected. Bowling. It was innocent enough.

No. It was never innocent when a grown-ass male vampire was spending one-on-one time with a young female werewolf.

"You two go bowling often?"

"Every Friday night. My parents say it keeps me out of trouble with the kids at my school."

"Were you getting into trouble at school? It's okay if you were. I did when I was your age."

"No, I wasn't. I didn't really have friends."

Green ticked another box on the Vulnerable Population Checklist he kept track of in his head.

"I'm going to ask you something, Cherie, and I need you to know that whatever you say stays between us. My whole job is to keep people safe, okay?"

She nodded.

"Do you feel safe with Lindale?"

Her eyes jumped to the vampire where he stood, chatting comfortably with Ridley. Then she said, "Yes."

That was a *no* if he'd ever heard one. But not a legal *no*, unfortunately.

"Okay, then. The last thing I need is your parents' phone number. I'll just give them a call, make sure for my own sake that they know where you are and who you're with, and then you can head out."

A minute later, keeping Cherie next to him, he had Mrs. King on the phone.

"It's totally fine. It's just Lin. They go out every Friday night. He's practically an uncle."

Oh, phew! Uncles never do anything untoward with their nieces. I guess there's nothing left to discuss.

Green's desire to lecture the woman on parenting decisions was strong, almost overwhelming. He let a little bit of it through to release some of the built-up pressure. "You let your teenage daughter go on unsupervised outings with a vampire once a week?"

"Officer Green, you said?"

"Yes, ma'am."

"Officer Green, I don't expect you to understand. Most

people don't nowadays. But vampires aren't our enemies here. If you ever want to learn more about it, we would be happy to have you attend a service with us at First Draculan Church. In a time when species have never been more divided, it's a weight off one's shoulders to have a place where we can all come together under one roof."

Green had a sudden urge to spit. He'd been in a Draculan church before; granted, it had been after hours, and he'd been chasing a naked man on drugs through the hallways. But he'd seen enough. Dark walls, decorative coffins. He thought his Christian church experience growing up had been a mindfuck, but worshipping *Dracula* was guaranteed to be a whole new level of crazy.

"Okay, Mrs. King. Thank you for confirming. I'll let Cherie and Mr. Cumberland get on their way. I suggest you wait up for them."

That was that, then. Nothing else he could do. The whole thing was wrong, but it wasn't *illegal* from what he could tell.

As the vampire and the teenage timberwolf drove off a few minutes later, Green sat silently in the passenger's seat, watching the single functioning taillight as it grew smaller and then disappeared around a corner.

"I forget this is part of the job, you know?" Officer Ridley was practically bouncing in his seat after having made a new friend. "It seems like it's all catching criminals, but sometimes we just get to help people out, let them know about their taillight or whatnot. It feels *good*."

"Protect and serve," grumbled Green. He turned his head to inspect the rookie. "You didn't think there was anything weird going on there?"

"No, I think it's great that a family of werewolves can be friends with a vampire."

"Species aside, then, you don't think it's strange that a grown man is spending alone time with a young girl he's not related to?"

Ridley jerked his head back, blinking rapidly. "What? It's not like he was pimping her out. The family gave permission. Can't people just be nice and get along?"

"No," Green said. "No, they can't. Not like that." He checked the clock on the dash. His favorite burger joint was still open for another half-hour. "You hungry?" He caught himself. "Oh, right. Well, *I'm* hungry. Let's call it for dinner."

Now that he had more experience under his duty belt, Green had an opportunity that wasn't afforded to rookies: overtime. Any time, any sector. That was the beauty of a perpetually understaffed department. The additional hours were there for the taking. The whole of Kilhaven was his oyster. And just like oysters, any of these extra shifts could ultimately be what killed him.

Regardless, the opportunity to work without rest had opened up a new world of financial security for him, one he didn't exactly know what to do with. He would have had to have a life outside of work to spend the money, so he simply saved. That was an easier option. Maybe one day he would take the time to shop for a new vehicle or a house in a suburb of Kilhaven.

For now, though, he just stockpiled.

But it wasn't solely the money or the distraction that drew him to OT. At least, not since he'd become an FTO.

Working on a different shift meant no idiot rookie in

tow. The odds of him getting killed were tremendously lessened by that fact alone.

Banshee sector wasn't his first choice to work, but he'd needed something on his day off, and it had been what was available. Dull even on a Saturday night during an all-out blood feud between species, there was little hope of this weekday day shift turning into anything other than a few noise complaints, downed trees after the previous night's storm, and perhaps some property crime reports.

Green cruised the sleepy middle-class neighborhood, knowing he was unlikely to find anything but giving it a shot nonetheless. There were no calls currently holding. Why they needed OT officers for a shift like this was beyond his pay grade to worry about. He knew most cops in his position would find somewhere scenic to park and wait for a call to come, but he couldn't stomach the thought of it. And besides, this was usually when he slept, and his circadian rhythms were screaming at him to maybe just shut his eyes for a minute. He knew what that would lead to, though. A cop found asleep in his car. The laughingstock of the department, assuming someone didn't come upon him, realize he was incapacitated, and murder him for sport.

Even as he hoped for a little action to pop off, he also hoped it was nothing too serious. Nothing that would make him call in the shift's corporal. Corporal Lawrence.

Jeremy Lawrence, his handsome former shift mate, made insubordination a knee-jerk reaction for Green. The two of them might've had a shot at a friendship following the shooting they were both involved in Green's second month out of the academy, but... things had gotten in the way. Namely Aliyah Brooks, the third officer involved in that shooting, and Lawrence's former FTO. An enmity had been struck up between the men instead. Though Green never doubted that Lawrence would have his back if and when things went sideways, it went unsaid that such a situation, should it arise again, would leave Green at a disadvantage later.

Also, Lawrence was a prick.

Yeah, that's it. He's just a prick. Period. A pretty-boy prick.

But all those petty nitpicks flew out the window of Green's squad car when a high-priority call popped onto the HAM's screen: *Aggravated assault, draining.*

Ah, finally some action.

And I hope no one's dead.

The second thought was mere professional courtesy; whether he cared about a death or not, death came. His emotions toward the victim were irrelevant. Superstition had bled out of him in the last few years.

It was hardly past one in the afternoon, and the sun shone down from a clear sky as he caught sight of the residence down the quiet street. It was a modestly sized two-story home, and he winced as if bracing for a blow to the chest when he noticed the freshly shorn lawn. The victim was likely dead inside that house—drainings rarely had survivors—but at least the lawn met the HOA standards. It was split seconds like this that could knock the wind right out of him. Not the death, the carnage, the grief of survivors, but the details that seemed to slash a hole through the veil that separated what society valued from what really mattered in the end.

His was the second car on scene as he pulled up to the curb and cut the engine.

Something about responding to these calls during daylight hours gave an unreality to a dead body on scene. Of course, there was no hard data from his time on the Force to back up that inclination. Murder happened 'round the clock.

The front door was already open, so Green let himself in, making a loop through the dining room and kitchen, both in a lived-in state but by no means filthy, before ending up in the living room, where he found the other officer.

"What do we got?"

From his crouch by the sofa, the other officer turned toward the sound of Green's voice. Green didn't know this guy. Probably fresh off field training, if the baby face and wide eyes were any indications. By this officer's shiny boots was a bleach-white body.

Yep. Unless they had four quarts of the right blood type on them at that moment, this vic was a goner.

He approached, and the officer glimpsed his name on his uniform. "Green? I'm Carriage."

"You check for a pulse?"

"Yeah. Shocker, none there. Just finished five minutes of CPR. Still nothing."

Green stared down at the stiff, cold body on the living room's shag carpet. No clear scent came from it, but the whole of the house smelled like werewolf, no doubt as a result of that same shag covering the downstairs. "You do tend to need blood in your body to have a pulse."

There was the sound of another vehicle coming to a stop, the driver's door closing, and a moment later, Corporal Jeremy Lawrence appeared inside. He made a vain attempt to hide his annoyance upon seeing Green already there, but it was no good. And pointless.

"What do we have here?" Lawrence said, sighing.

Officer Carriage, oblivious to the animosity between the

two other living people in the room, reported, "White skin, no pulse."

"Don't forget the puncture wounds on the neck," Green added. He didn't even have to lean over to see them; they were that big. He'd learned over the last few years of this shit that the size of the holes generally corresponded to the age of the vampire. Like rings of a tree. Whatever vamp did this had been around for a while. Not that clues like this even mattered. The department would have to be in the business of arresting vampires for murders for leads like this to make any difference.

Lawrence radioed for the ME and homicide to get over ASAP and then squatted by the body. Green crouched next to him. "Purple ooze, two holes in the neck spaced just over an inch apart, no blood to speak of in the victim's body. Any idea what it could be, Corporal?"

Lawrence hitched an eyebrow at Green. "Feeling a little sarcastic today, I see." He slapped his hands to his thighs and stood. "I don't blame you, Green. It's been one hell of a week. This is the third one of these in Banshee alone."

Green stood too.

"Carriage," Lawrence said, "keep a watch on this guy until homicide shows up. We're gonna search the rest of the house and property."

Shocked by the "we" of that, as if the two of them had any desire to spend time enjoying a shared activity, Green shot Lawrence a quick look.

But that deep-seated tension that had snuck through upon their first glimpse of each other on scene was nowhere to be found. If Green didn't know any better, he'd say that he and Lawrence had never competed for the affections of the same woman. Although, in the end, neither of them had won that competition, so maybe all was forgiven?

He followed Lawrence outside, waiting to discover a reason for the uncharacteristic... not *friendliness*, but neutrality.

The shifter kept his eyes on the ground, searching for the usual signs that were almost never there—bloodstains, shoe prints, dropped items.

Green had to admit that it was nice to hunt for evidence in the daylight for a change.

"Carriage is a good officer," Lawrence said. "He's got about six months under his belt. Hasn't shot anyone yet."

Ah, there it was. The jab was a return to normalcy and put Green's nerves at ease.

Lawrence went on, "You know how rare it is that we get a good one in lately, right?"

"Oh, I know. I'm training one who's not exactly on a path toward success."

"Then you know how crucial it is not to thrust your jadedness on the ones we want to keep around."

Green jerked his head up to glare at the corporal. "Are you... are you scolding me?"

"No, but let it be known that I could if I wanted to. I outrank you. You're working under me this shift."

Green rolled his eyes, making sure there was no missing the gesture, then returned his attention to the fresh-cut grass as they made their way around to the backyard.

A muscle in Lawrence's jaw twitched. "It's getting bad out here."

"No shit."

"It's not Valance's fault."

Green's eyes darted up to the corporal's face again. "Are you screwing with me?"

"No. It's not her fault. Sure, she may have pushed aside a screen that was obscuring the truth, but"—he jabbed a thumb over his shoulder toward the front yard—"she didn't just suck the life out of that poor werewolf. A vampire did that." He turned over a downed fence board with the toe of his boot. "I've thought a lot about this, as I'm sure you have. This mess is between vampires and weres. It's not our fight."

Rarely, if ever, had Green heard of humans and shifters being lumped into the same "our."

"What are you talking about? We're cops. This *is* our fight. Responding to crime is literally what we're paid to do."

"Right, right. I get that. I just mean this is what the world is like now. We have to forget about what it *was* like, because I don't think it's ever getting back there in our lifetime. Last time these two groups went after each other so openly, it had to get a whole hell of a lot worse before the treaty made it a little better. And that took decades, maybe even centuries—I dunno, I haven't read a history book since high school, but you know what I mean. You can't let yourself get jaded. This is a marathon now. And as long as you're on patrol, there's nothing you can do to change it, so stop trying. That's where the burnout comes from, the gap between what is and what should be."

Green couldn't keep from staring at Lawrence like he'd just spoken gibberish. Who the hell was this, and since when did this vacuous tool have anything resembling wisdom? Something had happened to this shifter, something major. An upheaval, even.

Then it clicked.

Jeremy Lawrence had been first on scene at the infamous family annihilation scene two years prior. What Green knew about it, he'd heard through the oft-incorrect news coverage and the even more oft-incorrect rumor mill at work. The incident started when a prosperous werewolf patriarch had lost everything he owned in a bad investment. Rather than confess it to his family, he'd killed them—wife, three children, even his own mother, who lived with them—and then turned the gun on himself. Rumor had it that the slayings hadn't been so simple. The family had tried to escape. That was guaranteed to make a real mess of a scene.

Lawrence had been pulling OT in Demon that night, had picked up an innocent enough patrol shift, and it'd landed him on the front page of the *Kilhaven Tribune*.

Now that the pieces were coming together, Green realized it was just a few months after that call when Lawrence had promoted. Probably not a coincidence.

"You've stuck with the counseling, I see," Green said.

"Yes, but I don't need a counselor to tell me all this."

"Yes, you do. You didn't know any of this shit before someone told you."

"I'm still making a valid point, asshole."

Green held up his hands. "Fine. I hear what you're saying. But if I *didn't* want to make things better, to close that gap between what is and what should be, why the hell would I be a cop?"

"I'm just saying, there's not a whole hell of a lot you can do on the street so long as we're all out here playing janitor."

"You trying to run me out of the Force?"

"God, you're an idiot. No. I'm not trying to do that."

"Then what are you getting at?"

Lawrence stopped walking and turned to face Green straight on. "I think your desire to make things better is noble. But it needs to be from the right position. I think you ought to consider promoting."

"You've been talking to Bannockburn." Not a question.

"What? No. I just think we could use some more good people handling that work at a higher level. God knows Organized Crime could use someone who's not morally compromised."

"You mean besides Brooks?"

Lawrence's expression tightened, "Yeah, besides her, obviously."

"Then why don't you do it?"

"I'm already doing something. I'm a corporal, if you've forgotten."

"How could I when you keep reminding me?"

It hadn't slipped past Green that Lawrence had called him "not morally compromised." That was almost a compliment. And such a thing only heightened his suspicions.

"You *haven't* been talking to Bannockburn?"

Lawrence huffed. "I just fucking said. You really are turning into Valance. Hey, I guess we all turn into our mothers eventually."

"You're one to talk, Oedipus."

To his credit, Lawrence managed to push through the jab. "What'd Bannockburn say? He suggest promoting, too? You're at four years, Green—*everyone's* going to tell you that you should consider promoting." He cursed under his breath again, shaking his head. "Two people you know mention it, and you think there's some sort of conspiracy afoot."

"You're an asshole. I'm nothing like Valance," Green said. "Now, if you'll excuse me, I'm going to search the house for clues so we can finally nail a fucking vampire on one of these crimes."

As he stomped away, Lawrence called after him, "Gonna blow the whole thing wide open, eh, Heather?"

CHAPTER SIX_

Maybe picking so much OT the last few weeks hadn't been the smartest idea.

Green pulled into his apartment parking lot, having narrowly avoiding falling asleep at the wheel. Had it been eleven, twelve days in a row he'd worked? Odd hours on odd shifts blended one right into the other, maxing out his allotted work time per twenty-four-hour period. He found a parking spot a building over from his and killed the engine. His hips and lower back throbbed angrily from all the consecutive hours in his duty belt. The mere thought of pushing himself out of his seat drained him. He dreaded lugging all his bags up the stairs. His eyes struggled to stay open. They closed.

A few minutes later, they opened again when he jerked out of sleep. "Shit." A thick strip of morning sun shone between two of the buildings, soaking his car with warmth that made it even harder to initiate any action. He'd regret it if he didn't get solid sleep in a bed, though. It may be a

Saturday, but with the rotation he was on, it wasn't his weekend yet. He needed to be back at the sub in just under ten hours.

He grabbed the body-size duffel out of his back seat and began to awkwardly climb the concrete stairs, the back of the bag clanking against the painted metal railings with each stair: *throng*, step, *throng*, step, *throng*.

When he finally reached the landing, the vivid image of his mattress on the floor—not exactly ideal for bringing the ladies home, but easy enough to literally roll out of on those days his whole body hurt—had established squatter's rights in his mind's eye. He could practically feel the cool, threadbare sheets on his skin...

And that was when he saw her. She was asleep on the raggedy welcome mat he'd inherited from the previous tenant. Her head leaned against where the door met the jamb. Her legs were bent, and an overstuffed backpack rested underneath her knees.

He almost didn't recognize her after so many years. Something about her looked completely different from the girl he'd last seen in a photograph.

He dropped his duffel on the landing and went to wake her. "Kim," he whispered.

She jerked awake and stared up at him, her gaze temporarily vacant. Then she blinked, and the vacancy was replaced by embarrassment. "Hi, Nor. Don't be mad."

"I'm not mad. But I *am* tired and confused. Why are you...?" His lagging brain caught up. "Whatever, come on inside."

So, rather than burrowing under his cool sheets, Green spent the next five minutes preparing coffee for the two of them, wondering only briefly if she was even old enough to be drinking coffee. Kim was lankier than the last time he'd seen her, no doubt about that, but he didn't want to go stunting her growth.

Ultimately, he decided he was too tired to give a shit, and he poured her some coffee.

He brought the mugs over to his fake leather couch, where Kim was sitting. She'd left her shoes by the door—a habit his mother enforced with her usual knack for martyrdom—and had tucked her sock feet under her butt. She hugged her backpack to her like he might try to steal it.

But when he held out her steaming mug, she released her grip on the bag. "Thanks."

"Smelled like the milk was bad, so I only had a little sugar for it."

"That's fine; I take it black."

He lowered onto the carpet on the other side of the coffee table and inspected her closely. "You're too young to have preferences like that. Does Mom know you drink coffee?"

Kim glared at her cup like she might be trying to drink the contents telepathically. "Who cares what she thinks?" Then, quickly, "Did you just move in here? I thought…"

Anyone who saw his empty walls might ask the same thing, but nope. "Same place since I came to Kilhaven."

"Ah."

The obvious question hit the sludgy surface of his brain like a slap. "Does Mom know you're here?"

"No. I promise she doesn't care where I am, though."

He set his coffee down so he could jam his palms into his eye sockets. This wasn't good. This had "Green family drama" written all over it. "Okay, why don't you *please* just tell me what's going on?"

"They kicked me out."

His hands dropped from his face. *"They kicked you out?"*

"Yeah."

"Why? What'd you do?"

She straightened indignantly. "Nothing! It wasn't my fault."

He'd heard that before. Frequently.

Green inhaled deeply, struggling to get his foggy brain to complete even the most basic of mental tasks, like following along to the important conversation at hand.

Sure, this was his sister, but he needed to switch from Norman Green to Officer Green if he ever hoped to get the full story out of her. "I'm sure it wasn't your fault, whatever it was. But what did they disagree with?"

She wouldn't look at him now, and he hoped that meant the admission of guilt was close. "I didn't mean to do it. I didn't even know I could."

"I understand." He nodded. "Just tell me what happened."

She pressed her lips together, and he hoped she wouldn't shut down. The sooner he resolved this situation and got her on her way back home, the sooner he could pass the hell out.

She inhaled the coffee, though, then dove into it. "I was throwing the football around with Keller in the backyard and... I shifted." She met his eyes over her raised mug, clearly trying to gauge his reaction.

But he had no reaction. The words hadn't landed. They felt like nothing more than garbled nonsense.

"I didn't mean to," she went on. "I was just sort of itchy all over, then suddenly I was a cougar."

He blinked. "A cougar."

"Yeah, you know. A mountain lion. A big cat."

"No, I know what a cougar is." Slowly, the reality seeped in. "You shifted?"

"Yeah."

"Into a cougar."

"I just said that."

"Yes. Yes, you did."

He paused, tried to corral his thoughts.

This was… surprising.

Not ideal.

But there was nothing *wrong* with it.

And this was his sister.

"What happened then?"

"What do you think happened?" she spat. "Keller ran inside to tell Mom."

"*God*, he's such a prick."

Her shoulders slackened the slightest bit. "No kidding."

"And then?"

"It's all kind of a blur. I was busy trying to change back, but I knew Mom would be out soon, so I ran into the woods until I could figure it out. When I came back later that night, she asked me calmly what happened, and I thought maybe she would understand. I don't know, just the way she was talking made me think that. So, I told her, and I apologized for it and said it wouldn't happen again, but she didn't care. She told Dad, and they told me I had fifteen minutes to pack my things and get out. They were fighting when I left. Dad thinks Mom cheated on him."

"She probably did, because she's a horrible person, but I don't think you're necessarily the result, Kim. This kind of thing isn't unheard of. It's a recessive gene. Sometimes it just happens."

She swallowed hard, then brought the mug to her lips.

The two sat in silence as Green felt his exhaustion double.

Kim had nowhere to go.

But what the hell would he do with a teenaged…

A teenaged what?

"Hey, have you shifted into anything else since then?"

"I'm a shifter, if that's what you're asking. I wasn't sure at first, but then I accidentally shifted into a moose."

"A moose?"

She seemed to shrink. "Are you mad at me?"

"What? Why would I be mad at you? It upset Mom and Dad, sure. But they're bigots, Kim. Scared, small-minded people. I don't care what you are; you're still my sister."

My sister who I don't have a clue what to do with.

She nodded and paused. "You're not going to kick me out?"

"Kick you out?" He almost laughed, but even his slow brain knew that wouldn't have been the right response in this delicate moment. "Of course not. But you gotta understand, I have no idea what to do with a thirteen-year-old."

"Fourteen. I just turned fourteen."

"I don't know what to do with that, either." An arrangement was in the works now, one he couldn't have fathomed twenty minutes ago, and one that would no doubt complicate everything. But he couldn't stop it. What other choice did he have but to let her stay?

"You don't have to do anything," she insisted. "I can take care of myself. I just need a place to sleep until I can figure out what to do."

"What do you mean, you can take care of yourself? You can't drive, and you don't have a job."

"I made it four hundred miles from Bowers to here, didn't I?"

He opened his mouth to dispute it, then stopped himself. "Okay, yeah, that's pretty impressive. How did you manage it?"

"I hitchhiked. It was—"

"You *hitchhiked?*" Horrifying images of all the possible outcomes of *that* nonsense flashed across his mind's eye. A young girl like her, clearly a runaway, lanky, dark skin, naiveté dripping from her—she shouldn't have made it this far. The odds of her getting stuck in an infinite loop of drugs and prostitution in some highway truck stop were astronomical. How—

"I didn't accept rides from any men. Only women."

"Oh."

"Sheesh, Nor. I'm not *trying* to get myself murdered."

"Then you're smarter than I was at your age." He paused. "All I have for you is a couch, but it's all yours. We do need to set some ground rules, though."

"Whatever they are, they won't be as bad as what Mom had."

"True. But we're keeping the 'no shoes' rule."

She arched an eyebrow at him, pressing her lips together —the first true sign of teenage attitude he'd seen since she'd arrived. "*You're* still wearing *your* shoes. And, ew, is that *blood?*"

He followed her gaze and saw that, yes, it was definitely blood. He wasn't sure whose…

He slipped his boots off and tossed them by the door. "I usually do it, but finding a little vagabond on my doorstep threw me off."

She wasn't buying it. And why would she? His was clearly the cheap carpet of a man who regularly wore muddy, bloody boots inside.

"You'll have to go to school," he added. "I don't have the time or desire to homeschool you. You start on Monday." She opened her mouth to protest, but he cut her off. "It's not the same here. There are plenty of shifters and werewolves and… all kinds. It's not majority human like back home. You'll be fine. No one will think twice about it."

She grumbled but nodded.

"And no leaving the house when I'm at work. You go to school, you come home. If I could put an ankle tracker on you, I would. That's how serious I am."

"What if I want to practice shifting?"

"You can do it here. But, you know, not when I'm around"—he held up a hand—"*only* because when you change back, you'll be naked, and that's… I don't need to see that. To be clear, though, I'm not ashamed of your ability to shift."

"You're just ashamed of my human body."

"Right."

"Anything else?"

"This can't be permanent. Sorry, Kim, but it just can't be. I don't know how to raise a teenager. I'll try to work on Mom and Dad and see if you can go back there eventually."

"No!"

"I won't send you back if they're going to be awful to you—"

"Then you'll never send me back. They're not going to change."

"You just shocked them. But they love you"—he struggled to force out those words against his absolute doubt of them—"and plenty of parents come around to this sort of thing. It just takes time."

"Nor, Mom is a fucking bitch."

"Hey! Watch your language."

"Is that one of the house rules?"

"I— No. It's not. Yeah, she's a fucking bitch."

"And when Dad's not totally checked out, he's the most hateful person in any room."

Green shrugged his agreement. There was no point arguing. After all, how could he blame her for ditching them the first chance she got when he'd done the same? And he hadn't even been a shifter.

He finished off the rest of his coffee and pushed himself to his feet. "Okay, I have to call Mom to let her know where you are, but then I'm going to bed. There are some microwavable meat pocket things in the freezer and the bathroom's right through there. Don't expect it to be clean... or stocked. We'll talk about this in the morning."

"It is the morning."

"*My* morning. Five p.m."

He shuffled into the bedroom, stripped down to his boxers, considered it, put on fresh boxers, and then climbed into bed and called his mother.

"Hello?"

"Hey, Mom. It's Norman. Just thought you'd like to

know that Kim showed up at my place this morning. She's safe."

"I don't know anyone named Kim."

The line went dead.

Okay, so maybe Megan Green *wouldn't* come around. Which meant he was now the adult in charge of a thirteen— no, a *fourteen*-year-old shapeshifter.

So that's *how life gets even more stressful.*

CHAPTER SEVEN

Green was startled awake by a knocking he couldn't quite make sense of. Only once he snorted and rolled hurriedly off his mattress, scrambling to his feet, did he understand why the sound had him so disoriented: it was coming from two sources.

He pulled on some gym shorts.

He responded to the first source by opening his bedroom door. Kim stared at him, wide-eyed. "I don't know who it is, and I wasn't sure if you wanted me to answer it or not."

The second knocking, no, *pounding*, pulled his attention to the front door. "Just hang out in my room for a bit." He grabbed his gun off his duty belt in his duffel just as a voice on the other side of the door called, "I know you're in there, Green. You're not on duty, and you don't have a social life. Open up."

Recognizing the speaker did not cause him to relinquish his grasp of the firearm.

He yanked open the door and glared at Heather Valance. "What do you want?"

She was in jeans and a black T-shirt and wore her backup in a holster on her hip, clearly visible. Must be her day off.

She looked him up and down. "Did I interrupt?"

"My sleep? Yeah, you did."

She shouldered her way past him into the apartment. "Close the door."

"Don't—" He pressed his lips together. If he started shouting at her, he might not be able to stop himself. Though so much time had passed since the raid on the vampire lab, fantasies of all the ways he'd like to tell her off still kept his mind racing when it should've been fast asleep at least one time each week.

He shut the door.

"I see you've redecorated the place since the last time I was here." She nodded at the single key hook he'd screwed into the wall by the door. "Is that custom, or…?"

"Just spit it out. What do you want?"

"How about I just wanted to see an old friend? Is that too—" She stopped speaking abruptly, and his gut twisted. She stared at something on the floor just behind him. She looked up. "Are you… fucking a minor?"

"Goddammit, Valance! Of course not. It's a long story. Just tell me why you're here."

"Then you're *living* with a minor. Otherwise, who the hell's shoes are those?"

He felt his blood boil even as he fought down his need to overexplain himself. "They're my sister's. *Why are you here?*"

She narrowed her eyes at him, and the corners of her mouth twitched as if she was fighting off a smile. "Sure. Your *sister*. Well, just don't get caught, I guess. But listen, I need you to promote the first chance you get."

He bowed his head and wondered briefly if she would leave if he stayed like that for long enough.

"I'm serious, Green. I need you to take the test."

He collected himself, then raised his gaze again to meet hers. "I don't give a cherub's shitty diaper what you need from me, Valance. How do you not understand that? You needed me to raid that leprechaun warehouse, and I did. And we both got cursed because of it. Then you needed me to storm the vampire lab, and I did, and—"

"And nothing bad happened. You got a little vacation time and got to be a hero."

He lowered his voice, hoping Kim wouldn't overhear. "We killed a *lot* of people."

"Not ones that counted. Not after what they did to those kids."

Movement down the hall behind Valance caught Green's attention as Kim cracked open the bedroom door. He shook his head subtly, which he hoped sent the message of "Stay the hell in there."

Valance must have taken it to mean he didn't agree with her argument. Which he didn't, after all.

She continued, "I only ask these things of you when there's something big going on. And, Norman, I need your help. I know I can trust you for this sort of thing. You always come through. However much shit I might give you for being a virtually useless human and having hips that would look more natural in an A-line skirt than a police uniform, I always know you'll show up when it comes time for it. And I'm here because *I need you to show up*. One more time. I promise this is the last time."

"Fine." He didn't trust a word of it, but he'd play along. "Tell me why, and I'll take the test."

She hesitated. "You know if I could tell you right now, I would."

He nodded. "That's what I thought. Yet again, you trust me to show up, but not to be in on whatever bullshit conspiracy you're cooking up."

"You kidding me? Since when has a single one of these turned out to be bullshit? I've been *exposing* conspiracies, not concocting them. The clowns? I was right there, wasn't I? They're still around."

Green's eyes flickered to the cracked bedroom door. Shit. This would require a little back-pedaling later on. Kim didn't need to know about the clowns.

"Wolfenvamps? Check!" she continued, only making things worse. "I was right about it all. I've never been wrong. You don't have to *like* it, but I should've earned a little of your trust by now."

"My *trust?*"

"Why don't you put down the gun, Green."

He'd forgotten he still held it and strode over to the coffee table, where he slapped it down before plowing on. "Your little crusades are why murders have skyrocketed in Kilhaven. We averaged a hundred and twenty homicides a year under Hornstooth. You know how many we've averaged since?"

"One thousand six hundred and five."

He had opened his mouth to respond, but that stopped him short. "Wait, really?" He was going to ball-park a number much lower than *that.*

"Yes, really. Don't try to out-statistic me, Rookie."

"I'm a fucking senior officer now!"

"Christ, you're acting hysterical. Are you... Is this a bad

time of the month for you?" He snarled, and she added, "What's your sister's name again?"

"Kim."

"Kim," Valance called over her shoulder. "Come on out, hon. I know you're here, and I'm a cop; you can trust me."

"No, you can't, Kim." But it was too late; his sister had already pushed open the door and was making her way to the living room.

Valance inspected her as she shuffled closer. "Oh, wow, she looks like you. I guess it really is your—" The werewolf swiveled abruptly toward Green, wide-eyed. Then she looked back at Kim, back to Norman. "Well, I'll be damned. You didn't tell me she was a shifter."

"I didn't know."

Valance's chuckle sounded like a butcher hacking at a hunk of meat. "Well, *shit*." She turned to Kim. "Hi, I'm Heather. I'm a werewolf. Sorry you have to stay with this guy. He's not a lot of fun. Hey, I bet you don't have much money, right? Yeah, you're too young for a job, and he's a cheapskate. Here." She pulled out her wallet, and from it slipped a stack of crisp bills.

"What the hell?" he demanded. "You don't get to just waltz in here and start tossing that casino boat money around."

She ignored him, grabbing Kim's hand and placing the cash in her palm. "Don't give a cent of it to him. He has money. And he had his chance at getting a lot more, but he blew it moping." She grinned. "You let Aunt Heather know when you run out of this and need more."

"Do *not* call her Aunt Heather, Kim. She's nobody's auntie."

Valance folded her wallet back into her pocket and faced

him with a dignified rigidness. "For your information, my sister has her thirteenth pup on the way, so I am *quite* the auntie."

"And do you give *her* kids wads of cash, too?"

"No, because she's a brainwashed religious nut, and she'd spend all the money on illegal firearms."

He held up a hand. "I don't want to know." He kind of did, though, and had wondered about Valance's family at various points of his career. Namely, how her parents could have screwed up so badly. But he'd never admit his curiosity, especially in a moment like this.

"I'm serious, Green. You gotta test this year. I need you in Vice."

"Vice?" He scoffed. "Not a chance. Get out, Valance."

"Fine, fine. I've said what I came to say. I hope you'll think it over."

"I won't."

Her gaze flickered briefly to Kim, and a strange shadow crossed her face. But it was gone so quickly that he might have imagined it. "You will," she finished.

And then she showed herself out.

Green stood silently, staring at the front door until a crinkle of paper pulled him out of his thoughts. "Kim, you can't keep that."

She clutched the cash to her. "Like hell I can't. Who was she?"

"She trained me. She's a lunatic."

"That's creaturist language."

"Huh?"

"Lunatic. It's a creaturist descriptor for werewolves. It promotes the false assumption that they act crazy during a full moon."

"But they *do* act crazy during a full moon. Everyone does."

Kim rolled her eyes and tucked the money into her pocket, but not before he got a glimpse of the denomination.

"Wait, were those *hundreds*?"

"I think you should consider what she said. Being a detective would be cool."

He stared at his sister, trying not to fault her for being so easily bought off. She was, after all, a vulnerable teen, easily exploited.

Damn, that must be close to a grand.

"I don't want to be a detective," he said.

"Why not?"

He passed her on his way to his bedroom. "The cash goes toward your school supplies, understand?"

"You don't get to tell me how to spend my money."

"It's not your money!"

He fell face-first onto his pillow, and the last image that appeared in his mind's eye before he finally drifted off was a single sparkling moment, one that had surfaced uncountable times in the past few years. Had it really happened, or had his memory painted it from some other material than reality?

Standing in that wolfenvamp laboratory, covered head to toe in blood, surrounded by heaps of unconscious leprechauns and slain vampires, his chest heaving, adrenaline lighting up every fiber of his body, the glorious tingle of earth magic flowing through him—his eyes meet Valance's. She grins.

And he grins back.

CHAPTER EIGHT_

The First Draculan Church of Kilhaven was an imposing
figure in an otherwise unimpressive neighborhood in Fang.
Many of the houses around it had historical designations, a
handy excuse for every fourth or fifth to exist in a state of
total disrepair. But the church stood out among all of it, a
white gothic structure with red stained-glass windows and a
large bell tower that rang at dawn every day.

Green hated it—hated the structure, hated what he knew
of the happenings inside of it. He felt about it the same way
he felt about drinking poison: *no thanks, and why would you
even offer?*

Ridley steered the car into the parking lot, and Green
realized with a twist of dread that they were the first on
scene. Shit.

Nothing about the call text had made much sense.
Whoever had reported it didn't seem to be entirely in touch
with reality and had called in a suspicious person, except
without having seen any actual person. It had looked like a
dud, which was the only reason Green assigned to it.

But now that he was here, the dense night clinging to the silhouette of the imposing building, he couldn't imagine why he would have agreed to even a dud call at this location.

"My family used to go here," Ridley announced. "I know the place. I'll take lead."

"No, you won't."

Green hurried out of the car, which Ridley had parked toward the middle of the lot, thirty yards from the building itself. To Green's relief, Officer Namises pulled up just as he shut the passenger door.

"Hold up," Green told the rookie. "We need someone else."

"It's just a suspicious-person call. It's probably nothing."

"Wrong attitude."

Namises hitched his belt up around his doughy middle as he walked over. "We first here?"

"Yep. You think we should wait for backup?"

Namises's eyes flickered to Ridley. "Probably."

From the direction of the church, a bang caused Green's hand to find the grip of his gun. He saw the source right away. Someone had flung open one of the old wooden front doors.

Namises aimed his flashlight at the source in an instant, and a single vampire staggered out in the path of the beam. The newcomer appeared dazed, clutching his left shoulder with his right hand as he stared into the light. Green could just make out the man's mouth moving, but whether he was trying to speak or simply gasping for air, it was impossible to tell. Suddenly a word made its way from his lungs and cut through the night air: "Staked."

He made it only a few steps before his knees went, and he collapsed.

Ridley charged forward, and Green followed a few steps behind.

The vampire on the ground was already gone by the time they reached him. A thick wooden splinter protruded from just below his shoulder. Perhaps it hadn't been a direct strike to the heart, but only a graze that took its time ending his un-life.

"Handle's been smashed," Namises announced, and Green looked up from the still vampire. One of the curved brass handles of the ornately carved wooden doors was dangling from only a single point, while the other had been dented in the middle to look like a butterfly wing. Clearer signs of a forced entry were a rare find. Someone had wanted desperately to get inside the church.

Green got Ridley's attention. "We have to secure the place before we worry about the wounded. Someone could still be inside."

He pulled his extendable stake from his belt and was annoyed that Ridley didn't do the same. If this guy was unwilling to kill his own, what good was he in a world where vampires caused so much violence? Killing your own wasn't ideal—Green knew that from experience—but species loyalty wasn't how this world was supposed to run. It wasn't part of this job of protecting and serving.

Green gripped his flashlight in his left hand as he stepped across the threshold.

A streak of white caught his attention at the edge of his beam. He turned his attention toward it.

Graffiti, the paint fresh and glistening, stood out against

the black walls. It was chicken scratch, as most was, but he'd grown better at reading it.

Kill the legion.

Liberate the children.

Drain the drinkers.

And there were symbols Green didn't recognize, but he tried to commit them to memory. Eden's Fist was the first likely culprit to come to mind. The human supremacist group had had it out for vampires for as long as they'd been around. It wouldn't take many methamphetamines at all to inspire them to try something this stupid and violent.

The officers proceeded through the halls in a V, Green in the lead with his stake, Ridley behind, being fucking useless and cocky, and Namises behind on the other side, gun drawn.

"Check the sanctuary," Ridley said. "It's at the end of this hallway."

The black walls gave their approach a never-ending feel. It was like floating in space. The door at the end of the hallway didn't seem to draw any closer. They hurried quietly toward it, Green's heartbeat staccato against his ribs, and he wondered if Ridley could sense the rush of blood.

Who was he really expecting to use this stake against?

No time to consider it. They reached the doors of the sanctuary, pulled them open, and stopped dead in their tracks.

"Oh my God," Ridley whispered. And then he screamed it.

And Green, looking around at the carnage—the overturned pews, the shattered lanterns, the bodies, and the blood, *the blood*—couldn't blame anyone for screaming.

CHAPTER NINE

A swarm of black-and-white vehicles descended upon the parking lot of First Draculan Church. As much as Green wished that meant he and Ridley were free to leave, he knew they'd be here for at least a few hours past the end of their shift. It was one of *those* calls. Too much to sort through. Detectives in from too many different departments, attempting to coordinate while also reluctant to communicate.

Sergeant Bannockburn was engaged in an intense conversation with one of the assistant chiefs over in a dark corner of the lot as Green waited patiently, leaning against the hood of his vehicle until the next person from leadership wanted to speak to him directly.

The excitement had long since overstimulated Ridley, and after an hour of trying to keep the vampire in one spot, Green had given up and allowed him to pace. The only question now was whether Green was under any strict obligation to stop the idiot from trying to insert himself into conversations with people who didn't have the least idea who he was. The rookie's badge number gave away his freshness, and Green didn't miss the dismissive glances from the detectives and senior officers whenever Ridley interjected.

Namises approached and settled in next to Green on the hood, taking it all in. Department personnel crawled in and out of the church in a steady stream that reminded Green's adrenaline-crashing brain of ants who's just found a bit of apple on the floor.

"Oh damn," Namises said, pulling his pant leg tight at the thigh to get a better look. "How did I get blood all the way up here?"

Green glanced over and saw the blotch by Namises's groin. "There was a lot of blood."

"No lie. I take it from your tone that this isn't the first time you've come upon something that bloody."

"Nope." A strange impulse came over Green. Maybe it was boredom, and he just wanted something to fill the time, or maybe something else compelled him to confide in the guy. Either way, he continued, "You know the raid of the vampire lab a few years ago? Where they were making those wolfenvamps?"

Namises eyed him skeptically. "Do I *know* it? The stake heard 'round the world? Yeah, I think I know it. I've never heard it called a raid, though. I thought someone called in something else, and a few officers just stumbled upon the lab."

Oh, right.

That was the official story. And thanks to that strange mistake, Green and Valance had possessed the perfect alibi for why they had rolled up to the empty retail lot that night. Only a few minutes after midnight, before Green and

Valance arrived, a woman had reported suspicious activity in the vacant shops across the street from her house.

Only, her house was on the outer edge of Banshee, not anywhere near Fang.

Somewhere along the communication chain of the caller, the call-taker, and the dispatcher, the original address provided had morphed into a completely different one: the exact address of the hidden lab. And then, a few minutes after it had appeared in the HAM queue for Fang sector, Green and Valance had arrived to check it out. Much to their surprise, reported the *Tribune* in the days following, they discovered much more than the usual amount of suspicious activity these calls tended to yield. They uncovered a whole gory operation that would ultimately pull back the veil on the long-running sham that was the Treaty of Hornstooth.

The timing of the miscommunicated call had been, unsurprisingly, a solid stroke of luck insofar as a reason why they were there in the first place.

Not a raid. Just a happy accident.

"I was there," Green said.

Namises's eyebrows shot up. "No shit?"

"No shit."

The shifter stared vaguely at the bustle around the church entrance. "I remember reading about it, but I didn't remember the officers' names. Who else was there?"

"Valance—she works on the Alpha 300s now—and Bannockburn."

"Bannockburn was there?" Now he sounded truly incredulous, and Green could hardly blame him. Being associated with something that high-profile was usually a dead end to any dreams of promotion. But not this time. Chief Spinner had taken a liking to the whole ordeal—after remaining mute on it for a solid week until the court of public opinion passed a favorable judgment—and touted it as an act of valor.

The only reason Bannockburn wasn't currently an assistant chief himself was that he didn't want the position. The sergeant was as high as he desired to climb.

"Who else?" Namises asked.

"Detective Felps was there at the end, along with Sergeant Montoya. He's a commander now. They showed up at the end."

"So, it was… just three of you against a dozen vampires?"

"More than a dozen. Plus, the leprechauns. And a magician dropped in with pretty good timing."

"But how…?"

"We got lucky."

Because Namises was such an attentive audience, Green kept going, starting with the leprechaun curse and continuing from there. He'd relayed these facts as needed on a few occasions, but he'd never *told the story*. This wasn't an official account. This wasn't a deposition. This was, finally, just a way to pass the time.

He was wrapping up when Robbery Detective Aliyah Brooks approached them. "Well, if it isn't Officer Shit Magnet."

Green, still chuckling with Namises, looked up. There was nothing he didn't like about Aliyah Brooks's face. He enjoyed himself every time he got to look at it. Perhaps it came down to a simple matter of its symmetry or her sharp but not unfriendly eyes, but he suspected it had more to do with the way he felt about her as a whole. Never had he felt so favorably about a woman he'd had so many near misses with. "Brooks. I thought I saw you pull up. What's it looking like in there?"

"Robbery-*ish*," she said. "Looks more like mass murder, as homicide keeps proclaiming. They're a little too excited about all this, if you ask me. Whoever caused that mess in the sanctuary might have taken a few things with them on the way out, though. And that's where I come in."

"Like what?"

"Hell if I know. Ornamental coffins? Blood decanters? We won't be able to start anything resembling an inventory until Sergeant Carrera's guys move out of our way."

"Wait," said Green, "isn't Carrera in charge of—"

"Missing persons, yeah. Looks like the intruders dragged some little people out of there. Some idiot said it might have been leprechauns." She shook her head. "I swear to God. Why would someone kidnap a bunch of leprechauns from a Draculan church? And why would a bunch of leprechauns even be *in* a Draculan church at this hour anyway?"

"Wouldn't be the first time we caught them hanging around vampires."

She braced her hands on her hips and sighed. "True enough. I guess they could be cooking up some more of that purple shit, but nothing else points to it. Can you imagine trying to drag a leprechaun anywhere against their will? You'll get a shillelagh up the ass just as soon as get cursed." She paused. "Ah, well, I guess I don't have to tell you that. Nah, I think someone came in and dragged out some children." She sniffed the air. "Elephant?"

Namises nodded. "Panther?"

"Sure thing. You're Fang 900s, right?"

"Yep. Fang 9-02."

She grinned. "No shit? That was my old call sign!"

"Wait," Green said, breaking up the quick-start friendship between the other two. "Go back to the part about children being kidnapped."

Her grin wilted. "What about it? It's nothing for Robbery to handle. There were some footprints through the blood, some dragging, you know, all that shit."

"Jesus," Green muttered. "No idea whose kids they might be?"

Brooks sounded uncharacteristically disinterested as she said, "Not a clue. All the witness said was that they were *not* baby vamps. Not pale enough, I guess."

"There's a witness?"

She rolled her eyes. "*Sort of*. It's a ghost. Lives in one of the old houses." She nodded across the street. "It's like getting blood from a stone, though. Her grudges run deep. She's demanding the department mete out retribution against all kinds of enemies before she spills what she knows."

Green leaned forward, making sure no one outside of their little triangle would hear him. "Does this seem a little familiar? Vampires possibly holding on to young people who are *not* vampires?"

"If you're talking about the wolfenvamps," she replied casually, "yeah, it sounds like that. Except there's no lab to be found there. And, really, so what if it is? You gonna bust in and expose it? Show the world, *yet again*, just how much vampires can get away with? Everyone's been outraged about that shit for four straight years. Finding more wolfenvamps might not even make the local news."

"Damn," said Namises, "she's not here to play, is she?"

Brooks flashed an unapologetic grin. "Playtime's over, I guess."

Green's mind, however, was on a new concern. Things *had* changed in the last four years. The public's tolerance for absolute nonsense on the part of vampires and werewolves, including brutal and brazen murder, was higher than it'd ever been in modern times. Only two days ago, this wouldn't have bothered him. But his situation had changed.

"Brooks, you got a second?" He pulled her aside, unsure why this, of all topics, left him feeling embarrassed to discuss in front of Namises.

They stopped a few parking spaces over. "What's up?" she asked.

"My little sister Kim showed up on my doorstep yesterday. She ran away from home, and now she's staying with me. She's fourteen."

Brooks failed to stifle her chuckle completely, and he didn't miss the way she had to bite her lip to keep from grinning. "Poor girl, if you're her only option."

"I'm well aware," he said. "Listen, she's a shifter, Aliyah. I don't know if my mom cheated on my dad or if it's just a recessive gene thing. But she shifted by accident, and my absolute piece of shit older brother ratted her out, and now she can't go home."

A softness appeared on that face he liked so much. "Aw, damn. That's rough. What're you gonna do?"

"I don't have a clue, obviously. But I'm wondering if maybe *you* could talk to her. You've been a teenage girl going through her first shifts. I—I don't have the faintest idea how to talk to her about that."

Brooks nodded. "Yeah, I can do that. Just let me know when."

He grabbed her shoulders but refrained from hugging her. "Thank you."

"In the meantime, leave some towels around your place, and make it look accidental. There's a good chance she'll shift a few times without meaning to, and she'll want to cover up quick."

"Yes!" He shook his finger at her. "That's the kind of pro tip I need!"

From across the parking lot, Ridley's voice cut unceremoniously through the general murmur: "Whatever bristle-haired mongrels did this to these elegant and brave vampires, they're going to pay for it!"

Green cringed. "That's my cue. I'd better subdue him."

Brooks glared at the rookie across the way. "Yeah, you'd better."

CHAPTER TEN_

The dining room of El Barrio del Burrito was way too colorful for Green's liking, but he put up with it to enjoy the delicious food that was half bacon fat, half horse tranquilizer, if his body's response to it told him anything. The offering there was, in short, culinary perfection. It was a drug that wouldn't show up on any blood test, except for one measuring cholesterol.

He tried not to stare over Namises's shoulder at the booth two down from theirs, where Brooks and Kim were chatting away animatedly. He'd invited Aliyah here expressly so that he didn't have to talk about teenage girl stuff, yet here he was trying to listen in.

Namises sipped his beer and waved a hand in front of Green's face. "Hey, I'm sure she's in good hands. From what you've told me, there's nothing Brooks could say that would be more damaging than what your parents have already said to her."

Green looked down at his plate to realize he'd already

eaten half of his enchiladas without remembering any of it. Damn. He really *was* distracted.

With his mouth full of food, he said, "Do you think there's any point to all this? To what we're doing?"

"How do you mean?"

"It doesn't seem like we're stopping all that much crime anymore, at least not the big stuff, and once we hand off the people we round up, it's rare that anything resembling justice is served. The vampires have old money step in on their behalf, and the werewolves have the politicians get them off the hook. Meanwhile, some meth-dealing shifter gets fifteen years."

"As he should. I don't mean to sound like a half-assed PSA, but meth is bad, Green. Cutting and selling it to addicts is predatory."

"Okay, fine. I guess it's not the punishment for the dealers I have a problem with. It's the lack of punishment for the others."

Namises sipped his imported beer. "Listen, I get it. But I think you're losing perspective. The bad calls, like the one at the Draculan church last week, we still only hit those maybe one out of every fifty or a hundred calls. Sure, that's *way* too often for my liking, but you gotta look at everything else we do. The victims we help. We get to be there for them in the worst moments of their lives; we get to step up and make a difference for them. Might sound weird, but I feel dang lucky to get to do this job. Let the upper echelons of society duke it out. Someone's gotta take care of the rest of us, and the rest of us is *most of us*."

Green smoothed out the surface of his refried beans with the back of his fork, treating it as his own personal gastrointestinal nightmare of a Zen garden. "I know you got a point, but I just don't know how to keep myself believing it, day in and day out. It's easy to forget about the smaller calls."

"Now, I don't mean to make assumptions about your friend Valance—"

"Not my friend."

"—but it sounds like she's got you mixed up. The calls that count the most are the smaller ones—the brave woman who calls in her boyfriend's abuse, the family who comes home to find someone's burglarized their home and desecrated the space they thought was safe, the overwhelmed mother whose car breaks down on the side of the road. Those are the calls where you change hearts and minds and where you make a difference. It's not the raids and the bloodbaths. That's just what they want you to believe."

"What *who* wants me to believe?"

"The folks who call us heroes so that they don't feel so bad playing fast and loose with our lives. Come on, Green. It's a well-known fact that people only ever deem a group 'heroes' when they need them as disposable pawns. Helps the 'she didn't die in vain' narrative go down smoothly."

Green narrowed his eyes. "Are you a conspiracy theorist? I wouldn't have pegged you for it."

Namises held up his hands. "No conspiracies. I've just been paying attention for a very long time. The bullshit wears thin when you do that."

"Whatever you say."

"You're a good cop, Green, and not because you have a good heart or whatever other poetic nonsense. You're a good cop because you'll take a stand against power when it's back on its bullshit. But more than that, you're not afraid to question the morality of your own actions. So, on the one hand, I'm glad to hear you're questioning if this job is worth it, but at the same time, I'd hate to see the Force lose someone like you. Too many conscientious cops leave because of what you're feeling, and you can guess what kind of folks take their place."

"People like Valance," Green grumbled.

"Valance? No. We'd be lucky to have more people like her. Yeah, she's crazy, but you can't say her actions haven't protected the public."

"I can. Her actions destroyed the Treaty of Hornstooth."

"If you say so. But she also made damn sure that bigtime leprechaun drug op got taken care of, and as you tell it, she kept vampires from making wolfenvamps. And she did it at great personal risk. She saw something was wrong and she went to fix it. Nah, I'm talking about the cops who see the stuff that's wrong and say, 'It's not my job' or 'I can't change it,' or worse, who see that it benefits them one way or another and turn a blind eye to it. Cops like Ridley. I'm sure you can think of a few more."

Green could without much effort.

"So, you're saying I need to stick around, even while this bloodbath continues."

"Especially while this bloodbath continues. Besides, what the hell else you gonna do?"

Green chuckled. His dream of being a janitor had disappeared long ago when he realized he was already a janitor in so many ways. But financially compensated better. "Nothing, I guess."

Namises tipped his longneck toward Green. "Exactly. This kind of violence touches every part of society eventually. You can't escape it. Might as well do what you can to protect a few people from it."

Kim's sweet, innocent voice rose in a peal of laughter, and Green's attention returned to her. Could he protect *her*, though? A young shifter in a violent city?

Namises interrupted his disturbing thoughts. "You're doing exactly what you're supposed to be doing."

"Huh?"

"You're taking her out, introducing her to the right people, getting her set up on the right track. You're doing all you can."

The waitress dropped off their check, and Green caught her before she walked away. "Actually, *they're* getting our check." He pointed to his sister's booth. The waitress looked over briefly, and when she returned her attention to him, it was clear that she was uncomfortable. But she went over anyway.

Namises glared at Green. "You're making Brooks pick up the tab? I take back all that stuff I said about you being an okay person."

"No, not Brooks. Valance." Green caught Kim's eye and gave her a stern look, warning her against reneging on their agreement—she could keep the rest of the cash if she paid for this one. Considering Valance had shelled out over a grand to his sister, he felt no remorse. This counted as teaching her about finances. The way they *really* worked.

"Why would Valance—" began Namises, but Green cut him off.

"The psycho is rich. Immorally rich. It's a long story that involves a riverboat casino and a few well-timed stock purchases." He sighed and shoveled rice into his mouth. "And yet she's still a cop."

Namises shrugged. "Sounds like she's found something to stay on for."

Green's mind traveled back to her request. She wanted him to join Vice. Why? There had to be a specific reason.

He finished off the last of his beer. "Let's hope to God that's not true."

CHAPTER ELEVEN

"Barricaded subject at the MacDougall's," Green announced from the passenger seat. "Might be a good one to jump on."

By "good one," he meant, *We might as well do it now, under my close watch, rather than letting you into a clusterfuck like this a few months from now when the other officers don't feel they have the authority to tell you to back the fuck off.*

"Let's do it," Ridley said. He reached for the button to the lights, but Green knocked his hand away.

"It's not an emergency. There are already a few officers on scene. We're mostly going to watch."

The vampire shot him a scathing look, and a moment later, he said, "Dispatcher just said it's escalated," and hit the button for the lights.

Green saw no such call text on the Human Accessible Monitor, and since he was impermeable to the telepaths, he had to either take Ridley's word for it or call him a liar.

There were three MacDougall's in Fang, but this one tended to require the most law enforcement to keep it from burning to the ground. It was the same location where

Green and Valance had arrested the protesting cow-shifter who was laying patties all over the dining room in protest.

Green counted five police vehicles in the lot when they pulled up. None had their lights on.

Through the windows, he spotted a cluster of late-night diners packed into the booths on the side of the dining room farthest from the restrooms. He appreciated their determination to gorge on pseudo-food despite the police confrontation happening only yards away.

As Ridley whipped the car around to nab an open parking spot, the swamp across the street caught Green's eye. He tried not to think about what he and Valance and Felps had found in there that night with disgruntled cow-shifter. He had a name for it now: wolfenvamp.

We did what we had to do.

He'd responded to calls at this location countless times in the years since that night in the woods, but he never forgot. And he never felt any better about it.

Only now, he needed to get his head on straight, because the rookie had jumped out of the vehicle with the engine still running and was charging toward the fast-food restaurant.

Green cursed, leaned over, and pulled the keys from the ignition. Then he locked the car behind him and jogged after his ward.

The screaming met his ears before he was even inside the building. Echoing from the women's room in erratic blurts, her demands made little sense at first blush and even less on the second.

Much to Green's annoyance, when he arrived at the start of the hallway leading to the bathrooms, Ridley caught his eye and nodded at him with an air of importance, like they were longtime war buddies with equal experience. The narrow space was crammed with their shift mates who'd been first on scene. Ridley filled him in as if he had arrived more than ten seconds ahead of Green. "Looks like she's refusing to come out. She thinks we're assassins here to kill her, sent by some alien race." The rookie nodded gravely as he spoke, affecting a sagacity that made Green want to punch him in his doughy chin.

Green decided to ignore him. He placed a hand on the shoulder of Officer Rachel Scorpio, an olive-skinned and soft-spoken nightmare who had transferred to the Fang 900s just over a year ago, looking for more action. She glanced over her shoulder and nodded acknowledgment before explaining, "Glitter Starr."

It was all she needed to say. The name was infamous in Fang. You weren't really a Fang sector officer until you'd had one of the many colorful encounters with Glitter Star. The quasi-transient shifter's offense of choice lately had been public nudity. Just last week, she'd jumped onto the hood of a cop car at a red light while completely pantsless. Officer Goforth had gotten an eyeful he'd never forget. And the substation had gotten a story they'd never stop telling.

She was already out of jail again.

Sometimes judges went with the "for fuck's sake" ruling on types like Glitter after they'd seen them for the fiftieth or sixtieth offense. The ruling, in so many words, was simply "Oh, for fuck's sake. Get her out of her. I have a lunch meeting at Coven Kitchen in thirty minutes, and I don't want to be late because of something like this."

But officers had to arrest these types anyway when they went and did things like touching themselves on a city vehicle or locking themselves in a MacDougall's bathroom.

Shankwright County Jail was often the safest place for someone like Glitter when they were in the middle of an episode.

"Oh, lord. Nope. Nope, nope," came a deep voice from somewhere near the bathroom door. Namises emerged from the small crowd a second later and caught Green's eye. "She's flooded the bathroom. We're gonna have to go in soon."

"I'll help," Ridley said, pushing forward through the group before Green could grab him and pull him back.

"You'd better get him on a leash," Namises warned him. "Glitter just said she's on her period."

"Oh, fuck."

Green pushed forward toward the front of the throng and grabbed hold of Ridley's collar just as he caught sight of the water flowing through the gap beneath in the door. It had a distinctly pinkish hue.

He tightened his grip and yanked Ridley away. The rookie glared at him viciously once they were clear of the hallway, but Green didn't miss the slight twitches of his nose; the vampire had caught the scent. "We're here mostly to observe, okay?"

"That's not how this is supposed to go," Ridley snapped, his words coming out petulantly through a sneer. "I'm supposed to be getting in there and doing all the dangerous stuff to get experience."

He wasn't wrong, but Green wasn't willing to risk his career on this call.

Green clenched his jaw to avoid saying what he was dying to say, to put the rookie in his place. But what would that accomplish? Nothing. And once Ridley was out from under Green's protective wing, he would be around blood on virtually a daily basis. Maybe he *should* start getting used to it in small doses. After all, Detective Felps could manage it just fine. Perhaps there was something to exposure…

But this wouldn't be a small dose, and Green knew it. Still, there were plenty of other officers around who might incentivize Ridley's restraint. The hothead wouldn't want to lose his cool in front of so many of his colleagues. The nickname earned from an event like that would stick for a long time.

"You're right," Green said. "You need the experience. Get in there."

Ridley nodded and headed back into the group for the tactical huddle.

A Plexiglas shield arrived, and Green knew what that meant: almost time to break down the door and pin the woman before she could fight back and earn herself further charges. Fast-food bathrooms were, as it turned out, prime real estate for complete mental breakdowns, so this was a well-practiced exercise for any officer who'd been around for more than a year.

Green noticed Namises staring at him.

"What?"

"Nothing, nothing." But the elephant-shifter shook his head.

"What?" Green demanded.

"Nothing. It'll just be interesting to see how this plays out."

A bang of metal like a cannon and the bathroom door swung open.

The real screaming began: "I got AIDS! I'm pregnant! You can't take me! I'll cut you!"

The water flooded down the hall, no longer limited by

the space underneath the door, and a small tidal wave of crimson splashed up against the toes of Green's boots. He cringed and tried to pull his feet out of the way on dumb impulse.

Glitter's words had ceased to be such, and now she sounded more like a feral cat, which made sense, considering she was a cat-shifter. But she didn't shift now. She was in no state to think of it, apparently, as the officers used the shield to pin her to the wall while they disarmed her of the pointy shard of glass she'd secured from the now-broken mirror on the wall. It clattered to the ground, then Officers Scorpio and Singh rushed in on Glitter's flanks and each grabbed hold of an arm. The hysterical suspect was cuffed a moment later, though that didn't take the fight out of her. And it didn't put pants on her, either.

Officers no longer needed for backup cleared out in a hurry once they caught sight of the blood running down her legs.

"Jesus Christ."

"Aw fuck."

"Not again."

To his credit, Ridley stuck around but did not start licking the floor or whatever other nebulous nightmare Green had expected. Did that mean he was free to leave the filthy splash zone as the four remaining officers—Scorpio, Singh, Ridley, and Ptarmigan—carried Glitter out of the restaurant?

He looked around. Namises was no longer loitering and had treated himself to a little fresh air, which settled it for Green. He was only in the way where he was, so he put his back to the fishy metallic smell and made his way over to the manager, sloshing through the pink water and then spreading it over the tile once he was free of the worst of it.

The manager looked to be all of nineteen and should not have been so unfazed by the scene unfolding in his establishment.

Green moved closer.

Oh, the kid was *very* high. Fair enough.

After a quick intro, which hardly seemed to register, Green said, "You probably want to shut down for the night. This is a health hazard if I ever saw one. I'm happy to help move people out if you—"

The screech of a barn cat pulled Green's attention toward the glass doors, and outside he saw Glitter thrashing against the officers attempting to hold her steady. His gut compelled him, and he sprinted toward the fray.

He shoved through one glass door, then the second just as Glitter wrenched free of Ptarmigan's grasp. She transformed her hand into a paw, pulled free of the cuff, and landed a solid swipe of her claws across Ridley's cheek.

Green was still fifteen feet away when the vampire's restraint visibly snapped.

"Stop him!"

But all that did was pull the other officers' attention in the wrong direction, and Ridley sprang, knocking back Scorpio and Singh until he had Glitter all to himself. His fangs burst forth like two deadly drill bits and sank deep into the side of her neck. She hardly managed to cry out before the toxins hit her system, and she went limp in his arms.

Green fired his Taser.

Ridley jerked, arching his back between where the prongs had lodged. A spurt of blood followed the removal of his fangs from Glitter's neck, and he fell awkwardly back onto the cement of the MacDougall's sidewalk.

The clattering of the pulsating charge died off, and Officer Ridley moaned before Scorpio and Ptarmigan were on him.

Glitter lay still on the ground, her head draped back against the curb as Green rushed forward. With her neck bared like that, it was easy to spot a pulse. It was also easy to spot the purple oozing from the two wounds. Well, there was a bright side. The venom had worked like a sedative.

And she was alive. But…

Green knelt over her body and radioed for two ambulances as the other officers piled on top of Ridley to secure him once he returned to his senses. Namises appeared on the other side of Glitter and helped move her to a more comfortable position in the grass.

Only once that was done did Green find the space to breathe and make sense of the jumble of danger that had just transpired. As soon as he was able, he muttered, "Fuck me."

CHAPTER TWELVE_

Since Green was unable to sleep after returning home that morning, he packed Kim's lunch for her first day at her new school. Getting Kim enrolled had been a nightmare that involved securing documentation from his mother for a child she claimed not to know. As a result, the process had dragged out for days longer than it should have.

Leaving Kim home alone each night while he was at work left him itchy and anxious, but what else was there to do? She had nowhere else to go, and while he had enough money socked away to afford the two-bedroom apartment down the breezeway when it opened up in the next few days, he didn't have enough socked away to become a stay-at-home brother.

As he packed her brown bag lunch, he could hear her clunking around in the bathroom. Did she wear makeup?

She'd made it plain that school was something he was inflicting upon her. How dare he not let her be a middle school dropout?

He didn't buy it, though. For one, the transcripts from

her previous school indicated that she was a stellar student. But it also made no sense why anyone would want to spend their days cooped up in his dingy apartment when they could be around people their own age. She'd probably like being surrounded by other paranormals. Though, honestly, he didn't care much one way or another how she felt about it. She was going. There would be adults there, real ones, and they could keep her safe while he slept each day.

She hardly spoke once leaving the bathroom (no makeup as far as he could tell), but she pushed past him and helped herself to some coffee in his to-go thermos before making to catch the bus. He stopped her just as she reached the front door. "You want me to walk down there with you?"

Her mouth fell open as she gasped. The horror was unmistakable.

"What?" he said. "I'm pretty cool. I'm a cop."

She squinted at him, the corners of her mouth pulling downward. "Exactly."

He waited thirty seconds and then went to the top of the stairs and kept an eye on her until she was on the bus.

And then his mind turned to the Internal Affairs interview.

Only as he was driving to work did he wonder, *Did I put any meat on her sandwich?* He was fairly sure he had not, which meant that on her first day at her new school, where she knew no one, she would be enjoying a cheese, lettuce, and mayo sandwich. He couldn't blame her for blaming *him* if her first day sucked.

But by the time he found himself sitting across the table from Detective Felps while sucking down his—fifth? eighth? —cup of coffee, Kim's sack lunch occupied no real estate in his brain.

When Green arrived at the Main and learned that Jason Felps was the IA detective assigned to Ridley's case, he almost couldn't believe it. Would this help or hurt his chances?

Felps would understand Ridley's plight of being a vampire in a job where their main food source was always splashing around. He might commiserate on the level of self-restraint it took to keep from draining people.

Fuck if Green knew anything about that, though. Maybe it wasn't as hard as Ridley made it look.

And Green didn't much care what happened to the rookie. Or rather, he didn't care if anything bad befell the asshole.

What he was most concerned about was that he would be speaking to a vampire detective after having tased not only his fellow officer, but a vampire at that.

At least I didn't stake him.

Then there were all the layers of history between him and Felps. It was not unlike having an abusive ex in common. Both had been manipulated by Valance, enlisted as sidekicks on her crusades. And one unspoken result of it was that Green had dirt on Felps. He'd watched Felps murder a clown that they'd disposed of in the swamp and failed to report. And even more damning was the fact that Felps had staked Melvin Brown in that same swamp, and hidden the evidence of *that* as well. A clown was one thing; a missing child was another entirely.

Valance's talent at making people complicit in her crimes was unrivaled, and both Green and Felps had been marked by it. It united them in mutual assured destruction.

"Looks like you missed out on your beauty sleep," Felps

quipped, kicking off with small talk after meeting Green in the hallway.

"Sure enough. Worked late, then my sister just started school today, so I wanted to see her off."

"Oh yeah, I heard you'd taken her in." He motioned to an open door, and Green walked into the cramped and undistinguished office ahead of him.

"You heard from who?"

"I'm IA. I hear everything from no one." Felps grinned and nodded toward the two empty seats at a small folding table.

Once they were seated, Felps opened the beige folder on the table in front of him. Inside was a stack of pink, green, and white papers beneath a scattering of evidence photos. Green's eyes locked on to the close-up of Glitter Starr's neck. He'd taken that picture himself.

Then the detective reached in his bag and pulled out a small silver device. Green had seen his fair share of these on tables in his career.

Felps pressed *Record*. "Okay, let's dive into it. I'm Detective Jason Felps with Internal Affairs speaking with Sr. Officer Norman Green from the Fang 900s…" He continued on with the date and case number as Green inspected the rest of the visible photos.

And then the interview began.

"Please, Officer Green, would you explain what happened last night at the MacDougall's on Trinity Street?"

And so, he did. He explained it from the start. He explained his hesitancy to let the rookie in on the action and why he ultimately decided it would be best if Ridley got firsthand experience in this sort of situation.

"And in the moments leading up to the biting, you were inside?"

This was the part Green had dreaded. He should have kept eyes on Ridley. Why hadn't he?

"Yes. I saw that Officer Ridley was surrounded by other seasoned officers, and rather than getting in the way, I made contact with the manager regarding health concerns involving the copious amounts of Miss Starr's blood on the floor."

"And walls," Felps added, looking down at his notes. "It looks like she smeared it all over the walls inside the bathroom, too."

"Ah. I wasn't aware."

"I wish I wasn't, to be quite honest." Felps paused. "Anything else?"

"I'd like to go on record mentioning the numerous reports I filed prior to this incident with my concerns regarding Ridley's ability to do this job properly. As I've stated before, I believe he's a threat to public safety, and more so when he's wearing a uniform."

Felps nodded. "I do see all those reports here, and they'll be taken into consideration. Anything else?"

Please don't fire me?

"No."

"Okay, then I'll end this interview at…"

Green's mind spun out as Felps concluded. It had gone by so quickly.

Felps stopped the recording with a tap on the device. "Sweet mother of God. I gotta tell you, Green, Ridley shouldn't have made it through the academy. He shouldn't have even made it through *recruiting*."

"That's what I've been saying! And now I'm going to get my ass handed to me because I couldn't control him."

"No, no, no," Felps said, waving a hand. "Ridley is suspended starting today, but you won't be. You'll be fine. I'll make sure of it."

Green paused. That sounded like a favor. Was this about their mutually assured destruction? "You'll make sure of it?"

"Yeah." Felps swept his hand at the papers in front of him. "Ridley was getting disciplined for impulsive behavior and creaturist language all through the academy. Unfortunately, the car dealership KPD contracts with for its vehicles? His sire owns it. I imagine that's the only reason he got through recruiting. He'd drained, like, five people before entering the academy. Allegedly, at least. It's a mess. I won't let him take a good cop down with him. We need all we can get."

Green nodded, trying not to show his horror at the information he'd just heard. "It's nice to know I was fighting a losing battle."

"And you were doing pretty damn well with it, too. I remember hearing about Ridley his first day in and thinking he wouldn't make it a day out on the streets. We've been keeping an eye on him, obviously, but you know how it is. The stack of papers has to be taller than the man before we can let him go without the union coming after us."

"Happy to have made my small contribution to the stack, then."

Felps nodded and shuffled the papers into a neat pile before closing the folder. "You been thinking about promoting?"

"No."

"You should think about it. You're good on the streets, *and* you have a head on your shoulders. You'd make one hell of a detective."

"That's what I've heard."

Felps chuckled. "Ah, yeah, I'm sure you hear it from everyone. You're at four years, right?"

"Just around there."

"That'll do it. So, are you? Planning on testing, that is."

"I like being on the streets."

"Hey, I get it. I pick up patrol OT whenever I can to get out from behind the desk. That's something you can do when you're jonesing for it. But being a detective means you get to make sure the important cases are followed up on, make it so the DA has no choice but to put the scumbags behind bars for a long time."

"Is that why you moved from Homicide to Internal Affairs?"

It was intended as a jab, but the vampire clearly didn't take it as such. "There are scumbags everywhere. Even in the department, as we just discussed. I don't favor one type over the next, frankly. You know, if you really like staying on the streets, you might consider something like Vice. Organized Crime could use a heart of gold like yours."

Green froze as a little alarm rang in the back of his head. *Was* it paranoia? Had he developed it as his sixth sense? "Why did you say that?"

Felps tucked the folder into the leather messenger bag by his chair and stood. "Say what?"

"Vice. Why did you say I should consider Vice?"

Felps blinked. "Because you said you like being on the street, and they do undercover work, so you could still be in the action while working at a higher level… Why do you look like that?"

Green realized then that he was glaring and tried to pull back. "It's just that you're not the first person who's told me I should consider Vice."

"Then maybe that's a sign you'd be good there. Who else suggested it?"

"Valance."

A moment of silence, then it seemed to click, and Felps tilted his head back with a drawn-out "Aaaahh" before adding, "Okay, now I understand why you looked like that. I promise you that Valance and I are not coming from the same place when we suggest that to you. I don't know *where* she's coming from; I just know it can't possibly be the same place I'm coming from."

"I hear you." Green forced his hackles down. "To be honest, Vice does sound kind of fun."

"Not kind of. *Super*. I worked it for two years before Homicide. Got to infiltrate a high-society vampire nest. They let you do *anything* you need to do to maintain your cover." Felps's accompanying grin spoke of some illegal-ass shit. And maybe some immoral-ass shit, too. "Anyway, you'd be good wherever you ended up. But I do think you should test. You can always turn down the promotion when it comes along. But it gives you solid options. And in this line of work, those aren't always easy to come by."

Green nodded. "Fair point. I'll think about it."

"And it doesn't have to be Vice."

"Right."

"Don't go creating a conspiracy just because both Valance and I mentioned it."

"I'm not the conspiracy theorist." But it hadn't just been

Felps and Valance now, had it? The numbers were stacking up.

Felps laughed. "Touché." He led the way to the door and held it open. "Is there a term for a conspiracy theorist who's always right?" He paused. "Ah, well, doesn't matter. Just something I've wondered on and off for years now." He clapped Green on the back. "Enjoy your freedom without Ridley."

CHAPTER THIRTEEN

Three of the roommates, all werewolves, had been slashed to bits in a way only vampire talons could accomplish, and the fourth, a human, lay drained on the floor next to the others. Green had taken the check-welfare call first, which meant he'd had the honor of finding the patio's sliding glass door ajar and discovering the bodies inside.

He wished he could have felt something akin to shock, but a part of him had known what awaited him the moment he read the call text on the HAM. This was the world now. This was Kilhaven, post-Hornstooth. Add these deaths to the pile. The officers in Fang were averaging about one murder call a month each. But he'd heard it was worse in Ecto, where a prominent vampire neighborhood butted up against a middle-class werewolf subdivision.

As he finished up his preliminary report to pass along to Homicide, rather perversely, his stomach growled. He checked the clock on the dash. Just after one a.m. Not too early to take his lunch break.

Inexplicably, his mind jumped first to Roman's Ramen. It

was just a seven-minute drive away, toward the edge of Claw sector. He hadn't been there in years, though, because there was no reason for him to. It was a werewolf place, and he wouldn't be welcome without the appropriate chaperone. But ramen did sound good. He must have sweated out a quart of water under his uniform already—it was another one of Kilhaven's infamously humid nights, and the heat from the day's sun was in no hurry to escape into the atmosphere. Hell, he might drink salt water straight at this point just to refuel. Throw a little sesame oil in there, maybe some fish sauce…

There was a pho place not far off, just a block outside of sector. That would do.

He was just about to leave Fang and cross over into Ecto when a call appeared on the screen. It was right next to him, across the dividing line. He was practically on top of it.

Damn.

Stolen vehicle. His finger hovered over the HAM as an ethical debate raged inside him. On the one hand, it wasn't urgent. But on the other hand, no other units were anywhere nearby, and he was right there. Maybe he could wrap it up quick, knock it off the growing list of holding calls.

Then he realized what establishment that address belonged to. It wasn't a residence of any sort.

Eden Men's Club.

He paused. The cherub-run place *never* called the cops. Or almost never. He *had* responded to one particularly memorable call where three leprechauns busted down the door of the covert game room and shot up the place.

A phantom whiff of blood and shit filled his nostrils as the memory came back to him. He'd packed one cherub so full of gauze that if the victim had managed to survive, he'd be tasting that stuff for years.

But a stolen vehicle?

He was officially intrigued. The cherubim mafia had called in… an auto theft? No, it didn't make sense. Something was up. He assigned to the call, then requested a backup unit.

The warehouse with its poorly lit Grecian facade appeared ahead, and he pulled into the dark parking lot. It was packed, so he ran a few plates for the hell of it, found one with felony warrants attached, and double-parked behind it.

Dinner would have to wait.

He looked around for the caller, but the lot was empty, so he snaked through some of the cars, his flashlight out. Not a single person sitting in their vehicle. But then again, if it was an auto theft, that meant someone would be *without* a vehicle to sit in.

You really are *detective material, genius.*

It was strange, though, that at a place like this, no one would be outside. Most petty criminals knew better than to run their hustles *inside* a mafia-run establishment, which meant the side action would have to take place in the parking lot. But there was no one here.

Maybe the cherubim have cleaned up their act. He chuckled at the thought. Yeah, the Greek mafia had a change of heart about illegal gambling and was running this as a legitimate business now.

And vampires could now be trusted within two hundred yards of a school.

He glanced toward the entrance. He could knock, but that would most definitely fall under the header of "initiating unnecessary contact." Maybe once his backup arrived, he could consider it.

For now, there was nothing to it but to return to his vehicle, look up the caller's information, and give a call back.

But as he crossed between the rows, the front door opened, sending a rush of jazz music and warm orange light his way.

"Officer?" came a voice, presumably from the silhouette in the doorway.

The cherub hovered a few feet in the air, his wings beating like a hummingbird's to keep the chubbiness aloft.

"Yeah, did you call in the stolen vehicle?" Green approached the front door.

"Yes. Would you come in?"

Green's eyebrows shot up. When was the last time law enforcement had been *invited* inside this place? He felt no fear about it, though, just good luck, like he'd been chosen.

Maybe I would *be good on Vice. No one suspects a human to be up to anything.*

Before he entered, the man at the door, dressed in an adorable little navy-blue suit, stopped him. "You requested backup. Call it off."

Green thought he'd misheard. "Pardon?"

"I'd like to speak to you, and you alone."

Some frenetic energy awoke just behind his sternum. Excitement, perhaps? It probably should have been fear, but it wasn't. He grabbed his shoulder radio. "Fang 9-07, cancel that request for backup."

The lobby of Eden Men's Club looked much like it had before, though there were far fewer bullet holes in everything. Expensive leather chairs and hand-carved wooden side tables lined the walls, and directly ahead of him, an ornate marble desk with a Rubenesque female cherub sitting behind it. Only lamplight lit the space, giving it a sensual feel that made Green keenly aware of how all the waiting clientele were men.

"Hestia, hold my calls," the well-dressed cherub said to the receptionist before leading Green past the waiting clients and through an oaken door. The last time he'd been here, this hallway had led to the slot machines, but he didn't see anything indicating that was still the case. Maybe they really *had* done away with the game room, which raised the question of what illegal trade kept the money flowing.

"Marcos Ambrosia. I run this place."

"Officer Norman Green."

The cherub opened a door off the hall, holding it for his guest to enter. "I know." He waved Green inside.

A woman, not cherub but something wingless and humanlike, was already in the room, lounging on a couch and staring at her cell phone. A full plate of nuts, cheese, and meat sat on a glass table that ran the length of the couch, and when they entered, she froze, a bite pinched between her fingers on her way to bringing it to her lips.

"Give us a minute," Marcos barked.

She pressed her lips together in agitation, but got up, grabbed the board of snacks, and headed for the door.

Green remembered he was hungry as he watched her go.

"Now, you have come for a stolen vehicle call."

"I take it that's not actually why I'm here."

"No, it's not." The cherub motioned to the empty chair in front of a sturdy wooden desk, and Green took a seat while his host settled into another on the other side. It was impossible not to notice that the cherub's wing-back chair was raised like a toddler's high chair. The boost brought him to eye level with Green.

"The cherubim have no side in this war between the werewolves and vampires," Marcos began. "Just as you humans have no side. This is not our war, you and I. But it affects us, doesn't it?"

Green nodded, wondering where in the hell this was going and feeling his heart race with excitement to find out.

Good God, am I an adrenaline junky?

Then an even more disturbing thought:

Am I hoping *for a conspiracy?*

"My people have not been sitting idly by. We've been gathering intelligence. And what we're seeing is... disturbing. We want to trust the police, but we know it would be foolish."

"Then why am I here?"

"Because we believe we can trust *you*."

"Hold on." He clamped his eyes shut for a moment. A conclusion had knocked on his brain, and he let it in. "You put that call out... when you knew I was close? You were cop shopping?"

Marcos smiled. "You know the reputation of Kilhaven's Organized Crime department, don't you?"

Green did. But he still felt the need to defend it. "There are a lot of good detectives there." He thought of Brooks in Robbery, of Felps, who'd been Homicide... maybe a few others he'd had brief encounters with. That was it, though. His defense fell flat.

"Not as many as you'd expect. They're not paid enough, Officer Green. *Others* pay them better. But it's the leadership that's the problem. They kill cases. We've known this for a while. The charges against those leprechauns who slew so many on these very premises four years ago were dropped before they reached the DA. And as we now know, those leprechauns had been working for vampires. You see how this goes?"

Oh my God, it's a conspiracy!

No, calm down. This isn't what you want. Police conspiracies are bad.

Green checked in on what face he was making. His eyes could probably be less wide and full of excitement. He squinted. "I do."

"We're familiar with your career. We've seen your name in the papers. You and an Officer Valance always seem to be where the vampires are while others turn a blind eye. And we need your help."

Green leaned back in his chair. "Listen, wherever this is going, I can already tell it's shaping up to be more of a Valance thing. She's—"

"She's a werewolf. We cannot take her side."

"If you're anti-vampire, then you're already on her side."

The mobster's adorable little nostrils flared. "We will not align ourselves with a werewolf."

"Fine, fine. Align yourselves with a human, then. But I'm not sure what you think I can accomplish for you."

"Like I said, we have information. And we'd like to give it to you." Marcos paused, steepling his little baby sausage fingers. "But we want to make sure you'll do the right thing with it."

"What do you believe is the right thing?"

"Not to let it be quashed this time. *Do* something about it. Correct me if I'm wrong, but you have been a cop with the Kilhaven Police for four years, correct?"

"A little over, but yes."

"Then you've seen things that those with elected power deny existing, haven't you?"

Green's mind sent in the clowns—their sharklike rows of teeth and the lime-green blood that dripped from their eyes when they got excited. Or when you shot them through the head.

He nodded.

"Would you be open to learning about more things that *do not exist*?"

He felt a craving inside him that couldn't be satisfied by a hot bowl of pho. "Sure."

Marcos bowed his head and was silent, giving his desk a strange, altar-like quality with its various trinkets—a gold pen in its holder, a small bronze statue of a minotaur, a rotary telephone, a polished wooden box with a numeric lock holding it shut.

Then the cherub broke the silence. "You are also eligible to test for detective soon, are you not?"

Green groaned. "For fuck's sake. Not you, too."

"If we're going to give you this information, we need you in a position where you can do something about it."

Green held up his hands, his intrigue quickly spoiling. He felt his sense return to him, clarity washing away his mucky desires for the clandestine. "Oh, and let me guess, you need me specifically in Vice."

Marcos cocked his head to the side. "How did you know?"

Green placed his palms flat on the edge of the desk, leaning forward. "Sorry, but you're not the first person who's suggested it to me. Not even this week."

The cherub's brows pinched together. "Really? Who else?"

"Valance, for one." He delighted in Marcos's obvious sign of shock. "Yeah. And a *vampire*, too. Ha! Can you believe it? You don't want to pick a side, so you wrangle a human to do your bidding, but the thing you want me to do is the same thing a vampire and werewolf have also told me to do." He stood and waved it all off. "No. No way. I almost fell for this, too." He chuckled dryly. "But if there's any reason *not* to do something, having a vampire, a deranged werewolf, and a cherubim mafia boss tell me to do that thing is definitely fucking it. Now, do you need anything else from me, or can I go take my dinner break?"

Less than two minutes later, he was back in his car. He assigned himself to dinner and pulled out of the parking lot of Eden Men's Club, feeling like he'd just dodged a silver bullet.

CHAPTER FOURTEEN_

Green wrapped up his portion of the call, handing the gas station clerk his card and letting him know that he'd be in good hands with Detective Brooks for the remainder of the investigation.

It had been a hell of a week for werewolf and vampire homicides in and out of Fang. Green was both relieved and unable to enjoy this simple armed robbery carried out by a couple of masked anarchist elves.

That was the rub, really. Calls like this, which could easily go wrong but hadn't, had started to bore him. But the calls that excited him, that kept his attention, collected over time inside him like a deadly plaque.

Maybe Bannockburn was right. Maybe Green was burning out. Maybe he *should* test for detective, get off the streets for a while. Not Vice, but something else. Human trafficking, narcotics, or even a community liaison spot.

You would kill yourself if you had to spend every day meeting with busybodies.

More likely, he wouldn't get the chance to kill himself because he would die of boredom first.

He laid his notepad on top of his car to jot down a few last notes from the scene. He'd parked in the fire lane, which was one of the small perks of the job he still very much enjoyed. Besides, Kilhaven was burning itself to the ground, so, in a way, that made him a firefighter. Except, unlike the actual firefighters, he didn't have time to earn his culinary degree during his shifts. Kilhaven could literally be burning to the ground, and the red curb of the fire lane would remain either unoccupied or occupied by a police vehicle. At least until the firefighters could pull their flaky pies out of the oven, hang up their aprons, and get their ass dressed for their one job.

He blinked, looked down at his pad, realized he'd written *firepie*, and scribbled it out. It was nearing the end of his shift, and his brain was officially mush. He checked his watch. Just before six a.m. Sun would be coming up soon, which meant it was almost time for him to get poor sleep in his apartment while Kim banged around in preparation for the school day, and the daylight managed to invade his bedroom despite the blackout curtains.

A big white whale caught his attention by the gas pump. No, not a whale, a van. And in it, four rows of seats were packed with teenagers not much older than Kim. One had brought a pillow with her and used it to cushion her head against the window, while around her the morning people chatted animatedly.

Most of the windows—the kind that budged an inch at the bottom, and that was it—were open, and a strong breeze was enough for him to pick up the scent. Werewolves.

Maybe a shifter or two? But definitely young weres. He suddenly found himself longing for his teen years. They hadn't been easy, but they were easier than this. The oblivion of it all was truly a gift. If only he'd known how much worse it could get. Adults had seen him struggling now and again and told him not to worry, that life got better. What kind of help was that? If only someone had said, *"Yeah, this is about as good as it gets, so maybe just enjoy what you can,"* that would have been some truth he might have used.

The driver's seat of the van was empty, but he caught sight of some movement behind the gas pump. Good on whoever was brave enough to cart around that many teenagers.

Green finished his notes, opened his door, and flopped into the driver's seat. It was somewhat astounding that in all this chaos, with all the killings and threat of violence and lawlessness, something as pure as a group of teens going on a retreat could still happen. Was it a youth group? Debate club? The van was unmarked, likely just a rental for this specific occasion. But regardless of where they were going, the excitement among them was palpable.

He aimed the air vents at his face and turned them on high.

Maybe things "out there" weren't as bleak as he'd begun to believe. After all, he lived in a bubble. Almost every interaction he had with others was amid a crisis. Someone had harmed or stolen from someone else. A victim and a perpetrator, always. *Of course* there were worlds other than his. Maybe the majority of the population still went on with their merry lives without batting an eye at the kind of violence he responded to on a daily basis.

It was a nice idea. It rinsed away the perpetually bitter

taste on his tongue. Maybe the world wasn't so doomed. Maybe it was still functioning much the same as it had. Maybe he and the rest of Kilhaven PD were doing such a stand-up job of it that the rest of the city didn't know the landmine on which they sat. They could remain blissfully ignorant. If the cost of that was his own festering cynicism, he was strangely okay with that. Only an idiot would join the Force looking for happiness or likability.

The driver of the van appeared from behind the pump and headed toward the convenience store.

Green glanced at him, looked back down at his HAM, then did a double take.

The driver was a vampire.

What in the ever-living undead fucking fuck was a vampire doing driving around a van full of young weres and shifters?

His hope for the future popped like a teenage pimple.

Nope, it was *not* right. There was no reason a vampire should be driving around a group like that. It was the disconcerting traffic stop from a few weeks back all over again.

Green stepped out of his vehicle and stepped over to the only patrol cop on this scene he was sure would find this as disturbing as he did.

Ivory Namises was camping in his idling vehicle, his head down, chowing on a home-packed sandwich. Green knocked on the window, and Namises's head jerked up toward the sound. He rolled down the window.

"Wah eh et?" he asked around a mouthful. He had a smear of what looked like mayo across his dark cheek but made no effort to wipe it away.

"Did you see that van?"

Namises's vehicle was ahead of Green's in the fire lane, which put the van in his blind spot. He twisted in his seat with a grunt, caught sight of it, and turned back to Green. "Yeah?"

"It's full of teenage weres and shifters."

"Uh-huh?"

"The driver is a vampire."

Namises's eyes went wide, and he swallowed down his bite in a hurry. "You don't say?"

"I do say. You find that as weird as I do?"

"I sure do."

"Can you press pause on that sandwich?"

Namises looked at it forlornly, but nodded. "Yeah, not like it could get any soggier anyway."

Back in his car again, Green waited until the vampire returned to the van and was nearly out of the parking lot before he began to follow. He glanced in his rearview mirror at Namises pulling out behind him.

The van turned onto the road, and Green gave it a little space. No need to alert this person to anything other than a coincidental police presence. Though the fact that the vampire had even left that many minors unattended at a gas station swarming with police showed a certain sense of disregard for law enforcement. Typical for that kind, really. So often, vampires thought they were above the law... because they were.

Something white on the back window of the van tugged Green's attention. A sticker. It stood out in his headlights against the black tinting, but he wasn't close enough to make it out. A symbol with some letters beneath it. A brand logo? The totally unnecessary identification of one kid's name and the best spot to lure them with? Maybe this wasn't a rental after all.

The game was to wait for any traffic violations, then he'd be able to follow his gut and make a quick check on the situation. He wasn't looking to write a ticket, but he needed to get his foot in the door here.

It wasn't easy at that moment to deny he was biased against vampires. But why wouldn't he be, really? And shouldn't *everyone* be? Copious laws kept them *away* from schools, daycares, and playgrounds without special approval from the Vampire Safety Council. That had to mean something.

The van signaled before changing lanes. Damn. It was heading for the highway. The odds of it doing anything other than cruising on for miles and miles beyond Fang were slim, but he would give it a shot anyway.

As the van accelerated onto the on-ramp, he sped up, closing the distance.

Now that he was closer, the symbol looked like someone had taken a Y and a B and smashed them unceremoniously together. And below it, the word YoungBlood.

"Fang 9-07 to Fang 9-02, any idea what YoungBlood is?"

There was a thick moment of silence, then Namises responded over the radio, "Fang 9-02 to 07. It's a youth organization."

"Religious?"

"Affirmative."

"Which church?"

"Draculan."

"Goddammit." Green didn't say this into his radio, just into his car.

Only three more exits until the van would cross over

into Alpha, and Green would no longer have any solid reason in a report for why he continued to follow the van out of sector.

Give me something. Failure to signal, swerving, anything.

The van exited the highway, and Green followed. Maybe this was it. Turn right, and it was still in Fang, but turn left, and it would be in Alpha as soon as it crossed under the highway.

It turned left through a yellow light.

Damn. He let it go and stopped at the red.

He checked his rearview mirror but couldn't make out Namises's face through the glare of the streetlights off the windshield.

A message came through the HAM, and Green read it off. *For what it's worth, I think it's fishy as hell, too.*

The sentiment wasn't worth much. Not when his gut was telling him more than half a dozen young shifters were in danger he couldn't fathom.

His eyes jumped to the HAM, and he tapped the button to bring up the map. The units were scattered around, some on the move, some stopped in clusters. Above each dot was the identification. He found the one he was looking for. *A305.* She was on the move, just a few blocks away. Had she just started her day shift in Alpha, or had she picked up OT?

If he filled her in on the van, she would follow up. There was no doubt in his mind about it. He wouldn't have to articulate why. She would know...

He pulled up the messaging screen and selected *A305* as the recipient.

The light turned green. He deleted the message and headed back to the substation.

Green was hardly a half-hour into his shift when the priority call popped up on his HAM. Shoot/stab hotshot. Twilight Delta trailer park. Group of shifters fighting.

He felt his heart skip as if he'd just laid eyes on a long-lost love. When was the last time he'd gotten to plow into a good old-fashioned shifter mêlée? He hadn't realized he'd missed it this much.

Lights. Sirens. Go time.

He *bwooped* his way through a busy intersection, relying on his peripheral vision to alert him to any vehicles that might be trying to beat him through, as he checked the new info that popped up on the call log: vic bleeding from the head but conscious.

Probably just a knife, then. Heads were always melodramatic with their bleeding. Didn't take much to prime the pump. There would be blood on everything, then. *Thank God, no Ridley.*

Twilight Delta was almost entirely shifter. Most trailer parks were. But unlike Shady Grove out by the swamps, the residents of Twilight Delta were more than happy to call the cops on each other, even as they themselves engaged in highly illegal behavior.

He checked his monitor, multitasking as he sped down a dark, empty industrial boulevard. He counted ten other units heading toward the call now. Hell yeah. Party time. Chaos that had nothing to do with vampires or werewolves? It wasn't even his birthday!

He pulled up, crushing his giddiness under the heavy burden of professionalism, just as Officer Scorpio was turning in. She'd transferred from Banshee to Fang for more action, and she appeared just as excited about this as he did. Their eyes met. A hungry smile turned the corners of her lips for a mere millisecond as she nodded toward the direction of the fray.

They found the particular spot among the trailers easy enough. String lights wrapped around the boughs of an old oak, illuminating the "yard," where an undulating mass of fists and fur could be both seen and heard at a distance. Fistfights like this usually meant no weapons, so perhaps it wasn't a stab so much as a claw. Either that or everyone involved was family and not actually looking to kill. Each seemed as likely as the next as Green and Scorpio rushed forward.

There had to be close to a dozen involved in the brawl. But to the side of the scuffle, a woman leaned over a bloody-faced man, and she switched between crying over him and hollering at the group fight.

Scorpio had a few paces on Green. "Police," she yelled. Her voice sounded like its own clenched-fist swing, and even over the sound of more sirens on the way, it caught the attention of the multi-person brawl.

Immediately, two of the fighters peeled off. "Stop!" Green shouted.

Unsurprisingly, they didn't listen. Those would be ones with outstanding warrants, no doubt. Or rather, with the *most* outstanding warrants. Those were always the first to split. They knew what was good for them.

Green got within sniffing distance. Definitely shifters. But because they weren't fully shifted, a regular Taser would do just fine, so that was what Green led with.

But Officer Ptarmigan came out of seemingly nowhere and beat him to it.

Only, he didn't opt for the Taser.

The particles of ricocheted pepper spray glittered under the many twinkling lights in the old oak tree, and Green cursed on reflex. Ptarmigan wasn't nearly close enough to the suspects for the jet to be especially effective on them, but he was far enough back to leave Green and Scorpio coughing, ducking, and putting distance between them and the brawl as they attempted to regain control of their breathing.

What exposure the suspects *did* get, though, worked as a wake-up call that, *ding-dong*, the police had arrived. And through teary eyes, the crowd untangled itself quickly and stumbled apart.

Then they began to shift—deer and pumas and hogs and even an alligator. Next, they scattered.

"They jumped him!" yelled the sobbing woman.

Who "they" comprised, though, Green had no idea. Officers were pouring onto the scene now, many already pursuing the suspects on foot into the dark nooks of the trailer park.

Corporal Laura King's voice rang out behind him. "Fang 9-80 to 9-90, requesting supervisor approval to shift."

Green made for the bloody man. The wound was bubbling blood, but he didn't see any brain matter.

Sergeant Bannockburn's voice came through the Fang channel. "Approval granted. Fang 900s may shift to apprehend the suspects."

It was on. Scorpio, who had managed to tackle a puma to the ground before it had taken off, passed the suspect off to the corporal before sticking her cuffs in her teeth and shucking her uniform. In a heartbeat, a gray wolf took off from where she'd just stood.

The corporal hogtied the puma, then did the same. The werewolf disappeared into the darkness at a full sprint.

Green knew his role now as the lone member of the shift who couldn't shift. He was on uniform duty.

But first, he needed to make sure the victim was in stable condition. The woman at his side hadn't taken off, but a part of him wished she had, as she continued to wail. "Ma'am, please just give me a little room."

The man on the ground was still conscious, but now he was shaking. Adrenaline crash or shock?

Someone else knelt beside Green. "Here, man." Namises pulled from his medic's bag a light blue terry cloth rag and soaked up some of the blood, attempting to locate the source.

Damn, it *was* a lot of blood. More than most head wounds, even. Probably had something to do with the dozens of beer cans scattered around the ground. Blood thinner.

"Here," Green said, reaching for the rag. "I got this; you go track them down. You can shift."

Namises pulled the soaked cloth away from Green's grasp. "Nah, they don't need me shifting right now. I got this; you go round up the gear."

It did look like Namises had the medical situation managed, so Green called for an ambulance then did his best to calm the hysterical woman. He ended up sticking her in the back of his car until she could cry herself into a state where she was fit to be interviewed. And while he waited, he used his flashlight to locate the myriad discarded uniforms and duty belts around the area. Next would be the roundup of officers as he helped them get clothed.

Officers continued to trickle onto the scene, ones from the evening shifts that were still on and a few from adjoining sectors. They'd missed the hunt, but they were happy to help pick the carcass clean.

He split the gear with Officer Singh, and after nearly five minutes of struggling to get out around all the vehicles that had blocked him in, Green began the slow process of tracking down stark-naked officers of the law. The recent addition of tracking devices in the cuffs certainly made the process much easier, but when he turned on the map and saw them spread out in every direction, he sighed.

God, how he wished he could be a part of the fun, but he never could be.

And in his rearview mirror, he caught sight of Namises helping the victim sit up and wondered why in the hell *anyone* who could shift wouldn't.

CHAPTER SIXTEEN

The clink and clatter of plastic chopsticks on ceramic bowls had a Pavlovian effect on Green, leaving him both salivating and extremely anxious. It was the orchestra of Roman's Ramen, and he knew it as the background track of conspiracy.

But with no clear conspiracy in mind, he couldn't help but wonder why the sergeant had brought him to this werewolf-owned restaurant.

"I guess we better just cut to it and save you the suspense," Bannockburn said once they'd placed their orders. "Looks like the review process actually worked this time around, and Ridley is out."

"That's good news."

Bannockburn pushed out air and nodded. "Yeah, it is. Seems a little ominous, given the state of the world."

"Like it'll come back to bite us all in the ass?"

"Exactly. The union will fight it because they have to, but I was talking to the vice president the other day, and he told me in so many words that they're on our side about Ridley.

At the end of the day, they know their ass is on the line if they protect rotten people like him. Loses them any credibility at all."

When their ramen arrived, each tended to it quietly, adding in the fixings and sauces ritualistically. It was Bannockburn who broke the silence. "What do you think of Rodney?"

"Who?"

"Rodney Namises."

"Oh! Ivory? He seems solid."

The sergeant nodded thoughtfully. "Yeah, he sure does."

If ever there was a time to ask this question, now, in the bubble of confidentiality the booth provided, seemed it. "Last week, at Twilight Delta, he didn't shift. I've never seen a shifter or were not shift when they got permission."

"And?"

"And what do you think that was about?"

Bannockburn looked up from his ramen. "You know what he shifts to, right? You think a big fucking bull elephant stampeding through a trailer park could ever, in any universe, be called 'de-escalation'?"

"Well, shit. I guess you got a point."

"Course I do."

Green wished achingly that he'd spent a little more time considering the question before opening his idiot mouth.

He opened his idiot mouth again, this time to shove in a sloppy mass of noodles. As his thoughts lingered on Namises, another recent call came to mind. "Hey, can I ask you something as, uh, *not* my sergeant?"

Bannockburn glanced at Green over his chopsticks, from which noodles quivered, stopped suddenly in their tracks on their way toward the sergeant's mouth. They slipped back into the bowl. "Go ahead."

"I was at a burglary call the other night at a gas station, and as it was wrapping, I saw this van full of teenage shifters..." He continued on, trying his best to highlight the shady bits so that he didn't seem like he was losing his mind and following around a bunch of youth-group teens for no reason.

And it seemed to work. Bannockburn forwent his food for the duration of the tale and kept his eyes glued to Green, though his expression didn't give away much more than attentive listening. That was something. A part of Green had expected to have his concerns dismissed right away.

But then again, this was Bruce Bannockburn, one of the sundry survivors of Heather Valance's psychological torture harem. In short, the sergeant's mind was clearly open to latching on to a solid hunch.

Green finished by mentioning the call weeks before that he'd taken with Officer Ridley, where they'd pulled over the vampire with the werewolf teen in the back seat. That hadn't sat well, either, and while two dots formed a line, not a pattern, waiting for the third to show up wasn't ideal either, if his suspicions of nefarious goings-on were correct.

"So, I dunno. I know it doesn't seem like much on the outside, but it sure doesn't seem like *nothing*, right?"

Bannockburn didn't respond right away, but it was clear his mind was active behind those dark brown eyes.

Finally, he said, "I don't think there's anything there, Green. I can see how you would, and I don't think you're crazy for thinking it, but I just don't see it."

The noodles turned to a lead weight in Green's stomach, and he felt shame heat up his cheeks. "Yeah, okay. That's why I ran it by you. I mean, it's just two somewhat similar events, right? Probably nothing. Just a coincidence. But if they *were* something, I'd feel terrible if I missed the signs."

Bannockburn plunged his chopsticks into his bowl again. "Like I said, it's probably nothing. You can let your conscience relax on this one."

Green nodded and was about to let it go, but… "I mean, doesn't it seem a *little* suspect to have a vampire driving around a van full of shifters? What would *ever* necessitate that?"

"You said there was a YoungBlood sticker on the back, right? There's your answer."

And now Green really did want to fall silent, because all the things he had to say about *that* were easily labeled as creaturist. Not that anyone would care if he talked a little shit about vampires in this establishment, but still. The more he let his suspicion of vampires flourish unchecked, the closer he became to being Valance but with a dick.

He stared at the cloudy surface of his soup. *You should embrace what the Draculan church is doing. They're uniting species in a divided world. That should bring you hope, you cynical fucking idiot.*

"However," Bannockburn said minutes later as if no time had passed, "if it doesn't sit well with you that the Draculan Church is putting vampires in charge of young shifters' and werewolves' religious education through the YoungBlood organization, there are legitimate ways to check in on that. Someone's gotta keep an eye on churches, since they do a piss-poor job of that themselves."

"What do you mean, legitimate ways?"

"It sounds like an operation that Vice might put

together." Bannockburn's eyebrows were near his hairline now, and he stared unblinkingly across the table at Green.

Vice? This shit again? Then the pieces clicked together: *You slow fuck, Norman.*

"Right. Vice." Green nodded, hoping Bannockburn would drop him another morsel if he didn't appear too excited that he'd *finally* found the thread.

Vice. The Draculan Church. YoungBlood. What else was connected to it? The massacre at First Draculan? More importantly, what the hell did the thread lead to?

Valance knew about this. Whatever was going on, it was the reason she'd insisted he test and try for Vice. Good chance Felps knew, too, as in-the-know as he was in IA. Did Lawrence? Brooks? Jesus, the *Greeks*?

The fact that none of them would risk saying it outright, that they all felt the need to hint and insinuate, didn't bode well for what Green might be up against.

"I have plenty of connections in Organized Crime," Bannockburn continued. "If you want to ride out with them for a few days, I'd be happy to recommend you and sign off on it."

Green imagined this was what it might feel like to be an archeologist and trip over a stone that turned out to be the tip of an ancient civilization. "Sure," he said, playing it as cool as he could, "I'd be up for riding out with them."

CHAPTER SEVENTEEN

Green's boots squelched on the concrete steps of his apartment building as he lugged his tac bag upstairs. He tried not to grunt with each step, but a muscle around his lower right ribs was screaming at him with every flex of it. Must have tweaked it in the line of duty. Probably while getting in and out of his vehicle or something similarly mundane.

What a hero.

It had rained off and on—mostly on—all night and into the morning. The second to last call he'd taken had required a trek through an overgrown green space to speak to a few homeless people regarding their dogs' recent aggression toward joggers. Nothing spectacular, the kind of tedious, low-key conversation that constituted most of his job, but the trip through the weeds and tall grass in this weather meant there was nothing below his waist that didn't end up soggy. And thanks to the humidity and no chance to change into his spare uniform, he'd stayed that way.

A late domestic disturbance had kept him out past the

end of the shift, and while the OT pay was nice, he could have done without. It was nearly eleven in the morning, and the hot sun made stale water vapors congeal on his skin. He couldn't wait to get inside, drop the bag, and unstick his balls from his inner thighs. But when he opened his front door and felt the air conditioning sweep over him, his moment of relief was short-lived.

The TV was on, and Kim sat on the couch. And next to her...

Green tossed his bag off his shoulder. "Kim!"

"What?"

"Who the hell is this?" He pointed to the boy on the couch.

The boy blinked at him, then looked back to Kim, clearly as astonished as Green was that Kim had not cleared this before inviting him over.

"Relax, Nor. It's just Jesse. He's a friend from school."

"He's a *boy* from school." He scented the air but couldn't get a read on the kid's species over the stifling smell of body spray.

Jesse scooted farther from her on the couch. "Uh, sorry, sir. I thought she'd asked. I thought it was okay."

"It's not!"

Jesse jumped up, his hands in the air. "We weren't doing anything, promise."

"Norman!"

"We were just watching TV. And drinking juice."

Green's eyes jumped to the near-empty glasses of orange juice, and he felt a deep stirring of hatred for this kid who came into *his* home, sat too close on the couch to *his* sister, and drank some of *his* orange juice.

Clearly, the anger wasn't well hidden, because Jesse

grabbed his backpack, mumbled a quick *see-ya later* to Kim, and then scurried toward the door. Green stepped aside to let him pass without taking his eyes off his sister. He stole a closer sniff—shifter of some kind—then closed the door behind him.

"Kim, what the *hell*?"

"Jesus, Norman!" She was on her feet now. "I just told you it was nothing! How can you—"

"No, how can *you*? I'm letting you stay here because you don't have anywhere else to go, but you will *not* get knocked up on my watch."

Her mouth fell open, and he saw the hurt well in her eyes an instant before the tears glimmered there. "We didn't even hold hands! And we never will, because you just ruined *everything*!" She sprinted off to her room and slammed the flimsy door behind her.

His hands on his hips, Green stared at the place the teens had just been. Then a sound from the television drew his gaze, and he turned to the screen. They'd been watching cartoons. On the screen, a strangely proportioned girl was fighting a sharp-toothed and half-shifted werewolf in a series of jagged *bangs* and *pows*. No gore, no cursing.

They were just kids watching cartoons together.

Kim's voice echoed in his mind: *"We didn't even hold hands!"*

He smothered the oncoming rush of shame with anger. This was *his* apartment. He paid rent. He'd stepped up to be responsible for her when he didn't have to. And it wasn't like she was six years old. She was fourteen. God knew he'd encountered his fair share of pregnant fourteen-year-olds on the job. And who the hell was that Jesse kid anyway?

Sneaking around while no adult was at home? Clearly untrustworthy.

He poured himself a tall glass of *his* orange juice, and by the time he was to the bottom of it, the adrenaline was wearing off, and he knew he'd messed up. Kim's sobs were slowly dying down from her bedroom near the kitchen.

He felt a squish, and with utter disappointment in himself, he looked down to realize his slushy boots were still on his feet. He bent down and removed them, peeled off his mushy socks, and tossed each where they belonged. And then he called Aliyah Brooks.

Her singsong country accent greeted him cheerfully, and that only made him feel more ashamed. "Hey, Brooks. I think I screwed up."

A tense silence on the other line, then, "Is it Valance? What'd she make you do this time?"

"Huh? Oh, no, no. I messed this up all on my own. It's Kim. I just came home and found her with a boy on the couch."

Brooks chuckled. "Good for her. Was it another shifter? Did they knot up when you surprised them?"

He pinched the bridge of his nose. "I'm only half sure I know what that means, but I'm one hundred percent sure I don't want you to explain."

"Well, it's just that sometimes when shifter men are having sex—"

"God, no. Please no. And they weren't having sex."

"Ah, handjob?"

"No! Brooks, stop! They weren't even kissing."

"You don't need to kiss during a handjob. Usually better if you don't."

He flopped down on his bed and tried not to raise his

voice and be overheard through the thin walls. "No, you don't understand. They weren't doing anything. They were just sitting there."

A pause, then, "I don't understand the problem."

"She didn't ask me if he could come over first."

"Mm-hm." She sighed. "You raise your voice at her?"

"Yes."

"Scare off the boy?"

"Sure did."

Brooks sighed again, heavier this time. "At least you realize you screwed up. That could have been her only friend at school."

He dragged a hand over his face. "Hadn't thought about that."

"Of course not."

A point like a thumbprint between his eyes started to throb. "I can't do this, Aliyah. I'm just not cut out for raising a teenager. I can hardly remember to feed myself. She needs so much more supervision than I can give her."

"You're probably doing just fine."

"I'm not! I don't know who any of her friends are. I don't even know all the classes she's in or a single one of her teachers' names!"

"You think she'd be better off with your bitch of a mom?"

"No. But there's gotta be somewhere else she can go, someone responsible who knows what it's like to be a shifter. I can't help her with any of that stuff."

"If you're trying to pawn her off on me, save it. Ain't gonna happen. But if you want me to talk— Oop! Hold on, I'm getting another call... Ah, it's her. Kim's calling me. Anything you want me to tell her for you?"

"No. But please don't teach her about handjobs."

Brooks scoffed. "She's fourteen, Green. She knows about handjobs." She switched over, and the line went silent.

He ended the call and was just about to fall asleep again when another person came to mind. He wasn't sure what he hoped to accomplish, but he called up his old friend Sammy Abernathy out in Pan City anyway.

"If it isn't Norman fucking Green calling me up on a beautiful Saturday morning."

Oh, right. It's Saturday. At least they weren't skipping school.

They danced through the greetings of childhood friends who hadn't spoken in a few solid years and then Green dove in with the reason for his call. "It's Kim."

"Your sister?"

"Yep." *Maybe only half-sister.* "She's a shifter." He waited for the sounds of shock at the big reveal, but none came.

"Ah, yeah, I had a feeling."

"You had a feeling?! When?"

"Oh, for a while. But you remember the last time we saw each other, back in Bowers at Harris's funeral? Kim was there. I could just sort of sense it. She wasn't fully human."

Green pressed a palm into the eye where the exhaustion headache was really settling in. "Both of your parents are humans, too. Was your mom... Was she faithful?"

"Dude."

"What? Sorry."

"You know it doesn't have to be like that. Shapeshifting is a recessive gene."

Green didn't know much about genetics, but he did know that. Still, it was hard to believe. "Yeah, I got it. I just... We don't have a single shifter in our family."

"You sure of that? I thought the same thing. Turns out, I

had an aunt *and* an uncle on my mom's side and a great-aunt on my dad's side who were shifters. I just didn't know about them because they split after their first shift and no one ever spoke of them again."

It wasn't a leap to imagine his own family doing the same. His aunt Laurie had used the Lord's name in vain to his mother once, and they hadn't spoken for a year afterward.

"It's gotta be hard, finding out you're a shifter," said Green, "when you're already in your teens." He thought of the way he'd secretly hoped to discover the same thing about himself growing up: to learn that he wasn't just some boring, useless human. But the only changes he'd gone through in those early teen years were acne, nine inches of height, and a deep voice that couldn't be relied upon to stay deep without cracking. Oh, and boners. Boners galore. He supposed that was a *little* like shapeshifting.

His desire to not be human had meant he'd never considered the downside of it much until now.

"It's excruciating," Sammy replied. "Not only are you getting used to your body changing from hormones, but you're also getting used to your body literally changing into an animal. I ever tell you what I shifted into my first time?"

"No, what?"

"Octopus. Big fucking octopus. Shifting into an invertebrate hurts like a motherfucker, let me tell you. All my muscles felt like rubber bands for a week after. The whole thing was a trip."

Green tried not to imagine it. "What do I do with her?"

"What do you mean?"

"My mom kicked her out, man. She's living with me now."

"For Christ's sake, Megan," Sammy said. "Of course your mom did that. She's always had a stick up her ass about paranormals. No offense."

"None taken—she's a bigoted bitch. But that doesn't solve my problem."

"Kim's problem. This is Kim's problem, and it's your job to help her with it."

Green had been fully prepared to continue his pity party for the remainder of the morning, but that stopped him in his tracks. *Dammit.* Finally, he said, "I don't know how to help her. I don't know what to do."

"Cut both of you some slack. I'm not a cop, but I know plenty of them here. If it's half as stressful to be one in Kilhaven as it is in Pan City these days, you gotta adjust your expectations for what you can and can't do. Listen, no matter how awkward you feel talking to her, and no matter how many times you screw up and forget to pick her up from piano practice or whatever, you're still doing more right by her than your mom ever has."

Green sighed, realized he had crawled into bed without having showered, and rolled off his mattress and onto the floor. Yesterday's discarded uniform lay in a lumpy pile beneath him. He racked his brain for the memory of having shucked those clothes but came up empty. The days really did blend together.

"I'm sure you're doing a great job with her, Norman."

He caught a strong whiff of yesterday's boxers. "I'm not," he said. "But I'll try to do better."

CHAPTER EIGHTEEN

Detective Deshawn Tyson relayed a license plate back to the station. *Alpha-8-5 Talon-Yeti-9-Quartz.*

The unmarked slick-tops didn't have a HAM to check it on—one of the many things Green had learned so far this week.

The owner of the plates got out of his sedan and walked into the grocery store as Green and Tyson waited to hear back on any involvement.

They'd posted up in this spot by the back of the massive lot almost an hour ago, ahead of the operation that was supposed to take place. It was day three of Green's ride-out with the narcotics team under Vice, and he was completely sold on the job. He would take the test. He would take all the tests. Whatever he needed to do.

He would miss being on patrol, but... not that much. He'd jumped in on the tail end of the planning for this operation, and the energy around it had charged neurons he thought had long since blinked out of existence. Thankfully, the drug supplier they were trying to nail wasn't peddling that purple shit, the stuff derived from vampire saliva that had swept through Kilhaven a few years back and occasionally made the end users go *boom-splat*. No, this was just heroin they were rooting out, and a good bit of it. High quality, too.

Detective Tyson checked his watch. "Jefferson should arrive anytime now." He grabbed his binoculars from the armrest beside him and aimed them at the rendezvous point: two dumpsters by the side of the grocery store. It was a common spot for low-level dealing, but this was not a low-level operation.

Green grabbed his binoculars, too. Sure enough, not thirty seconds later, he spied Detective Monte Jefferson, dressed in ragged pants, swiss-cheese shoes, and a makeshift poncho, strolling over from down the dark street. Green was the first to spot him, and he felt pretty fucking slick about that.

"I think I just saw movement behind the dumpsters," Tyson announced a moment later. "Probably the hook."

Green nodded. Of course it was the hook. And then the hook would meet Detective Jefferson, who had spent three weeks undercover, establishing himself as a lovable transient junkie just in town from Halcyon Falls, and, if the meeting went well, the hook would lead Jefferson straight to the dealer. Green checked on the white utility van parked at the strip mall across the street.

Once Green and Tyson got a location for the dealer, three tactical units would jump out on whoever had the drugs and see if they could flip him. The kingpin wouldn't be wandering around this neighborhood in the dead of night, selling dime bags, but they would get to him soon. One level at a time. Locate, threaten charges, flip, onto the next. Up and up they went.

"There he is."

Green snapped his attention away from the van, back toward the side of the building. A figure emerged into the halo of the parking lot lights. This would be the hook. They weren't sure who he would be, or at least they hadn't mentioned it in the planning over the last couple of days.

But Green recognized him. Years had passed, but he would remember this asshole until his dying day.

"Holy shit," he said. "That's not B-Rat, is it?"

Tyson looked over at his tagalong. "You two friends?"

"Met him my first week out. He was passed out on the sidewalk with his arms and legs stiff in the air."

Tyson chuckled but said nothing.

There was a smattering of characters across Kilhaven with whom everyone in law enforcement was familiar. Glitter Starr, whom Green had helped extract from the MacDougall's bathroom only a few short weeks ago, was one of them. There was also Scooter Cooter, who had legally changed his name to that from John Westover, and claimed the change had more to do with his being a turtle-shifter than the fact that he liked to yell, "Show me your cooter!" at women downtown. Last time Green had checked, Scooter Cooter had been arrested 249 times, but it was probably closer to three hundred by now.

But Boris Romanov, a.k.a. B-Rat, was not among the famous felons of Kilhaven. He was just your run-of-the-mill quasi-transient with a record that granted him credibility on the streets without putting him on a first-name basis with everyone wearing a badge.

"Don't worry, he's one of ours," Tyson assured him, as he kept a close eye on the situation.

Green tried not to let his surprise show. "He's an *informant?*"

"Yep. Officer Heather Valance out in Fang, she flipped him for us a while back."

"She's in Alpha now."

"Ah, you know her?"

"I do."

"She's got a real gift for getting people to flip."

Manipulation, that's the word you're thinking of. "If he's one of ours, don't we know already where he's going to take Jefferson?"

"Nope. Because he's not the only hook. He takes Jefferson to meet another guy—and we know where that'll be, over behind the nail salon—and then *that* guy takes Jefferson to the dealer."

"Ah." He struggled not to be bitter, but it was clear that certain key details had been kept from him during the planning stages. While he understood the logic of not spilling all the beans and informant names in front of an unproven entity— him—prior to the operation, his resentment stuck around.

"All right." Tyson set down his binoculars and started the car. "They're on the move. Try to keep eyes on them while I drive."

The detective pulled across the street and parked by the nail salon, not far from the white utility van where the tactical team waited.

B-Rat led Jefferson across the road, not bothering with a crosswalk when simply darting between oncoming headlights would do, and the two of them hustled to the alley between the nail salon and a small butcher shop. Green was able to keep eyes on them until they disappeared into the shadows. Then he followed Tyson's lead and put on the headphones. The detective turned the volume knob on the radio device and shut his eyes. Green did the same, focusing solely on the sounds now.

"How's it hanging, B-Rat?" came an unfamiliar voice through the headphones.

"Hanker, my man." A sound like hands slapping. "This is Grub. New in town out of…?"

"Halcyon Falls," Jefferson supplied.

Hanker spoke again. "Halcyon Falls is a real shithole."

"Not like the sparkling streets of Kilhaven," Jefferson spat back.

A paused, then Hanker cackled. "You always bring around the weirdest type, B-Rat. The weirdest." But he didn't sound upset about it. "You looking for it, Grub?"

"You know. B-Rat said it was good, but I dunno. The shit they have in Halcyon Falls was the real shit, man. The fucking realest."

"Might as well been smoking fucking dirt," Hanker replied. "Our shit's the best. You're not carrying, right? He don't like it when there's guns around that ain't his."

"Nah, but you can check." A moment of silence, some static and thudding on the mic as Jefferson was sloppily patted down.

"Yeah, okay, you stay here, and I'll be back with it. Cash first, though."

More shuffling, then quiet for a good thirty seconds. Green opened his eyes and caught sight of Hanker slipping around the side of the building, away from the others.

B-Rat was the first to speak. "Looks like he don't suspect nothing."

"Shut up," Jefferson said.

More silence. Green's ears strained against it as the disconcerting pause stretched long. He snuck a glance at Detective Tyson, who didn't appear concerned. Okay, maybe long pauses were a natural part of this.

Then Jefferson's voice: "Who is that?"

"No clue." But B-Rat's shaky tone indicated that he did, perhaps, have at least a single clue.

Green's heart began to race, and the pulsing in his ears made him strain harder to listen to the headphones.

"Is that… is that the *supplier*?" Jefferson muttered.

B-Rat said nothing, and a few seconds later, Hanker spoke: "He wanted to meet you."

Green's hair stood on end, and now Tyson *did* seem concerned. He palmed the headphones closer to his ears and leaned toward the audio equipment, staring without blinking.

"Who the hell is he?" Jefferson snapped.

"The boss."

"Why the hell does the boss want to meet me?"

Then B-Rat's voice, shaky, tight: "Yeah, why does the boss want to meet—"

But he didn't get to finish his question before a deep, silky voice like melted dark chocolate came through Jefferson's body mic. "Yes, he's one of them. Good job, Hanker."

"Hey, now," Jefferson spluttered. "You took my cash. Am I gonna get the drugs or—"

The deadly staccato of gunshots blasted the mic, and Green yanked his headphones off to protect his hearing. But he could still hear the report, tinny and distant, coming from his lap. Once it was over, he stuck them back on, his eyes wide, listening for what came next.

Hurried footsteps growing fainter.

Then B-Rat's voice. "Officer down. Officer— Oh shit, this is bad. He's—"

But what Jefferson was, B-Rat didn't say, and a second later, Green heard more echoing footsteps of someone leaving the scene.

"Shit!" Green threw off his headphones again and reached for the door handle. Detective Jefferson was down, shot to shit. The operation was blown. It was time to step in.

Please, no head wounds.

But a solid grip around his upper arm stopped him before he could open the door. "Hold up there."

Green whipped his head around, glaring at Detective Tyson. "He's been shot!"

"I know. The operation is blown. Goddammit."

"He's *dying!*"

Something seemed to click behind Tyson's mind then. "Ah." He let out a deep breath. "Okay, remember all that confidential paperwork you signed?"

Green nodded dumbly.

"Great. Jefferson is not dying. He *can't* die."

"He... can't die?" The confusion took the fight out of him, and he felt the grip around his arm relax.

"Yeah. Jefferson is, uh, immortal. He can't die. He can't be killed."

"The hell you just say?"

And now Tyson didn't blink. "That *cannot* leave this vehicle. Detective Jefferson is an immortal."

"No, he's not. He can't be. That's not—" A memory of a shark-toothed clown with powder-white skin grinning at Green in a dark swamp stopped him short of arguing further about what "didn't exist." Green whispered, "Holy hell."

"Yeah. We, uh, we suspect there are quite a few hiding out in Kilhaven. Usually, they grow bored and listless over the millennia and end up living on the streets, because why not? Ultimate freedom. But sometimes they don't."

Green stared blankly at the dark shadows where he knew an immortal lay bleeding. "Sometimes, they become a cop."

"Yuh."

"So… Jefferson is immortal. Why didn't he end up homeless like the rest?"

"You'd have to ask him, but I suspect it has something to do with the allure of a pension he can claim forever. Doing twenty-five years on the Force is nothing when you have eternity to look forward to. And if you can pull from the department's coffers until it inevitably collapses, that's a small price to pay for being on the right side of the law."

The idea of forever left Green dizzy. "Nothing can kill him?"

"Nothing we know about. And we've tried."

A rumble came from Green's headphones, and Tyson nodded for him to put them on.

"*Shit,* that hurt! Jesus fucking Christ. Bastard shot me in the balls. Sweet mother of God."

Green cringed, and Tyson mirrored the expression with slightly more reserve. "Can't die, but *can* feel pain."

"Do we need to, um, dig the bullets out of him or anything?"

"Nah, they'll just pop out on their own if they didn't already go clean through."

Jefferson came through the headphones again. "Coast is clear if anyone wants to *get off their ass* and bring me a stiff drink. Holy fucking hell. Goddamn. My *balls!*"

Tyson waved it off. "Tactical can do that." He started the engine. "You know, word on the street is that immortals are actually lesser gods and goddesses. But if that *is* true, gods help us all."

CHAPTER NINETEEN_

The drive home from the substation that morning was a blur. Immortals? Fucking immortals? People who couldn't be killed? What the hell? What the actual hell?

They were untouchable. Unstoppable. Could do anything they wished.

Instead, by and large, they did *nothing of any use to anyone else.*

According to Tyson, they usually became homeless, as if the lifestyle was some ultimate destination each immortal spiraled inextricably toward.

How many of the homeless Green had encountered were immortals?

And how could one tell if someone was an immortal? That was where he was stumped. What were the signs? Simply by not dying when, by all rights, they should have? In that case, a whole slew of people he'd encountered could be immortal beings... That man who was stabbed fifty times by his tent mate and survived to tell the tale? The junkies who could mainline fentanyl without their heart stopping?

Literally any of the homeless who survived last winter's unexpected five-day deep freeze where so many others had died in their hovels?

He sipped from his thermos of stale station coffee as he came to a stop at a red light. The hope was that the surge of caffeine would max out his overstimulated system and cause him to crash, preferably once he made it safely back to his apartment.

The light changed. He stuck the open thermos between his thighs.

The world was a different place now. There existed an invisible caste that had nothing to lose, who could get away with anything. Even "life in prison" was usually only ninety-nine years. When you had forever, that was a blink of an eye, a brief intermission in the production of doing whatever the hell you wanted. And perhaps they always ended at the bottom of the barrel, but before then? Did they climb upward and stay a while? Was the whole world run by untouchable beings who could do as they pleased and did? Was the *department* run by that? And how was an immortal made? What did they look like? Could a werewolf be immortal? Could a human? Did they know it about themselves from birth?

So many questions and no one to ask.

When he'd brought it up with Tyson hours after the botched operation, the detective had made it clear that the time for discussion on that matter was over. Not in the substation, not even when it could be safely assumed that everyone in the room already knew of the existence.

Could Green look it up on Kilhaven's mud-slow internet and expect to find anything beyond wild conspiracies?

But this is a conspiracy. It's exactly a conspiracy. A massive cover-up.

Now that he was venturing into this familiar territory again, a part of his mind awoke as if it'd never been dormant, sending chains of *What if... and then what if...* miles and miles ahead of him into the future.

What if he did an internet search for immortals? Would he be tracked? Cataloged in some surveillance system? It was clear that powers high up didn't want the word to get out about immortals. Or maybe it was the immortals themselves who maintained order by any means necessary. He'd more than learned his lesson that the strongest form of power was the one no one could prove existed.

Detective Tyson had mentioned Jefferson's immortality so casually, not only showing his own acceptance of the fact, but as if there were a vast inner group who knew of such things already. It was as if Tyson had forgotten there even was an outer group, people who *didn't* know. Green's mind became fixated on a single problem: how did he find out who was in and who was out?

And why was he out?

The main obstacle was that if he brought it up, he'd be violating the confidentiality agreement he'd signed to ride out with Vice. That would ruin his chances of ever getting in there, and it was looking more and more like he needed to take the damn test and put in for that promotion...

He shouldered open his front door while awkwardly clutching his thermos and managing his bulky tac bag and was met with silence. Well, it was early on the weekend. Kim was likely still sleeping.

He dropped his load by the door, finished off the dregs of his coffee, then shuffled to the kitchen, rinsed the thermos, and poured himself a glass of water.

Did immortals get thirsty? Did they have to eat?

Kim's bedroom door was cracked, and he crept over to peek in on her (and make sure an immortal hadn't stolen her in the night).

Her bed was made, and she wasn't there. "Son of a—" He shoved the door the rest of the way open. "Kim?" No answer. The clock told him it was a quarter till ten. Where the hell was she this early on a Saturday? Had she been out all night?

He called her immediately and heard it ring and ring. Voicemail. He didn't leave a message, just hung up and called back. Voicemail again.

"Kim, you need to give me a call as soon as you get this. You do *not* get to leave without telling me where you're going. Period. This is not okay, and—" And what? He'd kick her out if she did it again so that he'd *never* know where she was? "Just call me back."

His next call was to Aliyah Brooks, who answered with a voice heavy from sleep. She hadn't heard anything from Kim, but he didn't need to freak—

Who else?

The boy. She was with the boy. But how did he find the boy? Had she mentioned his name?

Shit, he was so out of touch with his own sister. No wonder she'd taken off without asking him.

He popped open his laptop and, without much trouble but with a lot of frustration at the connection speeds, found the school's email with the class list. This little punk was in her class, right? So, he just needed to contact the parents of every boy—

Jesse! That was the kid's name. It came to him in a flash the second he saw it listed, and in a few more minutes, he'd found the number of Mr. and Mrs. Montegue.

"Bob Montegue speaking."

"Hi, Mr. Montegue, this is"—he considered it—"Officer Norman Green with the Kilhaven Police Department."

A shuffling on the other side, then in a low voice, "Is everything all right?"

"I'm looking for my sister. Kim Green."

"Kim— Oh, Kimberly? Yes, she's here. Janice always makes a big Saturday breakfast to start the weekend, and we invited your sister over."

Green felt a nauseating wave of failure move through him, leaving him lightheaded with guilt. Had he even so much as made pancakes for her since she'd been living with him?

"So, she's safe?"

"Very much so." A groan and exasperated clucking, then, "Don't tell me she didn't let you know she was coming over." The soft tone of Mr. Montegue's voice made it clear he'd been through this kind of a scare himself.

"No, she didn't. Or maybe she did, and I forgot."

"You said you're with Kilhaven PD?"

Green paused a fraction of a second. Jesse was a shifter, if he remembered correctly. Which meant his choice of career might be a sticky subject with Bob Montegue. "Yes."

"Then, from the bottom of my heart, I say thank you. You do good work out there. I couldn't do it, but I'm glad there are braver men than me keeping us safe."

Despite himself, Green's mood lifted. "I mean, they pay me to do it. Hey, when should I come to pick up Kim?"

"Oh, we can give her a ride home, no problem."

"No, no, you already cooked her a pancake breakfast. I

can get her." Was his real intention behind the offer obvious? That he needed to scope out the place? Sure, Mr. Montegue had just done the *Thank you for your service* song and dance, but Green had heard that from people *while arresting them* for truly heinous crimes. He didn't mind an ass-kissing here and there, but you didn't trust ass kissers.

"Okay, I won't fight you on that, then," said Mr. Montegue. "I've got a golf game with some of the boys from work this afternoon, and I wouldn't mind getting there in time to stretch. Not as young as I used to be, you know! Torqued my T5 vertebra last month out on the course. Janice wasn't happy with me." He chuckled like what he'd said was actually funny instead of astounding.

Green chuckled along, and then got the Montegues' address. He ended the call and stared at his phone. Mr. Montegue seemed like no shifter Green had ever met. His T5 vertebra? Was he a chiropractor or just the kind of know-it-all that lectured his chiropractor? And *golfing*?

Knock it off, Norman. You're exhausted, and it's making you creaturist. You're a cop; of course *you don't know any shifters who play golf and know technical anatomical terms.* His mind cued up a montage of shifters he'd met in the line of work claiming they had the sugar diabetes and the liver bloat. It was as he recalled a call from the previous week out in Shady Grove trailer park, where two gator shifters were using small propane tanks as skeet shot, that he finally shook himself back to reality.

He worked in Fang. The only people with any money there lived in Crown Tree, and they were, by and large, werewolves. They tended to their own business, for the most part. The Crown Tree weres probably played golf and knew where the hell the T5 was.

And then he remembered for the thousandth time: his own sister was a shifter now. He needed to keep these biases in check. It would do no good to let her see them sneak out.

He treated himself to a shower before leaving. It didn't sound like the Montegues were in any rush to move Kim along, and if he let her stay a while longer, it would probably win him some points.

As the warm water washed over him, his armor ran off, and that bit of guilt he'd felt earlier returned in greater force. Kim was a good kid. She always had been. She'd seen through their older brother's nonsense and been able to value herself enough to leave when their parents turned on her. She deserved a stable home like what Jesse had, and she *didn't* deserve him yelling at her for having a boy over. She was craving some stability, and if the Montegues could provide that for her, he should simply find ways to support that and show his gratitude. He certainly was in no position to make her a pancake breakfast.

I bet Janice even wears an apron in the kitchen.

Meanwhile, *his* elegant solution to keeping food off his shirt had always been going shirtless. And the body forged in the fires of the academy had slowly softened and expanded like rising dough over the years since.

He imagined what he must look like in the kitchen each day: hunched, bleary-eyed, clanging pots around like the first humans trying to make fire, his soft body with a sheen of grease over it after hours of stress dreams.

The visualization knocked from his mind the half-formed idea of jerking off in the shower while he had the solitude, and he washed the suds from his body and toweled off.

CHAPTER TWENTY_

The sounds of enthusiastic life greeted him the moment he got out of his car at the suburban Montegue home. Squeals of joy and shouted orders—"No, now it's your turn!"—came from the backyard, and he distinctly heard his sister's laugh among them.

The Montegues lived in a part of Kilhaven that was hardly Kilhaven at all. It wasn't an old gated community like Crown Tree, but it still gleamed with money. New money.

It was on the outer edge of Alpha sector, squatting just inside the city limits, and he was sure that was no accident. New developments were well-plotted things, nothing left to chance. Annexed for property taxes, that was usually it. Maybe cheaper utilities. Some deal cut between the builders and city to line pockets by jacking up the house value for prospective buyers. There was undoubtedly a stringent homeowners' association out here, too, one that enforced everyone's lawns looking as they did: like emerald buzzcuts. Small lots, hulking houses, trees that were only getting started.

Pristine places like this ate at him, and he felt a sudden pride for Fang having nothing like this in it. Granted, that was probably in large part because of the sector's poverty, unsightly industrial lots, crime, and perhaps that one dumping site that was rumored to have been used for toxic waste a few decades before. But he'd take all that over *this*. This fake cleanness. This oblivion. This denial.

Green chuckled, remembering that this was Valance's new sector. No one would hate the sheer stability of a neighborhood like this more than she would. And it was as he was chuckling that a man opened the front door and grinned at him.

Green's humor died in his throat when he saw the fangs and pale skin. "Oh, sorry, I guess I have the wrong—"

"Norman! You sure got here fast. You're at the right place, son. Come on in."

No. *This* was Mr. Montegue? But how? A stepfather? How else could a vampire have a shifter son?

Green remembered he was a big, brave police officer and accepted Mr. Montegue's invitation inside. He passed the man and entered the home hesitantly. Was this a trap?

The door closed behind him, and then Mr. Montegue moved gracefully past, leading him down the entry hall into a wide-open space that comprised the living room, dining room, and kitchen. "Janice, Norman is here."

She had her back to him, scrubbing something in the sink, and as soon as she turned, Green's brain short-circuited. *She* was a vampire, too. And as if to add insult to injury, she was wearing an apron with *Doing dishes sucks* stitched across it in cursive, embroidered blood dripping from the last word. Like it was all one big fucking joke.

"You hungry, Norman?" Janice asked. "We still have

plenty of pancakes left. Your sister eats like a bird, so I totally overestimated how many we'd need."

"No, thanks."

"You sure?"

"Yep. Thank you."

She sighed cartoonishly, flopping her hands against her sides. "Then I guess we'll be eating pancakes all week, Bob. Pancake sandwiches, pancakes with hotdogs…"

He glided over to her and took her in his arms. "You know I love your pancakes, dear. I'll happily eat them for all eternity if that's what you want."

Green cringed. "Is, um, Kim in the backyard, or…?"

The Montegues broke off their kiss. "Oh, yes," said Mr. Montegue. "She's out in the backyard with Jesse and the girls. On the trampoline."

Green made a quick escape through the indicated door and was met with the squeaking of rusty springs. He turned the corner of the house and saw them, four children—that was all they were, just children—jumping like popcorn on the black trampoline.

There was a large net around it—safety first with bloodsucking parents!—and he felt like an ass for what he was about to do, the pure fun he was about to bust up.

But he had to. Something about the Montegues was *not* right. Something was off.

It's just your creaturist feelings about vampires.

No, it's more than that.

How are you so sure?

"Kim!" He marched forward.

Kim landed, planted, and wobbled up and down on the undulating surface. "Hey, Norm."

Her voice was saturated with guilt. No doubt the

Montegues had told her he was coming to get her, but the fact remained she'd failed to tell him about her plans in the first place. And she knew it. What she didn't seem to know was whether he'd give her a talking to here, in front of the others, or wait.

Only once he considered it himself did he realize he'd been heading full steam toward doing that very thing, embarrassing her in front of her boyfriend, or whatever this Jesse kid was to her, to the same degree she'd embarrassed him in front of himself when she'd disappeared.

But he refrained. Something about having just seen her bouncing so freely on the trampoline begged him to give her this one thing.

He'd let her have it on the car ride home.

"Time to go," he said, folding his arms over his chest.

The other kids had stopped jumping too, and they looked from him to Kim. Besides his sister and Jesse, there were two other girls in the group, younger, smaller, but unmistakably related to the shifter boy.

"Are you the policeman?" asked the tinier of the two.

"Yes, I'm a policeman. Police officer," he corrected himself, remembering the way the gender- and species-neutral noun had been drilled into his head at the academy. Not policeman, not policewere, but police *officer*.

"Do you arrest people?"

"Yes, sometimes. Kim? Can we get going here?"

His sister sighed and slipped through the opening of the net, then bent and grabbed her shoes. "Bye, Jesse."

He waved sadly.

"Will you come back, Kim?" asked the older of the sisters.

"Yeah!" chimed in the younger. "You do the best torpedo!"

Kim looked to Norman, who hoped his face didn't reveal the big, fat *no* just below the surface. "Yeah, Josie, I'll be back soon."

By the time they'd slipped away from the Montegues' overly hospitable offers and made it to the car, Kim looked like a completely different girl than the carefree one he'd spotted on the trampoline. She was hunched, staring fixedly at the air vent in front of her, and he almost felt bad for what he was about to do.

But he waited until they were on the road, and then he did it anyway.

"You *cannot ever* do that again, you hear me? As long as you're staying with me, I need to know where you are at all times. Kim, what the hell were you thinking?"

"It's not a big deal, Nor. I'm safe. It's the middle of the day. I just wanted to get some pancakes."

"Why didn't you tell me where you were going if it *wasn't a big deal*?"

"Because I knew you would freak out!"

He had her now. "And why's that? Because my sister was at the house of two *vampires*?"

"Yes! I knew you'd hate it!"

"Because it's dangerous, Kim! Do you know what vampires do to people?"

She threw her hands into the air. "Of course I do! They drink them! But not the Montegues. They adopted Jesse and his sisters when their parents died, and—"

"And how'd their parents die? Being sucked dry by vampires?"

She folded her arms again. "You're fucking impossible to talk to!"

"Watch your language."

"What are you going to do, kick me out? You gonna pull the same move Mom did?"

He swallowed down his next words because they would have been an incoherent jumble anyway. It was time for a different tack.

"There are all kinds of boys at your school, Kim. Can't you pick a *different* one for a boyfriend?"

"Ugh. He's not my boyfriend. And Jesse is nice to me. He doesn't make fun of me, and he listens. And I listen to him!"

"He's not your boyfriend?" Relief. Glorious relief. Maybe they were just friends. "But, uh, do you two like each other?"

He could feel her folding in on herself, and her shoulders slouched forward even more. "Yeah, but he's got a girlfriend."

"Then why's he having you over instead of her?"

"He *can't* have her over. She disappeared like the others, but he still thinks she'll come back."

"Hold on. Back up. What does that mean? Disappeared like all the others? What a creepy thing to say."

"It *is* creepy, Norman. Damn, I thought you were a cop. People disappear all the time."

"No," he said, "not really. Not teenagers." His heart raced as he thought of the last time young people had gone missing in this town. Just over four years ago...

But he hadn't seen any BOLOs for missing teens recently. He would have remembered that. "She probably just moved, or—"

"She didn't just *move*. Her parents still live down the street from him. But she doesn't come to school anymore, and they won't answer any of his questions."

Green was silent for a moment. He'd heard stories like this, mostly on daytime television, but it seemed unlikely here. Still... "Were Jesse and his girlfriend, you know, having sex?"

"Ew, Norman!"

"What? It happens! It's a beautiful..." He thought back to the last time he'd had sex: messy, drunk, disrespectful—what was her name, even?—and he dropped the lovey-dovey bullshit. "I'm only wondering if maybe his girlfriend is pregnant. That happens sometimes. The parents will hide their child away, give up the baby, act like nothing ever happened."

Kim rolled her eyes. "This isn't a novel. That doesn't happen in real life. Girls at my school walk around pregnant all the time. And she's not the only one who's disappeared."

"She's not?"

"No. Judith and Kyle left a few weeks ago, and then two other kids from another class disappeared last month."

"There's gotta be an explanation for it," he said. "Your school is right outside my sector. If that many kids went missing, I'd have heard about it."

She threw her hands up in the air. "I don't know what to tell you, then. They're not around anymore, and no one knows where they are."

"Their parents don't?"

She shrugged. "I don't know. I don't talk to their parents. But it sounds like the parents know and just won't say."

Green's sixth sense for conspiracy yawned and stretched,

but he ordered it to go back to sleep. He had enough to worry about. "Maybe they sent them away to a private school."

Silence fell in the car, but the question didn't go away.

He'd just learned that immortals were a thing, and he was ready to believe it. Why was he so set against Kim's story about missing teens?

Because you already know what it might be connected to.

His stomach clenched.

Not this again. Come on… Haven't I already done enough?

The vampire lab, the murders in the swamp—when would he be done with missing children? Or rather, when would missing children be done with him?

His mind jumped to the white van with the YoungBlood sticker on the back window.

There's more and I know it.

Otherwise, why would he have tracked that van?

He sighed. It wasn't over yet, no matter how much he wanted it to be. The showdown at the wolfenvamp lab wasn't the end of it. Would there ever be an end to it?

Now that he had Kim in his care, there damn well had to be.

Once they were back in the apartment and Kim had turned on the TV, Green grabbed his notepad from his bag, flipped to a new page, and went to stand between his sister and her show. This shouldn't be his problem, but it was. Plain and simple.

He held out the paper and a pen. "Just for kicks, would you mind writing down the first and last name of everyone in your school who's gone missing?"

CHAPTER TWENTY-ONE

The little image of an hourglass turned over and over itself on one of the substation's computer screens the following day. Green stared at the blank box where the results would display if any matches were found.

Hourglass emptied. Flip. Hourglass emptied. Flip.

Just when he was about to refresh the search, figuring the KPD system had glitched yet again, a little dialogue box popped up.

No results for "Kyle Fortune."

The computer lab was empty except for a single Demon 100s officer staring cross-eyed at a screen on the far side of the room, typing up what Green hoped for her sake was her last report of the shift.

He tried the next name on Kim's list.

The hourglass flipped, flipped, flipped…

No results for "Judith Mondragon."

Losing hope, he entered the next one.

Flip, flip, flip, flip…

And then line after line of results populated the screen for "George DiVinci."

Only, these offenses didn't seem at all appropriate for an eighth-grader. Soliciting sex from a prostitute, armed robbery, a few trespassing notices.

It was when Green's eyes fell upon the felony charge of carrying a firearm into a bar that he felt sure he was not looking at the same George DiVinci who had disappeared from Kim's school. The birth date verified it.

Not one missing-person report, either, which was not only unfortunate for the status of Green's query but was also a bummer, because the disappearance of someone like this older George DiVinci would seem like a big win for society.

He typed the final name from the list into the search bar and asked one last task of the overworked hourglass with almost no hope. As it continued to rotate, a voice from behind him made him jump.

"Great news, Green."

He turned to find Detective Jason Felps leaning against the doorframe of the computer lab.

"What's that?"

"Officer Ridley is *gone*."

"It's official?"

"All over but the crying."

Green tried not to think about vampire tears. He wasn't even sure they *could* cry. Would their eyes leak blood like a clown's did before it struck at its prey?

"Finally. Sounds like a win for all of Kilhaven."

Detective Felps laughed. "Definitely. And between you and me, it was only because of all your documentation. There were a lot of people in high places who wouldn't have had the nerve to risk the wrongful termination lawsuit without those details from you. By the time I had it all laid out, even the union chief was eager to get that guy out. I've never seen so many people wash their hands of a rookie at once. The politicians at the top of the department, sure, but the union?" He shook his head. "You saved everyone a major headache, is what I'm saying. I have no doubt Ridley would have killed someone in the middle of downtown before long, and you know how that goes. We would all pay for it."

"Protect and serve," Green said, deflecting the praise.

The Demon 100s officer muttered, "Fucking finally," gathered her things, and headed toward them, and Felps stepped out of the way to let her leave.

Green watched her leave. They were alone now, and his curiosity wasted no time in stepping up. "Hey, I don't mean to be weird," he began, "but are you... Are vampires immortal?"

Felps arched an eyebrow but showed no other recognition of the non sequitur. "No. That's not a term we would ever use."

"But I thought vampires could live forever if no one killed them."

"That's true enough. We live forever unless something kills us. Kind of like humans, don't you think? You live until something kills you."

"Right, but you don't age. Once you're turned, you stay the same age."

"We appear to stay the same age, sure. But we still age."

"But you don't die of old age."

"No."

"So… I guess I don't get it. Doesn't that make you immortal?"

"It makes us harder to kill, that's all. We have much less we can die from than other species. Sure, if nothing kills us, we could live forever, but have you *seen* the world we live in? There's a stake with every vampire's name on it out there somewhere. We just don't know when it'll show up."

Green let that settle in, and as he did, Felps pushed off the doorframe and nodded. "No such things as immortals, Green." And then he did something strange. He winked.

"Anyway," he continued, "Detective Tyson says you did one hell of a job riding out with them last week. He seems impressed. And I heard two of their guys are retiring soon. Once you test, I bet they'd snatch you up. I hope you consider it, too, because"—he cringed playfully—"I just don't know that you're FTO material."

He disappeared, leaving Green alone to ponder the words "once you test." No more suggesting, just assuming. That was how things happened around the sub. One person decided your fate and told so many people that you hardly had a choice in the matter. But did he *want* a choice in the matter? Hadn't he already decided he would test?

He turned back to the computer screen, where the dialogue box was waiting for him.

No results for "Katie Shah."

CHAPTER TWENTY-TWO

Green entered his apartment after work the next morning with a plan. It was one he'd begun orchestrating only moments after Detective Felps had left the computer room, and he'd fine-tuned it over the course of a shockingly slow Saturday night. It involved a folder of freshly printed study guides and waffles to go.

Kim wasn't yet up and about when he entered, and after a quick wave of panic that she'd disappeared again, he set down his load and peeked into her room. There she slept, snuggling one of her pillows with her back to him. It wasn't yet eight in the morning, so he decided to give her a little more time, no matter how eager he was to launch this plan.

He was on his second cup of coffee, deep into the sports section of the Sunday edition of the *Kilhaven Tribune*, when he heard a stirring. Kim emerged, dragging her feet over the carpet as she slogged into the kitchen. He waited until she'd passed him and was staring groggily into the open fridge before he announced, "I already have breakfast handled."

She blinked at him, and he launched into action, pulling the waffles from the oven where he'd kept them warm.

"Waffles?" She eyed him suspiciously, clearly identifying the source of his fresh inspiration, but nodded and flopped into a chair at the small table for two.

He brought over a plate of waffles with bacon on the side, the pad of butter in its plastic to-go ramekin, and a glass of orange juice from a fresh bottle he hadn't drunk straight from. Yet.

"Where'd you get these?"

"Harriet's Diner."

Her eyebrows rose. "Really? Isn't that… expensive?"

He grinned. "Only if you order the quiche." That was a lie, though. The waffles had run him a pretty penny, which he'd cursed at when he'd seen the total. But then he remembered this was important, and Kim deserved some overpriced waffles. And maybe he did, too.

"Mmm. Crispy." She crunched the strip of bacon and relaxed into it, and he was glad he'd spent the money.

He indulged in his own plate, soaking up the simple carbs his struggling nocturnal body craved after every shift. Once both siblings began to slow, he launched into it. "I looked up the names you gave me. No missing-persons reports."

She blinked. "Really?"

"Really."

"That doesn't make sense."

"No, it doesn't. But at least it means the parents know where their kids are. That's enough. You don't need to take on all that."

She bowed her head as if she understood.

"Hey, there's something else." He scooted his empty

plate to the edge of the table and grabbed the three-ring binder by his feet, setting it with a thump onto the table. "I need your help."

Kim narrowed her eyes at him. "Uh, okay?"

"I'm gonna test to be a detective, and I could really use your help studying."

A smile spread across her lips before she could restrain it. "You need my help?"

"Yeah. You get way better grades than I ever did. You're clearly smarter than me. I could use someone to quiz me on this." He held up the binder. "I mean, look at all this shit I have to learn. What do you say? I'd offer to help you with your homework in return, but I don't remember a single thing from eighth grade."

"I don't need your help with it," she said dismissively, her eyes still on the material. "You let me stay here, so I guess I can help you study." She looked up at him. "What kind of detective will you be?"

"No idea yet. Gotta pass the test first."

She nodded. "If I help you study, will you let me go back over to Jesse's house?"

"No. But I'll bring you waffles from Harriet's every Sunday."

She was silent for a moment more, then met his gaze. "And pizza from Franco's every Friday." He opened his mouth to explain that it would be tricky with his work schedule, but she cut him off. "They deliver."

She really was smarter than him, wasn't she? Shit.

He offered his hand. "Deal."

CHAPTER TWENTY-THREE

Green charged up two flights of stairs toward the third-story apartment, urged on by the distinct high-pitched squeals coming from the origin of the call. Family disturbance in progress, subjects with multiple violent priors involved.

Nobody told him that it was all women involved. If they had, he might have risked the delay to wait for backup.

The front door of unit 1831 was ajar. "Police." He pushed it open, using the doorframe as cover until he could get a read on the situation. The squeaking was louder than ever.

He almost laughed.

At the center of a cluttered living room, four—no, five—jackrabbits stood on hind legs, their little paws flying. It reminded him of a bunch of boxers warming up on an agility bag. Adorable little boxers.

He was instantly glad he'd maintained his composure when he noticed a human figure lounging in a Papasan chair in the corner. "'Bout time," she said testily. "You gonna break them up?"

The leporine mass continued to be a whirl of fluffy fists in front of him. They were all were-beasts if his nose wasn't deceiving him, but this seemed like the best possible way for them to work out whatever grievances were between them. No one could really get hurt like this, right?

"You called it in?" he asked.

The lounging woman, who was most definitely an adult and could have just as easily handled this herself, nodded like he might be dumb.

"Hey!" he called at the fluffle. It did nothing to stop them.

He clapped his hands loudly. Maybe that would do it. "Hey! Police!"

Still, they boxed on, squeaking and ignoring him completely.

Then one of the rabbits took a mean uppercut and was knocked halfway across the room.

Oh shit!

He rushed forward and grabbed at the guilty party, trying for the scruff of the neck. His fingers hardly touched fur before the were whipped its head around and sank its teeth into the soft flesh between his thumb and forefinger with shocking strength.

He cried out, yanked his hand back, and resisted the urge to send a boot into the mass. The sharp pain mixed with indignation at being so ignored, and he had to take a step back to keep from letting it amount to unlawful force.

"Fang 9-07, calling for backup with a—a net or something? I have multiple were-rabbits engaged in a domestic, and one just bit me."

Would this be the talk of the next show-up? No doubt.

Backup arrived in the form of Officer Scorpio, and she

had, indeed, brought a net with her. She flung it over the group, and Green helped her pull it tight around them until movement was so restricted that no more punches could be thrown. The net pulsed with the heaving breaths of little rabbit lungs, but at least they had no choice but to listen to orders now.

"Who are these people?" Scorpio demanded of the lounging bystander.

"My sisters and my mom."

"What happened? Don't even think about shifting right now, ma'am." A few human toes had popped out of one of the rabbits' paws, but they shrank back instantly at Scorpio's command. She returned to the witness. "What started this all?"

"My sister tried to kick them all out, and they wouldn't go. It just escalated, I guess. Y'all call it that, right? Escalated?"

With the suspects subdued, a deep throbbing in Green's hands pulled his attention, and he looked down at the bite. His whole hand was covered in blood now, and bits of the stuff had even transferred to his other hand in the process of tightening the rope. The net was made of black nylon, so at least it wouldn't show up there, though he couldn't see how he hadn't transferred plenty to it.

"Scorpio," he said, and held up his hand. "Gotta go take care of this."

She didn't even flinch at the sight of his red hand, just nodded and returned to her questioning of the witness.

Green stepped outside of the small fixed-rent apartment and inhaled the night air. From the third-story breezeway, the air was noticeably fresher than at the ground level. No scent of trash cans or the kind of sludge puddles that never seemed to dry in the muggy Kilhaven weather. Even the exhaust was less stifling up here. Just a breeze and the delicious scent of an impending storm.

"You'd better get that cleaned up," came a voice from down the breezeway. He looked, saw her, and tried not to flinch or groan.

Valance strolled over.

"You working OT in Fang?" he asked.

"Couldn't stay away. I'm with the 600s tonight. Was getting ready to head in, but I couldn't miss a call like this, and when I saw *you'd* taken it…" She nodded at his hand. "One of them get you?"

"Yeah. I guess I didn't grab it right on the back of the neck. She got her head around quick."

"You really ought to flush that out soon. You'll turn into one of them otherwise."

As much as he hated to recall it, he'd fallen for that bullshit before, in his early days outside of his mostly human hometown, where paranormals were more myth than reality.

But he'd learned. That wasn't how were-ness worked. Only in the scary stories he was raised on could it be spread any way other than heredity. The lore seemed to have been sloppily convoluted with how vampires were created. All part of the fear propaganda. Keep people misinformed to keep them afraid.

"That's why I came out here."

She leaned to her right to peek around him and glimpse inside the apartment. "Looks like quite the ker-fluffle."

He rolled his eyes. "Aren't you getting tired of the streets, Valance?"

She leaned against the cast-iron railing overlooking the

courtyard and sighed. "Of course. But I'm tired of everything. I'm tired of this half-ass guerrilla war we got going. I'm tired of having to grant vampires constitutional rights. I'm tired of the seams of these pants rubbing me in the same patch of skin for years and years. And I'm tired of taking shit from superiors."

"You ever think of promoting?"

Rather than answering right away, she shifted her weight fully onto her feet and eyed him closely. "Sounds like a hypothetical question. Sounds like you're finally thinking about it yourself. Are you coming to me for advice and wisdom, Green?"

"Maybe?"

"Need me to hold you to my bosom while you tell me your troubles?"

"Jesus fucking—"

"The answer is yes, I think *you* should. I thought I'd been pretty damn clear about that. You considering it?"

"I've already decided. I'm gonna test."

"Oh, wow. Proud of you. Takes some massive balls to risk failing a test where the scores are posted publicly for the entire department to see."

Green blinked. "They do what?"

"I guess you're packing more in those pants of yours than I thought."

"Only if you think ten inches is a lot."

"Of balls?"

He cringed. "Of course not."

"It's a lot of balls, Green. But I'm sure you'll get there with time." She nodded toward the stairs. "That hand needs some care. I'll *rabbit* up for you." She chuckled to herself and led him down toward the courtyard.

Once Valance had her medical bag laid out on the hood of her car, Green decided to resume the conversation. Not about the long balls, but the topic that had occupied his mind in powerful waves, like a leprechaun's curse. "You never told me why you wanted me in Vice. But I think I'm starting to get it."

She scoffed. "No, I guarantee you, you're not." He held his hand out over the hot asphalt for her to squirt water over the wound. She dabbed it dry and went for the antiseptic.

"I rode out with Narcotics. Did you know that?"

"No. Good for you. Playing grownup." She didn't look up as she worked, and he wondered if she was lying. Valance knew *everything* that went on in the department, didn't she? She even knew about things that went on in the department that weren't *actually* going on in the department.

He soldiered on. "What do you know about immortals?"

He couldn't be sure, but he thought her trained hands froze for a fraction of a second as she unwrapped a length of gauze. But then she grumbled, "I know they exist."

"I knew you would. What else do you know about— That's too tight."

"It's not too tight." She wound the bandage around again.

He pressed his lips together and resolved to take it off the second he got free of her. "What else do you know about immortals?"

"Enough to know not to worry about them."

"But... how can you not worry about someone who can't be killed? I heard they get bored after a while and start living on the streets."

"That's true enough. Do the bums living behind

dumpsters keep you up at night, Green?"

"If they're immortal, yes."

She brought his hand toward her face, and for the briefest of moments, he thought she was about to bite him just like the were-rabbit had.

She tore the tape with her teeth and finished up. "I'm going to tell you something, and I hope you listen close. You just said yourself they can't be killed. You can lock them up, but they'll just wait out their life sentences and then be back at it. Until it's formally recognized by the government that such beings exist, life sentences will continue to be too short. So, given that information, I ask you: Why in the hell would you waste your energy worrying about them? What good does that do? You can't do a damn thing about them." She nodded at his hand. "Don't forget to fill out the worker's comp for that."

"I know how to do my job, Valance. Jesus."

"Do you? You're welcome, by the way. I don't deal out my medic skills to anyone. Do yourself a favor and stop fantasizing about immortal beings. Unless we find a way to kill them, there's no point." She packed up her medical bag and loaded it into the trunk as he considered it.

Her last words echoed in his mind. *Unless we find a way to kill them.* But that would mean they weren't really immortal. Wait, was she—

He leaped up away from the hood at the sound of the car's horn. Valance was in her driver's seat, waving for him to get out of the way. She leaned out the window. "Earth to Green. I know you lose more blood than that once a month. Stop playing damsel and get out of my way."

He stepped to the side and glared at her as she drove off into the night.

CHAPTER TWENTY-FOUR

"Come on, Norman, you *know* this one." Kim held the flashcard at arm's length over the coffee table. She was surrounded by a jumble of his study materials on the floor, and she shook the flashcard as if that was all his memory needed. Green squinted at the scribbled words on paper from his place on the couch.

Silverton v. the State of Texas. He cupped his hands over his mouth, one still bandaged from the were-rabbit's bite, searching for any recognition of the court case. The name didn't even ring a bell, but that was his handwriting on the card, so he must have read it at some point.

Something to do with werewolves, obviously, but... what was it? Claw regulations? Shifting within the city limits? Buying property in vampire-zoned neighborhoods?

"I don't know," he finally said.

"You *do*! Come on."

"I don't. It's late; my brain is tired."

"It's ten a.m."

"You know what I mean, late for me."

"I'll give you a hint. Mail theft."

That did absolutely nothing for him. "I think I need some more coffee." But when he made it into the kitchen, he found the pot empty. *Damn. Must really be time for bed.*

"Hey, can I ask you something?" she called from the living room floor. Her tone made it clear that he wouldn't like whatever she was about to say, but he was too tired to be suspicious, so he merely braced himself on the half-counter to await whatever she had to say to him. "Of course."

"You know how I've been helping you study a lot?" She wouldn't meet his eyes.

"Yes."

"And you remember how you said I can't go over to the Montegues' anymore?"

He would have squinted at her at this point, but his lids were already drooping dangerously low. Any lower, and they'd be shut. "Yes."

"Well, Jesse invited me to go to church with him tomorrow. And I thought it would be fun. I know I usually spend Sundays with you, but maybe I could go to church with him in the morning, and we could do waffles for lunch or something."

Church. She wanted to go to *church*. And she was nervous about asking him.

He could have laughed. His mother had forced them to attend church every Sunday, and while he didn't miss sitting on hard wooden pews while a red-faced human in a holy muumuu shouted damnation at everyone, he could understand why Kim might miss the familiar ritual in her totally unfamiliar new life.

And with their family's history of church in mind, he recognized the courage it truly took for her to bring it up.

He considered it. Church with Jesse? Was that okay? There would be people around, and there was nothing wrong with the shifter kid. It was his parents that Green didn't trust. Granted, they would be going to church, too. That was how it worked.

But wait. Vampires at church?

It clicked.

"What church are we talking about here?"

She continued to avoid his eyes. "Uh, just some church nearby. I don't really know. I've just heard the youth group is fun. The kids at school are mean, but Jesse says the ones at his church are nice. They're from all over the city, and—"

"It's a Draculan church, isn't it?"

She wilted from her polite and proper posture and huffed. "Of course it is. What other church would take in a family like his?"

"You're not going to a Draculan church, Kim."

"Norman!"

"What? You're not!"

"You're such a bigot!"

"You're fourteen! How do you know that word?"

"You're a bigot, and you can't see that it's *good* that there's a place where all kinds of species can get along."

"That's not it."

"Then what is it?"

He clenched his jaw, wondering if he should even mention it. Those suspicions. The vampire and his teenage "friend," the break-in and massacre the church, the van of shifter teens. YoungBlood. More pressing concerns had shelved those mounting worries for a while, but he'd never discarded them completely. Something strange was happening behind closed doors in the Draculan church, but he had no idea what it was. Meanwhile, plenty of shit was going down *outside* the Draculan church in plain view. A man could only pursue so many leads at once. Especially one who wasn't yet a detective and was already swamped putting out urgent fires around town and pretending to raise a teenager.

He pinched the bridge of his nose and inhaled slowly. Maybe she was right. Maybe he *was* a bigot. Was that bad, though? His job was to keep people safe, not to build goddamn bridges.

He looked up again, and at that moment, seeing her sitting cross-legged alone in the middle of his study materials on a Saturday morning, it occurred to him just how many evenings she spent alone here while he was at work.

A stuck bit inside of him budged. "First Draculan Church?"

She nodded.

"Yeah, all right. But I'm going with you."

Horror overtook her expression. "You don't—"

"I do. The only way I'm letting you go is if I go with you. At least this first time. If it's as chill as you say, then, sure, you can go on your own in the future. Deal?"

She hesitated, still looked a bit sick, but nodded.

It was set. He would be going to church. With vampires.

Sweet baby Dracula.

CHAPTER TWENTY-FIVE

You're doing this for Kim. You have to stay for Kim.

Green snuck a peek at his sister in the pew next to him, and it was clear that she was *not* here for the religious experience. She sat so close to Jesse that the length of their arms touched, and he was sure they'd be holding hands if not for his proximity to them. And maybe Bob and Janice Montegue's too, farther down the row.

Nothing about this place seemed appropriate for minors —not the decor, the message, and especially not the nest of bloodthirsty vampires. Green had once chased a naked, drug-fueled man through the halls of this building, narrowly avoiding a collision with the ornamental coffins at every corner. And the last time he'd set foot in this sanctuary, the place had been painted in blood. Vampire blood. If he knew anything about the pervasiveness of the stuff, there would still be dried droplets of it hiding in nooks and crannies of this space, no matter how thorough the cleaning attempt. Probably some in the joints of the very pew he sat on with his little sister. The sister he was in charge of protecting. Surely being here, in this sarcophagus of a chapel, wasn't the best course of action for that.

At the front of the sanctuary, on the dais, the Holy Count wore a floor-length royal-purple robe with a black satin stole that ran down to his knees. Crimson light through the stained-glass windows painted his pale face as he waxed feverishly about the sacrifice of Our Lord Dracula, who gave of himself so that others could understand the power of the holy blood that ran through their veins.

Color palette aside, it wasn't that much different from Green's church experience back in Bowers.

Then, twenty minutes after the commencement of the service, the Holy Count held out his hands to the nest and invited all those of a certain age to proceed from the sanctuary to their youth-specific gatherings.

Kim rose without looking at her brother, and he grabbed her wrist. "Not part of the deal," he whispered.

Behind her, Jesse and his two sisters hovered impatiently, and she flashed Norman a look that said, *What do you want me to do?* As if this moment had come as a surprise to her. As if she hadn't been expecting this split all along.

As much as he dreaded separating from her in this creepy building with its bizarro ideas of holy and heathen, he couldn't bring himself to make her the sole teen left in here after the mass departure. Besides, the shit coming out of the Holy Count's mouth had every indication of getting weirder and weirder from here, and he didn't necessarily want her around for that, either.

What did he think would happen? It was just a little youth group. Maybe some scare tactics about how sex kills, perhaps a few poorly interpreted parables—it was nothing he couldn't sort through with her afterward over waffles.

He let go of her wrist and watched her walk away excitedly with Jesse.

The idea of escaping right then, hiding in the crowd of teens and children to slip out, was appealing. But then he remembered his secondary motive for coming, and it had nothing to do with worship. He was here for intel.

He had a suspicion—no, nothing so formed as that—and he needed to know more. This was what Vice did, right? And if there *was* something strange going on here (stranger, that was, than everything he'd witnessed so far), then wouldn't now be a great time to infiltrate the community? *Before* he was a detective? He could then promote with a unique bit of access already in his pocket. He'd imagined it clearly the night before: *"Oh, an op at First Draculan? Yeah, I can lead that. I know all about it, and they think I'm one of them. I can get you all the access you need. I'm already in the field. No big deal. Vice is a lifestyle, ya know? Not just a job."*

He stayed in the pew. And things did, in fact, get weirder.

When the blood communion rites began, Bob Montegue slid over and whispered, "It's just rabbit's blood. Not human, of course."

Green wasn't sure he trusted that statement. What was more, the alternative of rabbit's blood just made him think of the jackrabbit fistfight in that dingy living room. He had no desire to drink that blood, either.

When the congregants were called, one and all, to the dais to partake in their divine consumption, Green merely turned in his seat, moving his legs out of the way so Bob, Janice, and others in his row could pass. He felt even better about his decision to stay put when he saw that the offering wasn't served in any sort of chalice. It seemed that the Holy Count had been hiding a blood bag somewhere in those loose robes of his, maybe strapped to a clammy thigh, and a tube ran from it to a band on his wrist. From there, each member took their sip, latching their lips onto his skin and suckling.

There were so many visceral details of police work that Green never would have considered before joining up—how the homeless wiped or didn't wipe after a bowel movement in a storm drain, how drivers so obviously pretended not to notice when a police vehicle pulled up behind them at a light, things of that nature—and now he discovered one such detail about the Draculan Church: some people were slurpers. One by one, as the congregants stepped forward and attached their lips to the Holy Count's wrist, Green tried to guess if he would be able to hear distinct sucking sounds or not. Women, it seemed, had more control and knew how to drink the offering without being a slob about it. Most of the vampires, too. The non-vampire men, though...

His mind traveled to the last time he'd gone down on a woman. Had he made similar horrific slurping noises? Was that why she'd stopped him before she came?

You're not supposed to think about that in church!

Then again, how could he *not* in a church like this?

One portly man, whose species Green couldn't surmise from this many rows back, made such squelching noises that the choir, who'd been chanting a low, haunting melody, were forced to chant noticeably louder to spare the rest of the congregants.

Green flashed a forced smile at the Montegues as they

returned to their seats, and he couldn't help notice a drop of crimson drying on the side of Bob's chin.

After a half-hour dissertation on the parable of Van Helsing and the Texan, the service concluded with the Holy Count shouting maniacally about vengeance then wishing those in attendance a harmonious week of spreading the gospel.

Green hurried out into the lobby the first chance he got. Only once he was out did he realize that he'd expected the youth to be waiting outside in the entrance hall. But that wasn't the case. He was surrounded only by other adults.

One of whom he recognized, but not from this context.

Retired Officer Patrick Harmon spotted Green across the space, did a double take, then hurried over. "Norman! What a surprise."

They hugged, and Green said, "I wondered if I'd run into you here, but I didn't see you in the service."

"No, I don't do the early one. What's the point of being retired if you can't sleep in?"

Green and Harmon had worked together for almost a year and a half on the Fang 900s. While they'd taken plenty of group meals together and busted up some nasty stuff, Green had never held much common ground with the werewolf outside of the job. Especially considering how anti-vampire Green's OT activities had become, thanks to Valance. Harmon's Draculan affiliation had always caused him to opt out of those side projects.

And now here they were. Reuniting on unholy ground.

"I gotta say, Green, I never thought I'd see you here."

"Just between us, and I'm sure this comes as no surprise to you, I never thought I'd be here. But my sister wanted to come."

Harmon's eyebrows shot up. "You have a sister? I'd love to meet her."

Green scanned the crowd. "If she comes out here, I'll introduce you. She took off with the other kids."

Harmon's eyebrows rose. "The... the kids? She's young?"

"Fourteen. It's YoungBlood, right? Isn't that what the group is called?"

A slight glassiness eclipsed the werewolf's gaze. "Yes. Does, uh, does she know someone in there?"

"Yeah, her shifter friend from school. Jesse Montegue."

Harmon blinked and looked away. "Ah, the *Montegues*."

What was *that* tone? Green struggled to keep the conversation going. "She's a shifter, turns out."

Harmon looked at him again, this time appearing delighted. "You don't say!"

"Yeah, my parents kicked her out, so now she's living with me."

But as Green spoke, the brightness of Harmon's genuine delight darkened. "You know," the older man said, "YoungBlood is sort of a weird group. Very exclusive, can be a little snobbish. I didn't let my kids participate when they were young. Your sister might not be a good fit."

Green inspected him closely. "Really? The whole reason she wanted to go was that they're supposed to be really nice and inclusive."

"She hear that from the Montegue boy?"

"Yes."

"That figures." Harmon forced a conciliatory grin and clasped Green's shoulder. "Don't take this the wrong way, but I doubt she'll find much acceptance there. YoungBlood is usually reserved for the more devout families. Like everything, there's a hierarchy, and considering you're not exactly thrilled to be here, I wouldn't get my hopes up that she's found a place of belonging. You might want to steer her away."

"If you insist. But Jesse was recruiting her pretty hard. He's not her boyfriend, but he's *kind* of her boyfriend." Green rolled his eyes lightheartedly. "You know how that goes."

But whether Harmon did or not was unclear as a deep crease appeared between his brows. "She's spending a lot of time with him?"

"Not really. She snuck over to his house for pancakes a while back, and I told her she wasn't allowed—" Green stopped himself. How would he explain why he'd banned her from the Montegues' without exposing his own prejudice so openly here?

Harmon finished for him. "You don't let her go over there anymore?"

"You gotta have consequences for teenagers, you know? And she left without telling me where she was going."

The werewolf relaxed. "Totally understand. I would have done the same with my kids. They have to have consequences, or else they'll run wild."

Kim appeared out of the crowd on Green's left, and Harmon gasped. "You must be Norman's sister! You look just like him."

Green made the introductions, and then Kim looked up at him. "Waffles?"

He laughed and told Harmon, "We had a deal."

Harmon grinned and nodded at Kim. "Sounds like you came out on top, kid."

They said their goodbyes, and Kim led the way toward

the exit, but before Green could follow, he felt strong fingers wrap around his wrist. He jerked around, ready to fight, but it was just Harmon.

The man looked him square in the eye. "Your sister seems like a good kid, Norman, but I don't think you two are a good fit here. You understand me?" Harmon's stare pierced like a knife.

When Green didn't answer right away, the werewolf's grip tightened, causing the blood to pulse angrily in Green's wounded hand. "Yeah. I think I do."

He wouldn't have been surprised to feel Harmon's claws shoot out and sink into the soft flesh of his wrist, but that never came to pass. Instead, the werewolf's grip loosened suddenly. "I wouldn't say it if it wasn't important." Green nodded, then, massaging his hand around the aching were-rabbit bite, hurried after his sister.

CHAPTER TWENTY-SIX

Green waited until the rest of his shift left the room after show-up before he cornered the sergeant.

Sergeant Bannockburn had worked OT for a night shift, hadn't slept in over twenty-four hours, and it showed. The werewolf carried dark bags under his eyes, and his usual commanding presence had been absent while he read over the BOLOs minutes earlier.

And that was for the best, because Green preferred to catch him when his guard was down, especially for something like this.

"Sarge, can I talk to you for a second?"

Bannockburn looked up from the papers he was gathering and seemed surprised to find anyone left in the room. "Of course. What's up?"

Green moved in, not wanting to risk being overheard. He knew how the rumor mill worked around the sub. He'd never met any single group of people who were worse gossips than cops, and that included his mother's knitting club. Those biddies were still gossips, but they usually passed along more accurate information.

"Do you keep in touch with Patrick Harmon anymore?"

"Harmon? Not especially. He sends me cards each Halloween, pictures with his kids and grandkids on them, you know, that kind of thing. But I haven't spoken with him in at least a year. Why do you ask?"

Green hesitated. How did he put it? "Is it possible that he's sort of, I don't know, gone off the deep end?"

"Always possible when one of us retires. What do you mean exactly, though?"

"With his religion."

Bannockburn laughed, throwing back his head, and it looked like the werewolf had needed it. "Green. That son of a bitch has been off his rocker with the Draculan church for *decades*. How did you not know that?"

"No, no. I knew it, I mean, I saw it occasionally, but now that he has more free time, has he become especially involved?"

"I'm sure he has. What the hell else is he going to do? His kids have families of their own, he's past the point of no return on PTSD, and his wife is bedridden. Religion's all a man like that has."

"Wait, his wife is dying?"

"We're all dying. But no, it's not like that with her. She's been in bed for years. She's six, seven hundred pounds? Can't even shift anymore. Give me the truth now, why are you asking about Harmon?"

"There's definitely something going on at First Draculan Church."

The sergeant had hinted as much at Roman's Ramen the last time they met there, but this wasn't just a passing suspicion now. It was a real suspicion. And Green had just given voice to it, in the substation, no less.

Bannockburn's expression was unreadable. "There's always something going on there. You know they drink blood, right? Worship Dracula?" He rolled his eyes at that, adding as a footnote, "That vamp was a dandy by all accounts, not some hardcore evangelist."

"Yeah, I know that. Well, not the part about him being a dandy, but the other stuff. I mean, there's something weirder than usual going on."

"Something that pertains to our line of work?"

"Maybe. I attended a service on Sunday."

"Uh, *why*?"

"Kim, my little sister, she wanted to go. Her friend is in the youth group there, and he said she should come."

Bannockburn blinked rapidly. "You brought a *human* child into First Draculan?"

"No. She's not human. She's a shifter."

But this hardly worked to soften the worry lines around the sergeant's eyes. He pinched the bridge of his nose before looking back up. "Okay, let me get this straight. You took your shifter sister to a service at First Draculan, and you saw something unusually weird happen there that has prompted this conversation?"

"No. I saw the weird stuff before we went."

"And you still went? With your little sister?!"

When he put it like that…

"She wanted to go; she was practically begging me. I figured if I went, it might be safe."

"You were wrong, then. It's not safe."

Now they were getting somewhere.

"Harmon was there, Bannockburn. I saw him, and when

I told him I was there with my sister, he all but warned me never to go back."

"Then he's not off his rocker after all! Hallelujah! Praise Dracula!" Bannockburn's exasperation reverberated through the room as both men fell silent.

Green broke the silence. "You know something, don't you? Something big."

Bannockburn returned to organizing his papers as he grumbled, "I don't have to know anything particular to know you shouldn't go back. And for fuck's sake, don't take your sister there."

Green watched as his sergeant stomped out of the room, and he felt his heart racing after the minor tongue lashing.

Or maybe that was excitement.

Either way, he was definitely onto something. And if it was enough to keep Bannockburn from even hinting at it, then it was something big, explosive, dangerous.

Green knew he shouldn't be excited about the prospect. But he was.

CHAPTER TWENTY-SEVEN

It was a Saturday, not a Sunday, but Green stopped by Harriet's and picked up some waffles anyway. If Kim wanted some tomorrow, on their usual waffle day, he would make another trip.

He was in a rare good mood after a shift that had, all things considered, gone quite well. Two domestic abusers down, and one of the children on the scene of the second arrest had said she wanted to be a police officer when she grew up. Foolish, but both flattering and endearing nonetheless.

The warm sentiment had carried over and attached itself to his sister. He hadn't allowed that sort of tenderness, fearful as he was for her survival under his neglectful care, but it crept in now. Kim really was a good kid.

And then came the sadness.

She deserves so much more than me. Waffles were a piss-poor replacement for actual parental guidance.

He was thinking about calling his parents, really tearing them a new one for disowning their baby girl, when he entered his apartment. He was laden like a pack mule, takeout bags from Harriet's in one hand, his duty belt in the other, his tac bag over his shoulder. But as soon as he stepped inside, Kim's teen-sweet face beamed up at him from the couch. "Nor!" He felt a few layers of exhaustion peel away.

It was after they'd finished their waffles on the couch, soaking in a made-for-TV movie about a child superstar, when Kim changed the positive course of the day with a single request.

"Hey, Nor?"

He finished dragging a strip of bacon through the excess syrup on his plate and tossed it back. "Mm?"

"I was wondering… Jesse's family is going to the beach next weekend, and since I've never been to the beach, they invited me."

"Nope."

"What?"

"You're not going to the beach with two vampires."

"Norman!" She was on her feet now, her hands balled at her sides as she glared down at him. "Not fair!"

Whoa, that escalated fast. "Fair? That's got nothing to do with this."

"You already banned me from going to their house or their church, and now you're going to keep me from going to the beach with them?"

"Yes."

"What *can* I do with them?"

Green paused. "Nothing, I guess. I don't want you around them."

"You're such an asshole! A creaturist asshole!" She stomped to the window and flung it open.

The action hardly even registered. Somewhere in the back of his mind, Green assumed she needed some air to cool down, but that was all. "Aren't there other boys you can have a crush on at school?" he asked. "I'm only saying you can't spend time with this *one* family. I'm sure Jesse is fine, and I don't mind you two hanging out at school, but his— Whoa, what are you— Kim!"

But she was already halfway through her shift, and a second later, she was a falcon in flight.

He jumped up, discarding his sticky plate without a second thought, and hurried to the open window. By the time he got there, she was hardly more than a speck in the sky.

"Goddammit! Get back here!" His shout echoed off the apartment building across the way and returned to mock him. *Ack-ere ack-ere.*

He pulled his head inside the window again and let his eyes fall on the pile of clothes she'd left behind.

Fuck. She was probably safe enough as a bird of prey, but what would she do when it was time to land? Would she fly back?

She had to, right? Where else would she go? He was the end of the line.

But then again, she'd run away before, not from him but from his parents. Would she do it again? Would she go live with the Montegues?

He left the window open. Maybe she just needed to blow off some steam. He could relate.

But what now? Too early to report a runaway. Did he just go to sleep, hope she came back before he had to leave for work that night? There wasn't much else he could do.

He set out on his post-work routine, throwing his uniform in the washer, showering, and brushing his teeth.

He checked out in the living room, and her clothes were still in a pile. He left a note that said, *I'm sorry, let's talk,* on her discarded jeans and then crawled into bed. Then he picked up his phone and called the only person he would reach out to in this moment of despair, of utter failure.

Detective Aliyah Brooks answered on the second ring.

"I need your help, Aliyah. Kim's gone."

"What?"

"She flew out a window."

"When?"

"A half-hour ago."

"Maybe she'll come back."

He rolled onto his back in bed. "And maybe she won't. She's run away before. That's how she ended up here."

"You say she flew. What kind of bird?"

"Falcon."

"That's good. Not much will take after one of those."

"I don't know what to do. It's too early to report her missing."

"I take it you parted on less-than-ideal terms?"

"How'd you know?"

"I was a teenager once. Storming out was how I left every room for an entire year."

Green continued clutching his phone. "I don't know what to do."

"You already said that. Here. I know some hawk shifters in your part of town. I can give them a ring and see if they'll go looking for her. You remember any specific markings?"

"Uh, yeah, she had a black head, white neck, sort of gray and white speckled over the body."

"Great. I'll call them now. You owe me."

"Aliyah, wait. Don't hang up."

"Yeah?"

"What are you doing right now?"

"Uh, sitting on my sofa, drinking a beer on my day off?"

"You should, uh, come over. Just in case she comes back. She'd rather talk to you than to me."

She scoffed. "Oh, *sure*. That's why you want me over. On the off chance she turns up soon. Not because you finally have the apartment to yourself, and you haven't gotten laid in months?"

"That's not—"

"It is."

"Okay, maybe a little bit, but—"

"No thanks. I already have my day planned. Now, if you'll excuse me, I'm gonna call my hawk-shifter friends to help find your sister, then I'm getting back to my beer and porn."

"Porn? What kind of—"

"Get some sleep, Green." She ended the call.

CHAPTER TWENTY-EIGHT

Kim hadn't returned home by the time Green left for work that night. He thought about calling in sick and going to look for her or simply waiting around in case she came back, but what was the point of that? If she came home, she'd be safe. If she didn't, there wasn't much he could do about it. Brooks's hawk-shifter friends would call him if they found her, and he wasn't ready to report her missing yet and risk drawing attention to his poor guardianship skills.

Work would keep his mind off things, anyway.

He'd long avoided responding to clown sightings since he'd learned that the monstrosities still existed. But this call had come in too close to where he'd parked to finish up a report, and his conscience—or perhaps his pride (thin line)—wouldn't let him ignore it.

Namises had been in the vicinity as well when the call came through, and so, a few minutes later, the two of them stood just inside the home of the small, frightened leprechaun woman while Green forced a reassuring smile. "Don't worry, Mrs. O'Malley. Clowns were wiped out decades ago." Then he added, "But Officer Namises and I will go take a look. Probably just a dolphin-shifter. Sometimes the fins are mistaken for clown feet."

"I know what I saw," she whispered.

He hated to gaslight the poor woman, but what else could he do?

"I understand. Like I said, Officer Namises and I will go check it out."

They stepped out of the house in the quiet, densely wooded neighborhood. Green wondered how long he would have to stand in the shadows of the trees bordering the backyard before he could convincingly claim he'd done a thorough search and get the hell out of there. He had no desire to encounter a real-life clown tonight. And as far as he knew, Namises still thought the nightmarish things to be fake. Not even the savvy Detective Felps had believed it back when Valance had led both him and Green right into a pair of them.

That was years ago. Maybe they really are *extinct now.*

A boy could dream.

As he and Namises passed the O'Malleys' carport on their way around the house, Green glimpsed a YoungBlood sticker on the back window of their minivan. The *hell*? Leprechauns put their kids in that shit now, too?

Or perhaps Mr. O'Malley wasn't a leprechaun. Perhaps it was an interspecies marriage—rare even so many years after it was legalized, and especially strange for a leprechaun, but not out of the question.

"Hey, Ivory," Green said, walking lockstep with the elephant-shifter, "you ever see anything else weird going on with YoungBlood?"

"Nah. Last I even thought about them was when we followed that van."

"Did I tell you I took Kim to First Draculan?"

Namises, who usually moved in a slow, intentional way, jerked his head around to look at Green. "No kidding?"

"No kidding. It was *weird*. But then I saw this guy who used to be on the Fang 900s…" He continued his story as they reached the edge of the trees, and he didn't even notice they'd actually entered the cover of the canopy until they were already a good way in. Shit.

He did a three-sixty with his flashlight, still pretending this was only paying lip service to the 911 call—run a check, assure the caller there was no threat, write the report, forget about it forever. His beam didn't catch anything white and grinning with shark teeth, so he returned his attention to Namises, who said, "I think you should listen to your gut on this one. Doesn't even have to be something bigger going on below the surface there. Weird shit can just be weird shit, and that's enough to stay away from it."

"I hadn't thought about it like that."

Dried leaves crunched under Namises's boots as he trekked on (too loudly for Green's liking). "For what it's worth, I don't love the Draculan Church either. Don't trust it one bit. Maybe it's different here than it was in Pan City, but there… I tell you, the scandals never ended. Cover-ups and all."

"Cover-ups of what?"

Namises dragged his flashlight around, but he showed no signs of expecting to see anything. "I dunno if I should even say. It never came to light while I was there. Still hasn't, as far as I know."

"Let's wait, then."

Namises understood.

Green was happy to leave the woods without having to shoot anything. After reminding Mrs. O'Malley to simply keep her doors locked at night and call if she saw anything else, Green and Namises headed back toward their vehicles parked next to one another. They switched off their body mics, now that they'd closed out the call.

Namises leaned against the driver's-side door across from where Green waited with his arms crossed, leaning against the passenger side of his car. "So, the Pan City thing, it's weird, but I don't really know what to make of it. Never did. I told my sergeant, and he reminded me we're not paid to police what churches do."

Green narrowed his eyes. "You mean unless churches do illegal shit."

"Right. Of course. But I got the message he was sending: leave this alone."

"And did you?"

"Officially, yes. For a while. I haven't even told you what it was, though. Maybe you'll think I'm crazy once I do."

"I'm in no position to think anyone's crazy."

Namises nodded. "It was the kids. I don't know if it was YoungBlood or what, but the kids at the church started disappearing."

The hair on the back of Green's neck stood up. "Disappearing?"

"Yep. Well, sort of. It was never the parents that reported it, though. Aunts, grandparents, siblings, teachers. That's who started mentioning it. I don't even know who heard the first report of it, but it grew like this specter over all the patrol officers. Like a cloud that no one could condense into words. Until one day we could. And we did.

"It was at a cookout. My buddy was telling a story about some wild love triangle call he went to—you know, a typical go-to story like that—and then at the end... Man, I remember this so clearly. There were five of us sitting in a little circle on our lawn chairs, eating burgers. It was so sunny, that blinding kind, and it was February. Unusual weather, and we jumped on it. Anyway, my buddy finished his story, and then he added that when he was interviewing the woman with the shotgun later on, once she'd been disarmed, obviously, she mentioned her niece was missing. He said he looked into it, and nothing. No reports of a missing kid. Woman was crazy through and through.

"Ya know, there wasn't an obvious reason to add that last bit about the call, but he did. He was fishing. And we took the bait, but not at first. It was like the wall of silence cracked down the center the moment he mentioned the missing niece, and all it took for the whole thing to come crumbling down was for one of us to say, 'I had something like that happen, too.' I wish I could say I was the first to speak up, but it was my buddy Jane who did. And then another person mentioned it. And soon, all but one of us had shared a similar moment on a call, a missing kid who wasn't missing."

"So, what'd you do?" Green asked. "You come up with a plan?"

"We never talked about it again. In fact, once we'd shared our own stories, we never even mused on what it might mean." Namises shook his head. "God, I've always wondered how many conversations like that happened at cop barbecues all over Pan City."

And Kilhaven, thought Green. "But it sounds like you looked into it."

"I did. I had to. And I reckon other people did too, but no one talked about it. And over the years, I heard similar tidbits tacked onto stories. People were fishing, and when someone did bite, for whatever reason, they were thrown back into the water."

"The Draculan Church?"

"That's where these kids were going. It took me some time, but I tracked down a few of them. Their parents had given them up to the church, and they were never heard from again."

"Their parents *gave them up*?" Green was horrified until he remembered what his own parents had done with Kim. Wasn't *that* unbelievable, he supposed.

"Yep. They handed over their teenagers, signed them over to the church's care. Most of them wouldn't even tell their relatives about it, but a few did. That's how I found out. And then I took it to my sergeant, and he told me not to meddle, and the rest is unfortunate history."

"Sorry, man. That sucks."

"Yep. It sure does."

"What do you think the church did with them?"

Namises exhaled in a *whoosh*. "No clue. I wouldn't be surprised if some poor archeologist finds a mass grave fifty years from now, though. Don't get me wrong, I don't have it out for vampires, but let's not forget what they eat."

Green was beginning to understand something he wished he didn't. "Is that why you followed that van with me?"

"Maybe so. I don't honestly know why I did that. I always thought what I'd seen was limited to Pan City— couldn't tell you why I thought that. But, yeah, maybe that's why I followed the van with you, because of what I'd learned. And maybe because you seemed so set on it. No one I've met has a better instinct for danger than humans."

"Comes with having virtually no natural defense." Green paused. "Namises, I think what happened in Pan City is happening here, too. Kim says kids are missing from her school. Shifters and werewolves. Just gone. But I checked the names, and they're not reported missing."

"Goddammit." Namises sighed. "Then, Green, I'm sorry to say, but we've got a big-ass moral conundrum on our hands."

There was no denying that.

Green stayed put against the side of his vehicle as Namises loaded into his, assigned to another call, and then disappeared down the dark residential street.

The story of what was happening in Pan City was so familiar that Green would be a fool to think it anything resembling coincidence. That meant Namises was right. The two of them were in one big-ass moral conundrum. They knew—or strongly suspected—that something terrible was happening, something illegal, something led by vampires, and something the department would want no part of. And now that they knew about it, didn't they have to do something? Anything? Whatever it took? Kids were missing.

Again. Kids are missing again. Dammit. Why couldn't it be missing adults? I could ignore that just fine.

But he couldn't ignore this. More children.

The wolfenvamps had been children. Younger than the ones who were missing now by a few years. He still didn't understand the end game of that whole horrific mess. Had the vampires been building an army? An army for *what*? Who in their right mind thought they could control wolfenvamps anyway? There was no humanity left in them. The things would never follow marching orders…

He let that consideration drop as he had countless times since the raid on the laboratory. Goddamn that raid. It had turned the world upside down. *He* had turned the world upside down. Or, perhaps more precisely, he'd shown the world that it had been upside down the whole time.

And now here he was again, same dilemma, worse odds. Because as far as he knew, Namises was the only other cop who knew anything about the missing children and the connection to the Draculan Church. That made a pair. Two of them against an entire religion? They'd need more, but only a suicidal idiot would take those odds.

He stared into the deep, silent woods, a devious seed of thought sprouting.

Good thing I know just the suicidal idiot.

CHAPTER TWENTY-NINE_

The familiar smells of Roman's Ramen a few hours later felt like a salve over Green's frayed nerves. He was coming here too often now, and he knew what that meant, but the food was just so damn salty and flavorful.

Green was spotted the second he stepped inside. "Not you again," hollered Roman from the opposite side of the dining room.

It wasn't technically an ejection, and discrimination laws wouldn't allow it to be, so Green waved, looked around, and found an open booth.

He wouldn't have dreamed of showing up at this werewolf restaurant alone when he was early in his career, but now, clearly, the owner knew him. Did that make him a regular? Did he want it to?

He grabbed a spot by the window so he could see the comings and goings of the dark parking lot. The neon sign outside the front door glowed pink through the pane, bathing the condiment caddy at the edge of the table.

He saw her car pull up, watched as she assigned herself

to lunch with a few forceful jabs at her HAM, and then marched toward the restaurant like she was preparing to discipline it.

Valance came to an abrupt halt just inside the dining room, and Green waved her down.

"You're buying, right?" were her first words.

"Aren't you stinking rich?"

"I am. I don't see what that has to do with this, though. You called me here. You buy. That's how it works."

Despite her words, she didn't appear unhappy to be there, and why would she? Good food and the promise of something clandestine. All he'd told her over the phone was "I have something big I need to talk to you about," and she was in. The end of his night shift overlapped with the start of her day shift, and it was in that overlap when they met. The sun might be rising soon, but it gave no indication yet.

They put in their orders—not to Roman, but to a werewolf in her early twenties who gave every indication of being on cocaine—and Valance leaned back, clasping her fingers behind her head. "Okay, what do you got for me?"

The tone didn't seem right. It was too casual for what he was about to say. So, he leaned over the table, inviting her to lean in as well.

She did not. Damn.

"Okay, so I was talking with Namises yesterday."

She nodded. "Yeah, I met that guy, I think. He's the one with the dark skin and a few extra pounds."

"That's him. He transferred from Pan City." As he filled her in, much to his relief, her posture shifted. She lowered her chin. Then she unclasped her hands and set them on her thighs. And finally, she leaned forward.

"Let me get this straight," she said. "Namises says the

Draculan Church in Pan City was taking kids, but he didn't know what was happening to them." Green nodded. "And I assume you're not enough of an overachiever to try to fix something all the way in Pan City when you have no authority there." Green nodded again. "So that means there's something similar happening in Kilhaven."

"Yes," he whispered excitedly. "There are kids missing at Kim's school. And when I took Kim to First Draculan Church, I ran into—"

"The fuck?"

"Her friend invited her, and she wanted to go, so I insisted on going with her if she did. But listen, Valance, I ran into Patrick Harmon while I was there, and he all but told me not to come back and to keep Kim away."

She held up a hand. "I'm gonna stop you there. Patrick Harmon was *always* a weird one. A screw loose, truly. He joined the department back when the requirements for getting in were that you had one good leg and a trigger finger. And then they could never get him out. He wasn't a liability, per se, but I think we both know he wouldn't have passed the rigorous interview process you went through. So the fact that he's telling you you're not welcome at his church could just as easily be taken as a compliment as anything sinister."

"You don't think I have a case here?"

She didn't answer right away, but rather, she stared into his soul. "I didn't say that."

The server dropped off their meals and left without a word.

Green, fully starving, shoveled a few spoonfuls of scalding broth into his mouth before continuing. "I couldn't tie it all together until Namises said what he said. It all *seemed* connected, but it was just a gut feeling. Now, though…"

"Now, you have a story. I get it, Rook— Green. I do. You know that. And I think that's why you're buying me dinner right now. So you can stop trying to win me over. I'm in. Now, what about the kid who invited your sister to church? Where do you think he ties in?"

"Jesse. That's the kid's name. He's a shifter, but his parents are both vampires. I think he and his sisters are adopted."

"No shit? You don't think a shapeshifter is the biological child of two vampires?"

He scowled at her. "They invited Kim to go to the beach with them this weekend."

"And?"

"And I said she couldn't, of course." *And then she flew the coop.*

"Good. She shouldn't be traveling with vampires."

Hearing his own bias spoken so frankly stung, but it didn't change his mind.

Valance went on: "You think these vampire parents have something to do with this, don't you?"

"I don't know. I see it like this: if all the shifters and werewolves that are disappearing go to YoungBlood, and suddenly my shifter sister is being encouraged to go to YoungBlood, then the people encouraging her might know something about the disappearances."

"It's a good theory, but I need to hear this from you plainly: the thing that's going on in Pan City—parents giving their kids to the church—do you believe it's going on here in Kilhaven?"

He sucked in air through his nose, steadying himself. "Yes. I do."

She nodded and leaned back again. "Good. You're not a complete fucking idiot, then. And you might even make it in Vice." She grinned.

"*Goddammit*, Valance! Was this another test?" He slapped the tabletop, sloshing broth that was growing cold quickly. "You knew about it, and you wanted to see if I could figure it out?"

"Of course."

"Why can't you just *tell* me? How long have you been following this?"

"Oh, ages. I think I first caught a scent of trouble with the Draculan Church ten or eleven years ago."

He had to grit his teeth to keep from erupting. Once he could control himself, he said, "You've known about this that long? Why would you wait to do anything?"

"I didn't know *this* was what was happening. I just knew there was something fishy going on. Fishier than their usual nonsense. I didn't have specifics."

"And when did you learn what you now know?"

"I'm still learning things, Green. But don't worry, because this isn't like the wolfenvamps—I don't have any plan of charging into a church, stakes out. This isn't something we can bust open and everyone will openly condemn. This is a *church*, and we're in an unofficial war with vampires. We blow the doors off this thing, and we're not going to have the public behind us, thinking we're heroes, no matter how good of a show we put on. Nah, the Draculans are smart. They've positioned themselves as an institution of unity during a time of crisis. People need to believe it, so we're not going to make any friends exposing the underbelly of that. Not in the church, not in the government, and not in the department." She stuck a wad of noodles in her mouth and chewed a few times. "Assistant Chief Rugers attends some Draculan church just north of here. They have their followers everywhere. I can't go asking around about this. I knew that from the start. But I have a reputation, as you know. I don't tolerate bullshit, no matter who's behind it. I knew that as others in the department caught on, they'd seek me out. For something that runs this deep, I only want allies who really want it, who are willing to risk everything to get to the bottom of this. People who will do what it takes. And that's what I've got."

He nodded as a few things dawned on him. "Bannockburn? Felps? Brooks?"

"Yeah, they were a little quicker to the conclusion than you, but don't feel bad. They outrank you, and they see a lot more. But we need them to keep clear of this so they can be our eyes and ears."

He narrowed his eyes at her. "That implies you want me to get my hands dirty."

"Don't act like you aren't rock hard at the idea."

Green was about to respond, but before he could, someone else entered the restaurant. Green didn't bother *not* to stare. "Oh shit. What's he doing here?"

She looked over her shoulder toward the entrance. "Oh, he's with me." And then she waved over B-Rat.

The possum-shifter shuffled up, and Green could practically see the stink radiating off him like little heat waves.

"Nuh-uh!" Roman hurried over. "He's got to go."

"He's with me," Valance said.

"I can tell." Roman stopped within a few feet of B-Rat

then could go no closer. The owner reeled back, blinking against the body odor. "This is a health violation. Get him out."

Valance rolled her eyes. "He'll be gone in just a second. Stop making a show."

Green glanced over at a werewolf couple three booths over, both of whom looked like their delicious meal was about to come right back up.

Valance called his attention back to her. "You remember B-Rat, right? Your first night on the beat, I believe."

Green got to his feet, staring down at the shorter man. "And he took off as soon as that detective was shot. Fled the scene. Failed to render aid."

Valance stepped between them, and he didn't miss her upper lip as it curled against the thick cloud of must. "You need to take a seat, Green. B-Rat has done a lot to help us."

While he didn't want to back down, Green also realized he'd drawn unnecessary attention to them, and he needed that off him.

"Two minutes," Valance said firmly to Roman. "Then he's gone."

The owner threw his hands into the air, but he left, and Valance returned to her seat, staring up at B-Rat. "What do you got for me?"

"An address," he said. "We tracked one of the vans. Last spotted going into the Hemlock Pines neighborhood. I got a lady out there who found where it stopped. Didn't see no kids, though."

"They must've already been inside," Valance mused aloud. "The address?"

He reached into a crusted-stiff pocket and pulled out a slip of paper. "Right here."

"Any idea who lives there? I can look up the owner, but it might not be correct."

B-Rat shifted his weight and hitched up his sagging pants. "No need to look it up. We got a name. I may be pronouncing it wrong, but it's something like Cally-o-pee Athen-soo. It's written down."

Valance's eyebrows rose, and she looked at Green, who pretended to understand the significance of the name, though it didn't ring a single bell. She took the slip of paper from the transient, and when it was clear B-Rat didn't have anything else for them, Valance sent him off with a couple of wontons and a small stack of bills. Then she turned to Green. But before she could say a word, he demanded, "How long has that asshole been your informant?"

She rolled her eyes. "He's not *mine*, Green. I'm not his handler. He's *everyone's* informant. He's what we call a snitch. He loves it."

"But you were the one that flipped him."

"Yeah, I got to him first."

Another logical conclusion unfurled itself. "And you passed him along to Vice so you could stay in the know about what operations they were doing."

She shrugged. "Of course."

"Was he already an informant when I met him the first time?"

"No. But once I saw you gently cupping his balls during that pat-down, I thought, *There's a guy who knows how to get the police to do what he wants.*"

"Fuck you."

"He's worth his stench in gold. He's assembled quite the network of street spies."

"How does it even work? We're talking about a bunch of transients here—"

"And prostitutes," she added.

"Transients and prostitutes somehow organizing themselves to relay information across the city. The coordination involved—"

"It's called a text chain, Green. They have cell phones. It's not complicated. And is that really what you're getting hung up on? B-Rat just gave us the location of where the missing teens are being transported to, *and a name* to go along with it."

Right. The name. The name he was supposed to understand the significance of.

"I can't believe he got us a name," Green said as she finally unfolded the stiff slip of paper and read over it.

"And Calliope Athanasiou, nonetheless," she added.

"Right. That's so wild."

She glanced up at him over the paper. "You have no idea why it's significant, do you?"

He opened his mouth to protest but decided not to waste the time. "No, I have no idea."

"It's a Greek name."

"You sure? Sounds Italian."

"It's not Italian. Christ almighty. Maybe you're not ready to be a detective."

"Okay, so it's a Greek name. Is that important?"

"I don't know. But it's not nothing. The Greeks are always up to something in this town."

"Now you're just being—" His mouth fell open.

Maybe it was all the carbohydrates he'd consumed or the lingering specter of B-Rat's stink that had slowed his brain in making the connection. But he got it now. "The Greeks.

Over at Eden. They called me there. They wanted me to help them with something."

"Eden Men's Club?" she spat incredulously. "Wait, the Greeks called *you* out there because they wanted your help with something? Why am I just now hearing about this?"

He glared at her. "Sorry I don't tell you about every call I respond to, Valance. Shit. But I'm telling you now. They said they didn't trust Organized Crime, but they needed my help."

"And what'd you tell them?"

"I told them nothing. What *could* I tell them? They're the fucking Greek mob, and I'm a cop in a corrupt city who's doing his damnedest not to become a corrupt cop. I walked out of there. I put it out of my mind."

"When's your next day off? No, never mind. Take tomorrow off. It's my weekend anyway. We'll go talk to the Greeks."

"Didn't I *just* say I'm trying *not* to become a corrupt cop?"

"I'm not asking you to snort blow off a cherub stripper's baby belly, Green. This is an investigation. Now, are you going to take tomorrow off or not?"

"Not. I have the day *after* tomorrow off. It can wait another day."

She looked like she was about to argue, but then, for once, she backed down. "Fine, fine. That'll give me time tomorrow to prepare. Maybe scope out this address from B-Rat."

"Great, whatever. I gotta get home and see if Kim's back." He tossed his napkin and two twenties onto the tables and made to stand.

Valance grabbed his wrist before he could. "Your sister's

gone?" The intensity in her eyes knocked the wind from his lungs.

"Huh?" Damn. He'd let it slip. "Oh, uh, yeah. She wanted to go to the beach with the Montegues, but I told her no, so she turned into a falcon and flew out the window."

"When was this?"

"Yesterday. Just after lunch."

She loosened her grip. "Yeah, you'd better get back. If she's not there, file a missing-person report."

"She'll come back, I'm sure of it. She has nowhere else to go."

"File it anyway. I'll make sure it goes up the chain."

He nodded, committing himself to the shame of having to admit he'd lost track of the fourteen-year-old he'd been leaving home alone for hours at a time.

Valance let go of him, her eyes falling on the pair of twenty-dollar bills on the table. "You forgot to tip." She pulled out her wallet and slapped three twenties down. "There. Maybe he'll let us come back again in the future."

"Don't be mad, Norman."

That was how Kim greeted him when he entered his apartment later that morning. His sister was in the kitchen making breakfast, but had set a piece of toast and a butter knife down to hold up her hands defensively.

His relief at seeing her home made it incomprehensible that he would be angry. He was elated! She was alive. And fully dressed! But then, yes, there it was, the fear he'd been holding at bay.

The living room window was still open, and he dropped his bag by the door and stomped over, slamming it closed. "If you *ever* take off like that again, you'd best believe this window will be shut and locked when you come back." He kept his distance from her, knowing that a buffer was best when he was feeling this much manic anger. He planted himself in the living room and yelled at her over the half-counter that separated the space from the kitchen.

"Just listen," she begged. "I know I shouldn't have taken

off like that, and I should've let you know where I was, but I *couldn't.*"

"You're right," he snapped. "You shouldn't have taken off, and you should have let me know where you were. I was about to file a missing-person report. You were about to be on the fucking *news*! Cop's sister missing."

"Norman, I—"

"You know how that would have looked once it got out? Beyond being humiliating, my own goddamn coworkers would have interviewed me, maybe even arrested me. That shit could've ended my career!"

"Norman, just listen!"

"Why? Why should I? No, you listen to *me*. A teenage girl goes missing, they come after the man closest to her, and that's me. How can you be so *selfish*?"

She slapped the counter. *"Shut your fucking mouth for thirty seconds! Jesus!"*

He blinked, but he shut his fucking mouth.

"If you want to be mad at me after you hear this, fine, but let me say what I have to say. I meant to come back right away, but I saw something." Her voice wavered then softened. "I didn't know where to go, so I flew over to the Montegues'. I know! Just hear me out! I went to the Montegues'. I didn't really know what I was going to do because I didn't have any clothes, and I didn't want them to see me naked. So, I perched in a tree and tried to come up with a plan. And then this van pulled up."

The hair on Green's arms stood up. "Van? What kind of van?"

"A white one."

"With a YoungBlood sticker on the back window?"

She nodded, squinting at him. "How'd you know?"

"Doesn't matter. What'd you see?"

"A lot. I had falcon eyes, remember. A bunch of people left the house and got into the van."

"Was Jesse one of them?"

"No. I saw him step out to say bye, but it was just a bunch of other people I didn't know. Well, no, that's not true. I recognized a few from the youth group I went to."

"All teenagers?"

"Yeah." She crossed to the dining room table and flopped down in one of the chairs. "I was upset, you know? I thought he'd had a party and hadn't invited me. But then something just seemed off. So I swooped down, and I saw Felicity. She was *in the van*. She'd just come from Jesse's house."

"Wait, who?"

"Felicity! Jesse's ex-girlfriend who went missing."

Green joined her at the table. "And then what?"

She looked sheepishly at a juice stain on the tabletop. "Well, then I thought I'd investigate."

"And? What'd you find?"

"I followed the van, and it drove for a while. It ended up at this big, old-looking house. It looked like one of those haunted houses in the movies, with a big metal gate around it. The van parked around the back, and all the people got out and went inside the house. It didn't seem right, so I waited around for them to come back out. But they never did. Only the driver came out. And I recognized him. He's some college kid that helps with the youth group."

"Werewolf?"

"Vampire. And he left. I thought maybe he'd come back later, but he didn't. And I didn't see anyone else leave the house. They were all in there. So I swooped lower to get a look in the windows. I could see inside, but I couldn't see any people. Not on the first floor or the second. Well, I did see one person. A woman."

"What'd she look like?"

"She was pretty. A white lady. Or maybe Hispanic."

"Could she have been Greek?"

Kim looked at him like he was insane. "Maybe? Are Greeks white?"

"Yeah. Or… Maybe not? I dunno. Doesn't matter. What was she doing?"

"She was dancing in the kitchen. I heard some music, but not any voices. I don't know where everyone went."

"Did you fall asleep at all? Is it possible the teenagers left when you weren't paying attention?"

"I didn't fall asleep, but I guess they could have left out a back way when I was up in the tree in front. But I don't think so. I didn't see another van drive up or anything."

"No, I believe you."

They sat in a heavy silence until Kim asked, "What do you think happened?"

"I wish I could say." He let his mind wander through the possibilities. It was like walking down a long hall with doors on either side. Open one, see what was there, move on to the next. There were so many doors.

He focused again on Kim. "I'm not mad at you, okay? I was scared. But I understand you leaving, and now I understand why you stayed away. But I need you to promise me something. I need you to absolutely *swear on your life* that you will not do that again. You go straight to school, come straight home. That's it. If you leave the apartment for any other reason, I need to be with you. It's not punishment. It's to keep you safe. Something really weird is going on here, and for me to figure it out, I need to know you're safe so I can focus."

She nodded. "Can we still get waffles on Saturdays?"

He grabbed her out of her chair and pulled her into a tight hug.

CHAPTER THIRTY-ONE

Everything about this felt shady, but maybe that was because it was.

Green had no business visiting Eden Men's Club on his day off, except... he did. He didn't love the idea that he would need anything from the dirty-dealing and dirty-diapered cherubs, so he resolved to erase this visit from his memory as soon as he could, hopefully before it got within two hundred yards of his identity. He didn't want to be the *kind* of person who came to a place like this on his day off. For any reason.

Valance didn't seem to mind. She waved merrily at the security camera after knocking on the front door, and a few minutes later, the two cops sat in the office of Marcos Ambrosia as he smoked a cigar in a booster seat.

"Tobacco will stunt your growth," Valance said.

The cherub chuckled and set his smoke down on its stand. "It pleases me that you've both come. Good work, Officer Green."

"We can't be here long," said Valance, taking the lead as usual, "so how about we get everything out in the open?"

The cherub bowed his big old baby-proportioned head and flicked his wrist in a gesture for her to proceed.

"There are kids missing," she said. "You know something about it, but you don't trust OCD to handle it. Now, we've done searches for the missing kids we know about, and they haven't been reported missing. So we, *the police*, have a problem on our hands. What I don't understand is why it's worrying *you* so much that you would pull Green in off the street and ask for help. Are there missing cherubs, or are you suddenly a noble steward of your neighborhood, a benevolent shepherd who guards *all* sheep, no matter the species?"

"No cherubs are unaccounted for, but I think as you dig deeper into this, you'll understand why my interests are not best served by the current particulars of this situation you mention." He brought the cigar to his lips and indulged in another puff before continuing. "In my home country, half of my mother's side were devoured by werewolves in a midnight raid. While I don't hold that against *you*, Officer Valance, it hasn't especially endeared me to the species as a whole. I don't much care what happens to werewolf pups."

"I appreciate the honesty."

"You came to the table when you didn't have to. I owe you that much."

"I think you also owe us a more detailed explanation of why we got the invitation in the first place."

He fluttered over to a small bronze cart and grabbed a crystal decanter of amber liquid. Holding it up for them to see, he made the offer. Green declined. Valance accepted.

When Marcos handed her the tumbler a moment later,

the delicious scent of what was very likely the most expensive scotch Green would ever encounter met his nostrils, and he regretted turning down the offer. A sip wouldn't have made him lose his head…

"There was a woman who came to visit me four… maybe five years ago," Marcos said once he'd perched again on his chair. "She was new to town, from somewhere in the Ionian Islands." He added for Green, "That's part of Greece."

"I got it."

"Sure," muttered Valance.

Marcos went on. "This woman wanted to make contact with some of her people here. That's what she said initially, at least. But, of course, there were other motives. She wanted to set up a partnership. Something that she said would be mutually beneficial. Only, I couldn't see the benefit of it to me. The benefit was never specified, only implied."

"How do you mean?" asked Valance.

"Have you ever had someone demand you do something, 'or else,' Officer Valance? You do this for me, and *in return*, I won't make your life worse. It was immediately apparent that this was the kind of partnership she was proposing. We do something for her, and the *or else* was implied. It would only benefit us in that it didn't destroy us."

"And what did she want from you?"

"It was a strange request. She wanted us to forgive the debt of some of our frequent patrons at the game room. This was, of course, back when we still ran that operation. As I'm sure you've seen, we've evolved to something more sophisticated."

"Did you do as she asked? Forgive the debt?"

"No. I told her I would think about it, but I didn't." He

shrugged. "It didn't make any financial sense for us. I don't make business decisions based on threats from people I don't know. I just wanted her out of my building."

"If you'll excuse me, I don't see the relevance of any of what you're telling us."

"Because I haven't gotten to the relevant part. This woman, she wasn't saying we should forgive *all* gambling debts, but specific ones. The debts of clients who had teenage children."

Valance brought her drink to her lips and took a long swig, tossing back half of it in a single gulp. Still staring at the contents of her glass, she said, "She wanted the children."

"Yes. She asked us to forgive the debts if the parents gave their teenage children to her. The more powerful the children, the better. No humans, in other words. Shifters, leprechauns, weres, even elves—that's the kind of children she wanted.

"Now, I know you think me a low criminal, a predator even, but her proposal, aside from making no sound business sense, struck me as monstrous. Mostly because I knew how many of our regular clients would agree to such a thing to have their gambling debts forgiven. I couldn't dangle that in front of them. I couldn't play upon their desperation in that way. You must understand, family is everything to me. I won't be a party to destroying anyone's family in that way, werewolf or not. I wanted none of it.

"So, when she returned, I lied. I told her that we had made the offer to numerous clients, and none had accepted it. She said she appreciated the effort and was glad to meet some of her own people regardless. And then she left."

"Her own people. She was cherub?"

He scoffed. "No, not even remotely. She was abnormally tall—about your size, Officer Valance—and her species was unknown to me. If I described her more, you would think me stereotyping or making it up, because her most distinctive features were the ones so commonly associated with my homeland—spirals of thick, dark hair; olive complexion; dark green eyes. And no wings. She was beautiful, and I admit it nearly influenced my decision."

"So, she made you this offer," Valance said, "you told her you'd tried it, and it hadn't worked, and she appeared to be fine with that and left. I guess I'm still missing why you decided now was the time to tell us about it, years later."

Marcos nodded. "Less than a week after I told her there were no takers among our clientele, three armed leprechauns forced their way inside Eden and murdered many of my kin and clients."

Valance stared wide-eyed at the cherub boss. Green hardly dared to breathe.

All right, then. This changed things.

"Yes," continued Marcos, "the timing seems significant, doesn't it?"

"We thought it was the drugs," Valance said, her voice coming out slightly choked. "We all thought it was about the vampire drugs."

"Understandable. But my people never dealt that purple stuff. We wouldn't deal it to anyone, wouldn't allow it inside our walls. You know it makes people explode sometimes, right?"

Green nodded adamantly, and Valance said, "All too well."

The cherub sipped his scotch, then resumed his cigar. "I believe the shooting was the *or else* of her offer. We got the message loud and clear. It was our punishment for disobeying. I feared she would come back and make the offer again, and there was only one way I knew of to prevent that. I had to take away the bait. Once we rebuilt, we forgave all debts and began a legitimate business to avoid further attempts at exploitation."

"Bullshit," Valance said. "No way she scared you straight."

"Fine. *Mostly* legitimate. Everyone needs a side hustle *just in case*. But then, months after the shooting, I read something in the newspapers. And your names were there with it."

Valance nodded. "The wolfenvamps."

"Precisely. Children on the precipice of puberty, stolen from their homes, turned into a creature so powerful, so deadly, that no one could truly control it. Why would someone try that? Why would anyone play with fire like that? What potential gain outweighed the risk?"

It was a question Green had never found an answer to, but he suspected that was about to change.

"Everyone pointed fingers at the vampires," Marcos continued, "but you know as well as I do that vampires were already in a position of great privilege in this country. They could do as they pleased so long as they pretended otherwise and paid lip service to rules. Why would anyone risk losing that cushy spot atop the ladder and devolving to what we have now? Open warfare? Their numbers are being systematically diminished by roving bands of criminal werewolves. People say the vampires were building an army with those mutants." He scoffed. "An army for what? What did they need to take over that they didn't already control? What did they need to defend themselves against that they hadn't already murdered into submission generations ago? To what aim would they create something so lethal and abominable as wolfenvamps?" He looked from Valance to Green and back, scanning their expressions. "Are you beginning to see? *She* wanted it. *She* was behind the creation of the hybrids. The more powerful, the better; that's what she'd said to me. I believe that when I failed to give her what she desired, she went to those who would have no qualms doing it for her. Those vampires. What is life to them? What is family?" He spat on the floor to the side of his chair. "And then you busted up the lab. You two exposed and destroyed it. If any true wolfenvamps had been created, they were taken where she could not get them. I spent many sleepless nights wondering where she might go next. And then my daughter mentioned that children from her school were missing." He paused, and the shadow of a smile appeared. "I hope it comes as no surprise that I have useful connections among your colleagues. And those connections informed me that none of the names of the missing had been reported as such. It all but confirmed my suspicions. And there was another commonality among the missing."

Green said, "The Draculan Church."

Marcos arched an eyebrow and looked from one officer to the other. "Ah, you do know more than you let on. I see we've arrived at the same place from different directions. Good, good. I knew I could trust you two. You prefer justice over peace, and that is, I believe, what we need here."

"This woman," Valance said. "Did you get her name?"

"I did. But I'm guessing you have it as well. Do you also have her address?"

"We do. What's her name?"

"It's an interesting name. I'm sure you've run it and it's

come back clean, because I had my man do the same. Calliope Athanasiou. Very interesting name, indeed."

"That's the one. But humor us. What's so interesting about it?"

"Are you familiar with the story of Calliope in the Greek tradition, Officer Valance?"

"No. I was too busy getting laid in high school to learn that kind of thing. Green probably knows all about it, though."

Green sat up straight. "What? No. I'm not familiar with it. I, uh, had too much sex, too."

Valance nodded at Marcos. "Will you honor us with a summary?"

"Calliope was the daughter of Zeus and Mnemosyne; she was also the most powerful among the muses."

Green looked to Valance to see if she was getting more out of this primer than he was. She yawned. Marcos glared at her.

"Apologies," she said, stifling a second, larger yawn, "go ahead."

He did, but his voice was tighter now, his words clipped. "Calliope is a common first name for girls where I come from. But when combined with the last name, well, I don't mean to weave a conspiracy, but—"

Valance leaned forward. "Go on."

"Athanasiou isn't an especially uncommon name, either. What's notable is that it comes from the Greek word for 'immortal.'"

"Immortals aren't real," Valance said flatly, then leaned back in her chair and took another swig of her scotch.

"Right," Marcos replied. "Immortals aren't real. So, the fact that we appear to be dealing with one must be false."

"Hold on," Green said. "You said you didn't know what species she is. But now you're saying you think she's an immortal. This seems like a leap."

"I never said that I believed she is immortal. I merely laid out some of the etymology of her name. And immortal isn't a species. It's a status that can cross all species. Officer Valance, for instance, could be immortal, even though she is also a werewolf."

Green shot her a glance. It certainly would explain a lot of her more reckless behavior.

She frowned at him then addressed the cherub. "Let me get this straight. You think an immortal muse strolled in here and asked you to gather up teenagers for her."

"Close. Except, as you said, immortals don't exist."

"Right. They don't. And neither do muses, as far as I know. But let's pretend for a second they do. You turn her down, so she goes to a clan of vampires with the offer that if they make her wolfenvamps... what? That's where I'm stuck. You think she gave them an offer like the one she gave you? Do it *or else*?"

"I don't suspect so. Vampires aren't easily intimidated. And while it's not hard to know what a vampire wants—blood and the freedom to take blood as they wish—they already had that when she would have approached them. I suspect she offered them something even more enticing. Something she had that they did not."

There was only one thing he could mean. "True immortality," Green said, recalling his last conversation with Detective Felps.

"Imagine," Marcos said, "if vampires could not be staked. The last restraints upon them would be cut. They could drain as they pleased, and no one could do a thing about it."

"I can see the appeal for them," Valance said. "But what in rapist Zeus's name would an immortal want with a bunch of paranormal teens?"

Marcos held up his hands, his cigar, mostly ash now, pinched between his index and middle finger. "That, I don't know. But I assume she's not just looking for friends to braid her hair."

Valance met the cherub's eyes, but her words sounded like she was somewhere far away. "No, I don't suppose that's it." She stood so suddenly that Green flinched. "I appreciate your time, Mr. Ambrosia. This has been most helpful."

"I thought it might be of interest." He fluttered out of his chair, hovering at eye level with Valance. "And if I'm not mistaken, you're now in my debt."

She scoffed. "Not a chance, short stuff." And then she shoved Green ahead of her, and they left the club without another word.

CHAPTER THIRTY-TWO

Ten minutes later, Green pulled into the MacDougall's drive-thru and put the car into park behind a minivan packed with children, knowing their order would take a while.

"We're in way over our heads," Valance said.

These were not the words Green ever wanted to hear from the most terrifying person he knew.

She stared straight ahead from the passenger seat. They hadn't spoken since leaving the club, outside of deciding that a high-sodium bite was in order.

He glared at her. "You said not to worry about immortals."

"I'm not *worrying*. I'm not busting out my knitting needles and clucking my tongue. I'm just stating a fact. You and I, both undeniably killable people, are in way over our heads if we take on an immortal."

"Then, I dunno, Valance, maybe we shouldn't take her on. Maybe, for once, we should just say, 'This isn't our problem. It's too big for us. Our time is better spent helping other people.'"

She waved him off. "Don't be stupid. You know as well as I do that we won't be able to stop thinking about this. Missing children, Green. We've done this dance before. We know the steps, and none of them involve putting one foot in front of the other with our backs to it."

Ahead of them, a woman hung halfway out of the driver's window to shout her order into the box while one of her kids screamed in the back seat.

"Okay," Green said, "but what the fuck are we going to do?"

"Here's the thing. We don't *know* she's immortal yet. We just know she's a fucked-up Greek who's into children. She could just be a run-of-the-mill pedophile."

"But her name."

Valance nodded. "You're right. No getting around that. For instance, your last name means *Green* in English, and you have green skin."

He groaned. "Obviously names aren't *always* literal, but hers translates to 'immortal muse.'"

Valance appeared to be thinking deeply about it, so he didn't interrupt her. Finally, she came out with the fresh idea that had formed behind those piercing eyes: "If you and I ever got married and I took your name, I'd be Heather Green. Ever think of that?"

"Uck!" He jerked his head away from her. "Hell no, I haven't thought about that. Besides, you would *never* take my last name."

She nodded. "True. Norman Valance isn't a bad name, though. Stronger than what you have now, at least."

"I'm not taking *your* last name."

"If we got married, you would. You'd take whatever I gave you, and you'd like it."

"We're not getting married!"

"Now that I know how much you don't want it, it's gotta happen. Sorry."

"Valance. Stop."

She didn't. "Mr. Heather Valance has a nice ring to it. Never thought much about marriage, but maybe it's time I settle down, take a few husbands, break them in."

"Jesus fucking…" The van ahead of them started forward, then stopped abruptly, and the mother began shouting some last-minute additions into the speaker box. "Can we please get back to the dangerous immortal?"

"We should make sure she's immortal before we do anything crazy."

"And how do we make sure of that?"

"Great question. We could shoot her. Surefire way to know. Unfortunately, there are no good outcomes for that. Either we murder someone in cold blood, or we piss off an immortal, since she can't be killed by bullets."

"You sure?"

"Why would bullets be the thing that could kill them? Doubt they'd earn the moniker of 'immortal' if they could be killed by the thing that regularly kills ordinary people."

"No, I mean, are we sure immortals absolutely cannot be killed?"

She shrugged. "Oh, I've heard stories of it, but I don't put much stock in that. Sometimes people say they killed one by using iron or silver or whatever else. One idiot claimed he drowned one. Most likely, the immortals just played possum until they could walk away and start a new life somewhere else."

"How many do you think there are?" Before she could answer, he said, "God, this sucks."

"It does. I have no idea how many there are. There's not exactly a check box on the census for it, and it almost never comes up. Once they opt for a life in the gutter, they're just a minor nuisance, something to be managed. It's when they get big ideas that we see trouble. And it sounds like this Calliope cunt has big ideas."

"What if we go to the church? Tell them what's going on? Expose it from there?"

Valance shot him a glance of pure pity. "They already know. Trust me. You ever cracked open a church cover-up?"

"No. Of course not."

"Well, I have."

"In Guatemala?"

"Close. Panama."

"Do I need the story?"

"No. You wouldn't be able to eat if I told you. Just know that the problem with church cover-ups isn't that the shitheads involved are too slick. Everyone already knows to some extent what's going on—not just the leaders, but the congregation. And because they know, they're culpable, and they fight like rabid bat-shifters to keep it from seeing the light of day. Because they can't feel like superior pricks to the rest of us if they have to come face to face with the evil they've been aiding and abetting."

"So you think Harmon knows about the missing teens, then?"

"You kidding me? Of course he does. He wasn't exactly subtle about running you and Kim out."

"I guess I should take it as a compliment. He was trying to protect me."

She exhaled in sharp exasperation. "Yeah, some saint he is. And what about all the kids he's letting disappear without a word? No, fuck Harmon. He's complicit. His spine always turned to jelly whenever vampires were involved. Mass brainwashing, that's all religion is."

"It's not *all* bad."

"Right. Some brainwashing can feel good. It's still brainwashing all the same. They tell you what to think and believe, so you don't have to do the work of it."

"Not everyone is a natural at making up conspiracies like you are, Valance."

They pulled forward finally, placed their order, and stopped again as the van waited for its food at the window.

"What option do we have, then?" he said. "Can't take on an immortal, and can't take on the church. Don't tell me you're going to take this up the chain and try to get some real firepower on it."

"I would never tell you that because that is the most insane idea you could ever have. Ha! Can you imagine Chief Spinner lifting a single one of his eight legs to put a stop to this? No, not politically expedient at all."

"Then what? What are we supposed to do?"

"First, we confirm she's an immortal. Once we do that, we need to get into that house. We find the kids, and we extract them."

He let his head drop into his hands, and almost immediately, the car behind them honked. He looked up. The van was gone.

Once they had their food, he parked and started in on his curly fries. "I can't do this again, Valance. I'm sorry, but I can't. We only survived the last time because of our good luck. We don't have that this time, and we'd need it *more* than before. And my situation has changed, you know that. I'm in charge of Kim now. If I die or end up in the hospital for weeks, she's got no one. I think we have an aunt somewhere near the Pacific, but if I don't know where she is, a fourteen-year-old sure as hell won't be able to track her down. I have to think of Kim. I can't die."

Valance chewed a massive bite of burger, then took a swig of her soda. "Suit yourself."

"Excuse me?"

"I said, suit yourself."

"Right. But… what does that mean?"

"It means whatever you want it to mean, Green. Jesus. You do what you need to do. I'm not going to pressure you here."

"Thanks…" He kept his eye on her, ready for the jab he knew was coming.

"It's only the lives of innocent children we're talking about. Nothing to keep you up at night."

"Goddamn, Valance."

"Yeah," she said. "He sure does."

CHAPTER THIRTY-THREE

Green couldn't shake the guilt of leaving Kim home alone. It was one of his evenings off, and he should have been spending it with her, studying for the detective's exam, or simply being a good big brother.

But she'd understood his justification. "I have to check on the missing students," he'd said.

"Good," she'd replied.

And with another promise that she wouldn't leave the house, he'd grabbed his keys and headed to the rallying point.

The sun was starting to set when his cell phone rang, and Valance skipped straight to it. "Having trouble getting the connection into the truck, so we're running late."

"Everything okay?" he asked.

"Definitely not. I just had to threaten his life. But we'll be there."

The line went dead.

A half-hour passed, then an hour. Green vacillated on a minute-by-minute basis whether it would be smart to call her back or if waiting was the best approach. So he did nothing. And almost two hours after the phone call, he caught a glimpse of headlights coming down the dirt service road on the outskirts of Alpha sector.

Valance was in a new truck he didn't recognize, and even in the now-dark sky, the paint on it gleamed the color of fresh blood. It was the kind of model with rear-wheel wells so wide that it gave the vehicle a curvaceous frame that bordered on pornographic and said, *I could crush you, and you would like it.*

She hopped down from the driver's side and slammed the door, and the sound of another door shutting on the other side caught his attention. A few seconds later, a small man shuffled around the front and into view. Green got out of his car in a hurry. "Wait… No, no, no. Valance, tell me that's not the same guy."

The leprechaun folded his arms crossly and glared as the three of them faced off in the middle of the dirt road.

"You want me to lie?" Valance said. "Then sure, it's not the same guy."

"He *cursed* us! Don't you remember how many times we almost died because of it? How is he not still in jail?"

"Didn't do nuttin' ya didn't deserve," the leprechaun spat.

"How do you *think* he's not in jail?" Valance answered.

It took Green a second, then he groaned. "You flipped him? *This* one?"

"Of course I flipped him. *We* flipped him, cut him a deal, and now he works for us."

Green continued to gape. "Does he? Does he really? Then how come you had to threaten his life to get him to come here and— Is his eye swollen shut?"

"Stop being dramatic, Green," she said. "There's a big difference between swollen and swollen shut. He can see just fine. He's agreed to our terms."

"'Less harm comes to me shillelagh, then I'm cursin' ya both into te next life."

"You'll get it back when we're done," Valance griped at him. "Quit bitching. You agreed to these terms fair and square."

"Under duress!"

"You were only under duress because you cursed me, and I had to force you to remove it. You did it to yourself, little man."

Green stepped in. "Hey! Can we focus on the task at hand?"

Valance and the leprechaun both shrugged.

"What's your name?" Green asked.

"Jack."

"Jack?"

"Yeah, 's 'at okay? I suppose ya expected some'in' like Darragh O'Kelley. But it's just Jack, if 'at's fine by ya, *Officer*."

"Jack. Did Valance catch you up on the plan already?"

"If ya can even call it a plan, sure. I go up tere to the front door, say I have a telegram from Crete to hand-deliver, ten I give'r tis letter." He pulled it from his breast pocket and flicked it. "And in ta meantime, I hit'r with a curse and see if it sticks or no."

"Then you haul ass out of there," Valance added. "Won't take her long to realize the telegram is complete bullshit."

"Why don't ya just go an' ask'r yourself wheter she's immortal? Don't see why ya need me."

"We just do," Valance replied, then she nodded toward their target location. "We'd better get a move on."

A late-afternoon shower had made the ground soft beneath them as they cut through the overgrowth, approaching the Hemlock Pines neighborhood from the rear.

The manor was just as Kim had described, and Green and Valance parted ways with Jack shortly before they reached the outer gate. The cops made their way around the perimeter to creep in for a closer look while Jack played the role of a certified mail carrier.

If anything were going to make Green feel entirely inferior to Valance, it was this particular activity, creeping in the shadows. This was her element. She *was* a shadow. She made no noise at all as she moved.

He'd crept around with her before, more times than he'd like to admit, but never had she been so unencumbered, free of not just the weight and bulk that came with a police uniform, but the official nature of it as well. She wasn't Officer Valance anymore; she was La Tunda, the nightmare moniker she'd earned in Guatemala.

And she was leaving him in the dust.

He hurried to catch up with her, painfully aware of his own clumsy sounds.

Her head remained on a swivel as they approached the side of the giant home. Green decided to cut himself some slack for his inferior abilities, remembering that even though she wasn't in her wolf form, some of the lupine night vision remained, helping her find just the right placement for her steps, allowing her to agilely duck below low-hanging branches rather than being bitch-slapped by them, as had happened to him multiple times already. Lights were still on inside, and they glowed through the first-floor windows, allowing for an easy peek into Calliope Athanasiou's home. Valance got first look, then motioned that the coast was clear, and he could peep in too.

He stared into an ornately decorated dining room, a long table with place settings for a dozen guests, but no guests and no Greek woman. He leaned from side to side to take in as much as he could. Two rooms branched off the dining room on opposite ends. The one at the back of the house seemed to be the kitchen, and the one closer to the front of the house appeared to be a sitting room. Perhaps it was more, but all he could see of it at this angle was one and a half wing-back chairs and the outer edge of a dangling crystal chandelier.

The sound of knocking caught him off guard, and he dropped low, out of view of the window. He'd been so absorbed in scoping out the place that he'd forgotten the most important part of the plan: Jack needed to come face to face with the suspect. The leprechaun must have already been buzzed past the gate.

Valance stayed low and hurried toward the corner, and Green followed as quietly as he could. Positioning himself so he could see above her lowered head, Green managed to get a clear line of sight of the front step. The door was inset, though, so he couldn't see who answered, only a profile of Jack as he said hello and announced the certified telegram from her home country. The conversation was muted from this distance of perhaps ten yards, and the wind wasn't on their side, carrying Jack's words away from them rather than toward. But Green didn't miss the leprechaun's slight hand motion, hardly more than a twiddling of his fingers. The curse was cast.

Was it the same one Jack had put on Valance and Green after their bust of the drug warehouse? He hadn't even thought to ask what kind it would be. Had Valance? Or was she so convinced they were dealing with an immortal that the degree of the curse was irrelevant because she knew it wouldn't stick?

Jack continued to chat cheerily with the person at the door, presumably the suspect, though Green couldn't confirm, and then the door closed, and it was over. Jack took a step back, glanced over to Valance and Green, and shook his head.

But what did that mean? Did it mean she wasn't an immortal or that the curse didn't stick?

Valance had no patience for the ambiguity and threw her hands up in a silent question.

And then, as Green watched closely, the leprechaun clearly mouthed, "Im-mor-tal."

It was the last thing he ever mouthed.

The door opened again, causing Jack to jump and turn guiltily toward it. And then something that would assuredly visit Green in his nightmares emerged from inside the home. It was large, a grayish brown, tubular and pulsing. Green caught a gleam off clown-like teeth in the opening that might constitute a mouth before the creature whipped out, came down upon Jack like a gnashing vacuum attachment, and swallowed the leprechaun whole.

It was gone in an instant with a crack of the front door closing again.

Green couldn't move, couldn't even flinch at the touch of Valance's hand on his arm as she gripped him and pulled him back, back, back, into the shadows and away from whatever the fucking hell had just sprung from inside Calliope's home and put a swift end to their informant.

"Valance," he whispered hoarsely once they were back at the vehicles. He didn't know what else to say. He just needed an anchor, and she was it.

When she didn't respond, he said it again.

"I know," she said. "I know. That was... Fuck me."

The frozen feeling in his chest began to melt, and on the horizon, a tidal wave of hysteria loomed. His heart beat so quickly that each thrum blended into the next. "Fuck you and fuck me and fuck *everyone*," he said.

Their eyes met, and he saw the shock and fear and relief in her face, and she must have seen it all in his. A second later, both erupted into manic laughter.

"What... the fuck..." she wheezed.

"We... are so... fucked."

Tears shimmered in her eyes, and she wiped them away. "So fucking fucked. Guess we should've learned a little more about muses."

"Rest in peace, Jack," Green said, starting to catch his breath.

"Yeah, *one* piece. She swallowed that fucker whole."

Their hysterical laughter started all over again, and a strange idea intruded on Green's adrenaline-overloaded brain: *I'm going to die with this woman by my side.* Then another thought let itself in: *That's fine.*

CHAPTER THIRTY-FOUR

Green hadn't slept more than four hours since he'd witnessed Jack the leprechaun swallowed whole down the gaping, jagged maw of the muse. He'd taken his full three-day weekend rather than picking up OT on the last day as usual, and he had wiled away the extra waking hours by pretending to study with Kim and suppressing the scream that attempted to claw its way up his throat every time he thought too hard about what he'd seen and what he was up against if he wanted to interrupt whatever horrific kidnapping scenario was taking place.

While Kim was at school, he'd visited the library, wanting to read up on muses but suddenly too paranoid to allow his browser history to log any such search.

In none of the volumes did he see anything resembling the tubular protrusion that had shot out from the doorway and enveloped the leprechaun, but he did see plenty of other unsettling depictions of firsthand encounters. Muses, it seemed, didn't just inspire beauty; more often than not, they opted for inspiring terror.

His reading hadn't left him in higher spirits, and he hadn't found a single thing that might indicate with any certainty why Calliope would want a bunch of paranormal children shipped to her home. But the reason for it couldn't be good. He'd left the library convinced of that.

By the time he made it to the substation the following evening, the familiarity of it made him feel much more himself. Yes, muses could be horrifying, but add it to the pile, really. He encountered dangerous things every day, and there was nothing like his job to remind him of that. So, he loaded up his cruiser, like always, and rolled out to find some deadly situations no one else wanted to deal with.

Fang sector didn't disappoint, and a few hours later, he got his first break from the action as he shuffled slowly through the undergrowth next to Ivory Namises, each dragging their boots in case they made contact with the ditched knife that had brought them out into this overgrown field. Officer Scorpio had hauled away the suspect, and the ambulance was long gone with the victim, so now all that was left was gathering this last bit of evidence. If they could find it.

The night air was unusually dry but hot. The aggravated chirping of the cicadas rose in heat waves now and again, and grasshoppers launched themselves this way and that in the scanning beam of Green's flashlight. Out here in the relative isolation seemed as good an opportunity as any to bring up the thing that weighed so heavily on his mind. "I was talking to another officer the other day about immortals."

Namises didn't even look up. "You're really interested in them, aren't you?"

"She said they can't be killed. No matter what. But that doesn't make sense."

The shifter chuckled dryly. "You mean it keeps you up at night. Not quite the same thing."

"When you were in Pan City, did you *ever* hear about an immortal being killed?"

Namises was silent, the swishing of the stiff weeds at their ankles sounding suddenly louder as a chorus of cicadas quieted. "Yeah, they can be killed."

Green whipped his head around. "They can?"

"Yes, but it's not public knowledge."

"That immortals *exist* isn't public knowledge either. And yet everyone seems to know."

"You don't understand; they might as well be unstoppable. You, for instance, could never kill one."

"Why's that?"

"Forgive me for the presumption, but you're mortal, correct?"

"Is that it? Mortals can't kill immortals?"

"That's the word on the street."

"No way. That's all? It takes an immortal to kill an immortal? You just hand a gun to an immortal and have them pull the trigger?"

Namises sighed. "I doubt it's that simple. Maybe it is, maybe it isn't. I've never tried it myself. Never seen it done, rather. I've only heard it could happen. In my old sector, we had an immortal banshee we were dealing with once. She became a spree killer. Went around screaming and killing. A few of my buddies on a different shift finally went to arrest her—we didn't know she was immortal at the time—and she started her screaming. They knew ahead of time she was a banshee, obviously, so they were wearing heavy-duty earplugs for it. At most, they'd get a few extra cancer cells or maybe some diarrhea from what sound got through.

"Apparently, she didn't like that. Really pissed her off that she couldn't kill them with her shriek. So she attacked them. They thought they were ready for that, too. Shot her with salt and holy water, but it didn't take her down. She kept coming. So they shot her with bullets. Also didn't take her down. Nothing they tried would. It was a close call. She ripped out my buddy's left earplug before someone else showed up and finally killed her."

"Wait. So another *immortal* showed up and killed her?"

"That's the rumor."

"Someone on the Force?"

"Who knows? I certainly don't. Everything about that call became classified, locked up, beyond the reach of public records requests, even."

"And your friend?"

"He had a massive stroke, but he survived. He can't work anymore, but I think he's okay with it. You have a close enough encounter, and spending time with your family starts sounding pretty good."

Green's mind began weaving new possibilities. For once, Valance was wrong. They *could* kill an immortal if they had to. Not that he was especially keen on killing anyone else in the line of duty, but to know it could be done if push came to *ka-pow* while they were evacuating the teens was definitely a comfort.

Now all they needed was an immortal on the rescue team.

And that was where the real problem was. The only other immortal he knew about was Detective Jefferson on

Vice. Green highly doubted he could enlist the man on an unsanctioned mission like this.

Not for the first time, Green wondered if this was something they could run up the chain. Of course, Valance thought not, but that was part of being a paranoid lunatic whose conspiracy theories had caught a few lucky breaks.

But he didn't have to be like that. He could tell Bannockburn, right? The werewolf already knew that something fishy was going on. And then it would just be a matter of Bannockburn relating it to his lieutenant, and her relating it to the commander, and eventually…

Spinner wouldn't do shit. That was the end of the line for command, and it wasn't a great one. It seemed far more likely that Chief Spinner was in on the cover-up than it did that he would do anything to put a stop to it. The arachnid got along too well with the vampire community to push a topic like this into the public eye.

Besides, Green would do just about anything to be forgotten by the chief. He hadn't forgotten his last encounter with the man—the offer to snitch on Valance, the veiled threats if he didn't. He also hadn't forgotten the simple fact that someone in high places had intentionally withheld when his leprechaun curse would be lifted. If Valance hadn't been tipped off by Bannockburn, she and Green wouldn't have survived the lead-up until midnight when their luck flipped. Of that, he was certain.

Having his name in the papers had made him a bit of a local hero for a few weeks, and that provided some safety; if anything mysterious happened to him, the public would ask questions. But it hadn't endeared him to anyone of importance in the department that had worked so hard to ignore the obvious problem of the missing children.

And now more children were missing, and if the elves at the paper learned about it, they might also realize this wasn't anything new, and the police department hadn't so much as lifted a finger.

Could he go to the paper? Could he do it that way? Valance had leaked to them before, the last time.

No, because he couldn't risk tipping off the immortal that they were onto her. Calliope. A muse. A nightmare.

Jesus. Why is it always me?

"Think I found something." Namises reached down into the grass and pulled up a silver spoon with dark discoloration at the center of the bowl. "Nope. Wrong evidence." He tossed it and kept on shuffling.

CHAPTER THIRTY-FIVE

"You didn't bring us here just for the pizza, did you?" asked Aliyah Brooks as she took another slice from the top box on the kitchen counter of Green's apartment.

"There's beer, too," Valance said, pulling two from the fridge and holding them up.

Brooks accepted the offer eagerly.

Sergeant Bannockburn, however, did not partake in the free food and beverage. It was almost as if he *knew* something terrible was coming, as if there were no scenario wherein Norman Green and Heather Valance would rally this particular group of people without needing them to do something stupid, illegal, and life-threatening.

He wasn't wrong, of course. He sat on one of the dining room chairs with arms folded across his chest, staring at the other three helping themselves to the grease and alcohol for lunch.

Valance walked over, grabbed one of his knees, and wobbled it. "Oh, come on, Bruce. Whatever happened to the fun-loving risk-taker?"

Around a mouthful of dough, Brooks said, "He got promoted."

Bannockburn continued to be sullen, and Valance groaned. "Is the stick up the ass included in the benefits package?"

"No, I had to pay for it myself," he snapped, "but it's tax deductible. Now, are you going to tell us what you're about to drag us into?"

Green kept his distance in the kitchen with Brooks while Valance took a seat at the table next to the sergeant. "You already know what this is about," Valance replied. "Why are you so grumpy? You knew it would come to this."

"I *didn't* know that. I don't know how many ways I have to say it, Heather. I'm sick of your conspiracy shit."

"And I'm sick of people orchestrating conspiracies. Also, I call bullshit on that, Bruce. If you were really sick of it, you wouldn't have come at all. You get as much of a hard-on for this as any of us. Stop pretending."

He said nothing, and Valance nodded for Green to start with the rundown.

"We've learned some things about the missing teens," he said.

"There are no missing teens," Bannockburn barked. "You can look up the reports yourself."

"I have, and there *are*. No one's reporting them missing. The parents are covering it up."

"That's their right."

Green jerked back like the sergeant had taken a swing at him. "What? No, it's not. Not if where the kids are going is dangerous. We don't let parents beat their kids, do we?"

"He's got a point," Brooks said, and Bannockburn was forced to concede with a minute nod.

Green went on: "There's a woman named Calliope Athanasiou who owns an estate out in Alpha"—Bannockburn shot Valance a sharp, suspicious glare, and she shrugged guiltlessly—"where the kids are being taken. We have, um, intelligence that a van associated with the Draculan Church's youth group, YoungBlood, dropped off a group of teenagers, mostly shifter and were, at Athanasiou's address a few days ago, and none of them have been seen since."

"Have you gone to the house? Check welfare, anything?" Bannockburn glared at Valance now. "After all, it's in the sector you requested to be transferred to."

"Green and I went two nights ago, actually. With an informant. And— Well, just go ahead, Green."

"We have reason to believe Calliope Athanasiou is immortal."

Brooks gagged and beat on her chest with a fist until she was able to breathe again. She tried to speak, still couldn't, and waved for them to go on without her.

"What makes you think she's an immortal?" Bannockburn asked, sounding unconvinced.

Green said, "There's the name, for one."

The sergeant arched his eyebrows. "What about it?"

"It's Greek. Comes from the word for 'immortal.'"

Bannockburn leaned forward, pinching the bridge of his nose. "Holy hell, you two." When he looked up again, he shook his head. "We don't build cases off names! One of my first arrests was of a hag named Heaven Blessings, who murdered ten of her eleven family members. You remember Trombolo the Tremendous? Not so tremendous. Mostly just stole bags of chips from the corner store and shot bunnies out of his pants. Aliyah, are you, I dunno, extra fond of babbling brooks?"

"I am, actually."

He grunted. "My point is that we have nothing to go on. We bust in this woman's home assuming she's immortal and then end up killing her; we're going to make the entire department look like a bunch of jackasses."

"Hold on there, Bruce," Valance said. "The rookie—"

"I'm not a rookie," Green said.

"—the *junior-most* member of this group really buried the goddamn lede on this one. Yes, her name means immortal, but when we went to her house the other night, it was to check this theory."

"Do I even want to know how you went about that?" Bannockburn asked.

"Most assuredly not, but you need to know anyway. We took Jack O'Shea with us. An informant and a leprechaun."

The sergeant's mouth dropped open. "The one that cursed you both?"

"The same," said Valance.

"Goddamn," murmured Brooks.

Valance continued, "Immortals can't be cursed, so I asked him to knock on her door and throw something minor at her, a belching curse or whatever. If it stuck, she wasn't immortal. It's a simple enough tactic."

"Huh." Bannockburn's dark mood seemed to lift slightly. "That's not a bad solution. I figured a plan out of you two would involve more firepower and gore."

"Nope," Valance said. "It was pretty clean."

"And the curse?" asked the sergeant. "Did it stick?"

Valance cleared her throat and took a long swig from her beer before saying, "It did not. And the suspect ate him."

"Ate him?" Bannockburn looked desperately from Valance to Green for some sign that he'd misheard, but Green only nodded to confirm.

"Swallowed him whole," Valance clarified.

Brooks got up from the table and began going through Green's cabinets. "You got any liquor in here?" She pulled out a bottle of cheap scotch and inspected it. "This'll do." She took a swig straight from it. Then she brought it back to the table and shoved it into Bannockburn's hands.

Brooks asked, "How'd she eat him?"

Green and Valance exchanged a look. "It's a little hard to describe," she said. "Aside from being immortal, we also believe Calliope Athanasiou is a muse."

Brooks shook her head. "Never heard of one of those."

"Then you must've gotten laid in high school."

"Big time."

Valance turned to Bannockburn. "Sarge? You know what a muse is?"

"Yes, but I also got laid in high school. I just read books now. Muses aren't real."

Valance scoffed. "We're still playing that game? Okay, fine. Suit yourself."

"There's more," Green said, and the sergeant took a swig. "We have reason to believe Athanasiou might have been behind the laboratory where the wolfenvamps were created. We think she might have promised the vampires true immortality if they helped her create powerful teenage creatures. She wanted them for some reason."

"And where are you coming up with this new intel?" Bannockburn sounded more exhausted by the second.

Green swapped a look with Valance, who mercifully took over. "The Greeks. We went and talked with Marcos

Ambrosia at Eden Men's Club." And as she told the story, Green watched the others' expressions change. Brooks's eyes grew wider, and Bannockburn's narrower.

"You trust the Greeks?" he asked, once Valance had recalled that particular conversation. "You believe they don't have some ulterior motive for dragging you into this? Maybe this Calliope woman owes them money."

"The ulterior motive is pretty clear," Valance said. "Ambrosia believes, and I agree, that Athanasiou was behind the leprechaun shooting there. His motive for telling us is revenge. I don't think we need more beyond that. You ever pissed off a cherub?"

Bannockburn held up a hand. "Yes, and I don't need to be reminded of the headache it became." He took another swig from the bottle. "Okay, fine, I'll bite. We're dealing with an immortal who's taking teenagers and not returning them. What do we think is happening?"

"Are they still in the house?" Brooks asked. "Have we confirmed that? Maybe she's just making them do her chores or whatever."

Valance said, "We have intelligence that once the last known load of teens went in, they were nowhere to be seen a few hours later."

"Oh, damn," said Brooks. "What are you thinking, a portal?"

"It's possible," Valance replied. "I've definitely considered that."

"What?" said Green, feeling panic rising. "I've definitely *not* considered that. You mean an interdimensional portal? Like the one that opened up when that idiot threw an Aztec brick into the scrying mirror?" The suppressed memory from years before of his hand slipping through the sucking hole and touching something warm and hairy on the other side caused his left eye to twitch like he'd bit into a lemon.

"Could be," said Valance. "But it's not my first guess."

Bannockburn had set the scotch bottle on the table, and his arms were folded across his chest again. "What are we supposed to do, then? We can't kill her. And say we somehow manage to subdue and cuff her. What's stopping her from just breaking her hands and getting free? And you said she *ate* a leprechaun—which we'll be circling back around to; don't think I'm not going to need more info on that—who's to say she can't eat us? What are we supposed to do against a dangerous person like that who can't die?"

Valance opened her mouth, but Green beat her to it. "I think I know how to kill an immortal."

The rest of the group fell silent.

"You can't kill an immortal," Valance said. "That's why they're called immortals. We've been over this."

"You're right," Green said. "*I* can't kill an immortal. But Namises knew about one that was killed in Pan City. She was killed by another immortal. So if we can get another immortal to help us, we might be able to pull this off."

"Hold up." Bannockburn waved it off. "No, we can't just go in there with the plan to kill someone. Contrary to what Valance thinks, kill-now-ask-questions-later is not a part of this job. Killing can't be part of our plan. We only get to defend ourselves and others."

Valance glared at him. "Yeah, we're defending the world from an immortal who is stealing kids. I don't… What am I missing here?"

Brooks added, "More importantly, we don't have an immortal we know of, do we? I mean, all of us are mortal, right?"

Valance wouldn't meet anyone's eyes.

"Uh, Valance?" Green said. "Is there... something you need to tell us?"

Finally, she looked around, realized everyone was staring at her, and said, "Oh, it's not *me*. I'm mortal, just like you. But I do know someone who only plays dead."

"Go on," Bannockburn said impatiently.

"B-Rat."

Green shouted, *"B-Rat?"*

Bannockburn muttered, "Sonovabitch."

And Brooks said, "Wait, the possum?"

Valance held up her hands. "I didn't want to say anything, but yes, he's an immortal."

"How do you know?" Green asked.

"I might've hit him with my car once. What! He was playing dead in the middle of the road, and it was dark."

"For the love of..." Bannockburn groaned.

"And you're sure it woulda killed him?" Brooks asked.

Valance chuckled. "I felt him go underneath the tires. Drove all the way over him. His insides were hanging out. And then suddenly they went back in. It was one of the most disgusting things I've ever witnessed."

"He didn't report that?" Green said. *"A police officer ran over him."*

"Report *what*, exactly?" she said. "I captured the whole thing on my dashcam. His intestines were hanging out all over the asphalt, and then they just sucked back in, like someone slurping spaghetti. You don't get a clearer sign that someone's immortal than that. He begged me not to let anyone know what he was. At first, he said he'd tell everyone I ran him over if I let it slip what he was, but I explained to him he was lying in the goddamn middle of the goddamn road, and I wouldn't get in trouble for it. And so we struck up a deal."

Green shut his eyes. "That's how he became an informant."

She pointed at him. "You'll make a great detective after all, kid."

Brooks helped herself to another slice of pizza. "Great. Let me make sure I have this straight. The four of us plus fucking *B-Rat* are going to take on an immortal... in her own home? Is that what we're thinking?"

"Not what *I'm* thinking," Bannockburn said.

But before Green could find a way to say that, yes, that was what he was thinking, but it wasn't as dumb as it sounded, Kim poked her head out of her bedroom. "Sorry, but, uh—"

"Kim?" Green hurried toward her. "When did you get here? How did you—"

"The window. I left it open this morning so I could fly home if I needed to. And I needed to."

"You're supposed to be at school."

"It's my lunch break. And I really needed to talk to you."

"How long have you been listening?"

"A while. Don't be mad, Nor."

Brooks called, "Hey, Kim. We got pizza."

Kim looked at her brother for approval, and he sighed and nodded for her to go ahead. This was bad, but it was too late to undo it.

"We got beer, too," Valance said.

"She's fourteen," Green snapped.

"So? I had my first beer at nine."

"That explains so much," said Bannockburn.

"Hey." Valance nodded at Kim, leaned to the side, and

pulled her wallet from her back pocket. "You need some more allowance from Auntie Heather?"

Kim's eyes lit up, and she went to grab the proffered stack, but Green stopped her first. "You said you had to come home. What happened?"

His sister seemed to wither and grow more self-conscious in a heartbeat. "I, uh, it's nothing."

Brooks handed her a slice of pepperoni pizza on a plate. "No secrets are too confidential or dumb for this group. Come on out with it."

Kim's eyes darted to Bannockburn, the only face in the room she didn't know.

"He's fine," Brooks assured her. "He's not a whole lot of fun, but you can trust him."

After another moment of hesitation, Kim addressed her brother. "Jesse says there's another YoungBlood field trip coming up soon. I asked if I could go, and he said it was only for official members."

"Field trip? Where?"

"Camping, he said. They call it a Ren-field trip. I don't know if that…"

"Sickos," Valance muttered. "You know I love a good pun, but hell."

"When *exactly* are they going?" Green asked. "Do you know?"

"I think it's this weekend," Kim said. "He said something about Minamas?"

Bannockburn groaned, and Valance mumbled, "For fuck's sake with these people."

Kim looked startled.

"They're not annoyed with you," Brooks assured her.

"It's that demented religion. Listen. You've done a good thing by telling us."

"I'm afraid they'll never come back."

"That's not unfounded," Brooks replied. "But by telling us, we'll make sure they're safe. Do you know how many kids are going?"

"No, but I can find out for you."

"That'll make you the youngest informant I've ever had," Valance said. "Good work, kid. Will you keep your brother updated as you find out more?"

"Valance!" Green said. "No. We're not getting her involved."

"Put your hackles down," Valance said with a dismissive flick of her wrist. "She's already involved. She's dating the bait."

"I'll be careful," Kim said. "I won't ask too many questions. I'll just listen when Jesse mentions it."

"See?" Valance said. "She's smart. She's already better at this than you are, Green."

"She's not going on the payroll," Bannockburn grumbled.

"No need." Valance grinned. "She's already on it." She held out the stack of cash again, and this time Kim managed to swipe it before Green could stop her. "Hide it where your brother won't find it."

Green's annoyance threatened to get the best of him. "Finish your pizza and get back to school, okay?" he snapped.

Kim nodded, noshing on her slice, looking satisfied with herself. "I gotta get back to my other clothes before someone finds them anyway."

She returned to her room, leaving the grownups alone.

"I guess we have a deadline," Valance said. "Minamas. Fuck's sake."

Bannockburn looked like he was about to say something, but he stopped himself. Then he got up without another word and stomped out of the apartment.

"Everyone processes their own mortality differently," Valance said, looking unfazed by the dramatic exit. "I've known Bruce since we were kids, though. He's in. And he's gonna love it. Anyway, guess the planning comes down to us three. Aliyah, will you bring that second box over here?"

"Beer too?"

"Might as well."

CHAPTER THIRTY-SIX

"I'd say there's a good chance the clerk knew the suspect."

Officer Namises's voice caught Green, whose mind was on something completely different that would take place in another sector, by surprise. "Huh?"

Namises eyed him. "You all right, man?"

"Yeah, fine." They stood on the sidewalk just outside a liquor store, the silhouettes of bottles standing out against the broken windows where the suspect had entered, taken all he could, including cash from the register, and left.

"You've seemed distracted the last couple of nights. Is it your sister?"

"Yeah, sorry. She's just acting out," he lied. "Normal teen stuff. A little bit of an attitude." He forced a smile.

"She's fourteen?"

Green nodded.

"Sounds about right, then. Seems like it's really getting to you. Whatever you need to get you right back here, you let me know. The public needs you present, not stuck in your feelings."

Namises was right about that. So, Green sighed and *did* try to get his head back into the present. "You're right, you're right. Thanks for pointing it out. Not looking to get myself killed doing something stupid."

Another lie.

By the time he was back in his car, his mind had fled the scene again. He pulled up the city map on the HAM and zoomed out for a bird's-eye view of the police units sprinkled around his sector and those surrounding. His thoughts projected themselves at an old Victorian house in Alpha...

Green tapped aimlessly on the dots, and as he did so, the call each was on popped up, this one a shoot/stab hotshot, that one a domestic violence with kids involved. His dot was hard to pick out among the clump at the liquor store, where the armed suspect had managed to get in and out *without* earning buckshot to the face, something the clerk could have easily pulled off with the shotgun hidden below the counter.

He zoomed in until he could make out the *F907* above his dot. There he was. Just a speck in the universe. Hardly even visible from this close distance. A single point.

If only he got to live his life that way. If only he weren't such a shit magnet and could go about his dotty little life without worrying about immortals and missing children and cover-ups.

He searched and found the dot marked *F990*. It was the call sign Bannockburn had inherited from Montoya when he'd replaced him as sergeant on the Fang 900s. *F990* was responding to a request for a supervisor just a few blocks north. But Bannockburn wouldn't be there long. He would find an excuse to take a call at the edge of the sector soon. It was just a matter of time.

The dot for *A305* moved in jerks across the screen as the lagging system refreshed in fits and bursts. If Green's guess was correct, the psycho werewolf that dot represented was prowling for a little action in just the right location. Valance would find it soon. That was part of the plan.

He spotted *R802* in a far corner of the oddly shaped Alpha sector. Brooks had picked up patrol OT on her day off, but kept her Robbery call sign. In a city as chronically understaffed as Kilhaven, there was plenty of OT to go around, even in a relatively quiet sector like Alpha.

There was nothing more for Green to do here, but he didn't yet remove himself from the current call. He needed to wait for the right one to come out. He couldn't let himself get stuck on something stupid and time-consuming when the *final* call came through.

Was he now part of a conspiracy himself? There were more than three of them involved, and they were absolutely breaking a few laws in the execution of it.

He concluded that it was, in fact, conspiracy. The notion didn't particularly bother him as it might've once.

Did that make him a dirty cop? He was trying to do the right thing, trying to help people that so many within this system had written off as collateral damage, not worth the trouble of looking into. He'd have to break laws to save lives. It was muddy, for sure. But perhaps a sense of moral purity was a privilege only afforded to those who sat on the sidelines.

He thought of Kim. If she'd gone missing in this Calliope bitch's house, he would burn down heaven and hell to get her back. What was *wrong* with these kids' parents that they would forfeit their children willingly? What did the church have on them? Was it blackmail?

That seemed a generous assumption. More like the parents had offered up their brain as a sacrifice, and the Draculan Church had bathed it in blood squirting from a tube on a creepy zealot's wrist.

Any laws or policies that kept people like him from rescuing children who'd been abandoned to who-knows-what were laws and policies he didn't much care about. Someone had to *do* something, and if that made him a bad little dot, he could live with it. Not everyone got to feel morally superior all the time when the real shit was going down. He already had blood on his hands. What was a little more if it saved some teenagers?

He switched his screen away from the map and to the holding calls, scanning the text lines. The one he was looking for wasn't there yet.

B-Rat would have his guy call in a suspected Peeping Tom, but there was no telling for sure what the telepath dispatcher would translate it to for the HAM. So Green looked for keywords and phrases that fit.

A few minutes later, a suspicious-person call caught his attention, but it was the location that cemented it. Greenview Apartments. All the way on the edge of Fang.

He assigned to it, and his part of the plan kicked off.

He was doing this again. It was happening: with or without him, this shit was going down.

And, God help him, he loved it.

He had no desire to get himself killed by an immortal terror. But that outcome seemed unlikely—or not entirely likely, which was a thin line to skate—when he had Brooks, Bannockburn, and Valance with him. They'd managed to escape the drug warehouse, hadn't they? Sure, he and Valance had been horribly cursed, but no one got their head cracked open with a shillelagh, and that seemed like a win, considering. And the laboratory worked out, too. Yes, they had earth magic on their side, but they'd still had to do some of the work, and Brooks hadn't even been there. It had just been three of them.

Truth be told, he probably only needed Valance by his side in situations like those, like the one he was up against now, to feel like it might work out. Her ability to slaughter an entire building may not result in a promotion, but when it came time to slaughter an entire building—he was well aware that it shouldn't happen as often as it had in his career—she was his first pick for that every time.

But they wouldn't be slaughtering an entire building now. That was the opposite of their goal. This was a rescue mission, even more so than in the lab. How would she fare when the objective was as few deaths as possible? He didn't figure she was assigned to many operations like that in Guatemala. From what he'd heard, Valance, *La Tunda* as they called her, was somewhat of a human wrecking ball. Slip in, light the place up, slip out.

But she wouldn't kill childr—

The pale face of Caitlin Holloway in the swamp came to mind.

But Holloway wasn't a child. Not when they'd found her. She was a failed wolfenvamp experiment. That was all. She had no future, not like that. She could never return home, would have had to spend her days eating rats in the swamp until a gator got her...

No, he couldn't morally rationalize it.

He white-knuckled the steering wheel as he snaked

through the neighborhood streets toward Greenview Apartments.

Caitlin Holloway would always be a weight attached to his ankle, among his accumulation of necessary regrets.

More and more, he spiraled toward the macabre conclusion that there was no getting out of this line of work morally spotless. Not when the department cared more about reputation and maintaining the facade of peace than it did defending the public and attaining real justice. Someone had to *do* something while the rest, like Patrick Harmon, Carlos Montoya, and Jeremy Lawrence, turned a blind eye and refused to get their hands dirty. What did they think their job *was*? Who did they feel responsible for in the end?

He reached the location of the suspicious person and slow-rolled through, looking for a suspect whom he knew wouldn't be there. The only suspicious person on this street was him.

Then, through the HAM, a message popped up. It was from Namises.

Just pulled into Greenview apts. Thought I saw someone slip behind trash cans. Might be a possum.

Green braked. Damn. Possum? Had B-Rat actually been in the area when his guy called them in, or was that just a strange coincidence, and it was a natural possum Namises saw? It was enough of an oddity to worry him.

Green jumped on his radio. "Fang 9-07 to 9-02. Just pulled into the complex. What building are you near?"

He'd been so lost in his thoughts that he hadn't noticed Namises had assigned himself to the prowler call, too. All the way on the other side of the sector. Why had Namises done that?

He felt like smacking himself because the answer was so

obvious. Green was a piss-poor actor. He may be developing Valance's addiction to unapproved ops, but he still hadn't learned how to lie straight to people's faces about what was going on without making it obvious that something else entirely was going on. Namises had sensed something at the last call and followed him. Of course he had. Green must have had the same faraway look in his eyes as the night he spotted the YoungBlood van at the gas station and asked Namises to follow it with him. The elephant-shifter wasn't an idiot. He'd been around a long time, seen a lot of things. And in Pan City, a lot of those things were probably cops on a crusade that the department wouldn't handle. He must have recognized the flu-ish symptoms.

Green coached himself on how to play it cool as he searched for the building Namises had specified.

The complex was old but upscale, which meant Green had only been there a couple of times. "Established" was probably the word the management used on the sales material. The buildings were cut stone, and thick vines crawled up the sides. Finally, he spotted the other police cruiser and parked at an angle to join the shifter, who waited by the hood of his idling vehicle.

"You say you spotted something behind the garbage?"

A large concrete receptacle was off to their left, obscured from the security lighting by a low-hanging bough. But Namises's headlights were aimed right at it, casting deep shadows where the light couldn't reach.

"I think it was just a possum." The words sounded scripted, and Green realized the other officer was staring at him with a disconcerting intensity.

"A natural one?" Green asked, trying to act like he hadn't noticed.

Namises shrugged mechanically. "Could have been a shifter, I suppose."

Green nodded toward the spot. "Shall we?" He needed to wrap this up, so he was ready for the next part of the plan. The arrival of the other officer had thrown far too much up in the air for his liking.

But he hardly made it a step before Namises gripped his shoulder firmly. He jerked around, spinning free of it. "What?"

"What aren't you telling me, Green?"

"I have no idea wh—"

"Don't bullshit me." Namises's voice carried a command Green hadn't heard in it before. "Don't you *dare* bullshit me now. The way you been talking and acting lately, I can't help but think you might be in over your head. And with something big. Because it's never something little for us. Not on this job."

"It's just Kim, man. Just Kim."

"Stop. Lying. To. Me." Namises's eyes had gone black now, cutting into Green like sharpened onyx. "I've seen too many good men and women get killed on this job. Too many. Pan City is a mess of secrets, everyone working their own angle. I didn't expect Kilhaven to be different, but it is. With one exception: you."

"Me?" Green didn't mean to scoff, but Namises had it all wrong. It wasn't *Green* who ran on the fuel of dangerous secrets but Valance. *She'd* dragged him into this. She dragged him into everything. Didn't she?

"Yeah, you," Namises continued. "You and that Valance woman. The two of you are always up to something. You told me a little about the other stunts you pulled together, and I went and read up on them. Figured I should know who I'm working alongside. And then you're so distracted lately? Asking about immortals? Shit, Green. Whatever's got you this nervous, it's gotta be serious. And if it's that serious, seems to be like it could take us all down with you. Don't you think I deserve to know?"

"I won't take you down with me."

Namises's eyes grew large. "But there *is* something going down."

Dammit. "No, there's nothing going down right now."

"But it'll go down soon?"

"No. Listen, you don't need to worry about it."

"But I do. Let me help. You know I'm a good shot. I got your back. Whatever it is."

Green set a hand on the other officer's shoulder. "I know you've got my back. But you don't want within a thousand feet of this. It's localized anyway. No public danger or anything." Namises clearly wasn't buying any of it, but Green felt a clock ticking down in his brain, so he added, "You'll be the first one I tell about it once it's over, all right? Can we look for whatever was moving behind the cans now?"

Namises sighed. "There was nothing moving behind the cans."

"Huh?"

"C'mon, man. I lied to get you where we could talk. There's nothing back there."

Of course. Green was more than ready to jump into his vehicle and search for the final call, but he had one more risk to take here. "Hey, man. Do me a favor?"

Namises had already walked around to the driver's door and was about to load in when he stopped and nodded for Green to go on.

"If you really want to have my back on this, don't follow me around all night."

Namises agreed with a grunt and a dismissive wave of his hand.

Green acted busy in his car until the other officer drove off. He watched the dot for *F902* head back toward the heart of Fang.

Then he waited.

The radio lit up a second later. "Fang 9-90. Alpha could use an extra unit at the Hemlock Pines call. Neighbor reported screaming coming from the address in question. Possible domestic dispute—9-07, looks like you're nearby."

"Fang 9-07 to 9-90, got it. Switching to Alpha radio now."

Green assigned himself to the call then pulled up the map on his HAM. Valance and Brooks were already en route. Once they were there, they'd put in the call for a supervisor, and Bannockburn would head over.

Ready or not, here comes F907.

During the entire drive over, the warning of Namises echoed in his ears.

CHAPTER THIRTY-SEVEN

No sooner had Green arrived down the street from Calliope Athanasiou's home than a direct message popped up on his HAM.

It was from Namises. *You're in Alpha? Remember what I said.*

Green, who had thought of nothing but on the drive, selfishly wished he *did* have the added backup of the elephant-shifter's marksmanship. Not that it would help against an immortal, but bullets still carried quite a force with them, one that could knock someone on their ass and allow others enough time to run the hell away.

He was nervous, no doubt. More so, even, than before the lab or the warehouse. After all, vampires, leprechauns, and even wolfenvamps could be killed.

So can immortals, he reminded himself. *Just not by me.*

B-Rat was their only hope, and the second Green laid eyes on Brooks and Valance huddled by their cars, that hope seemed flimsy at best. All of them were relying on a transient possum-shifter to keep them alive for this extraction.

They were all going to die, weren't they?

A sudden streak of protectiveness rolled through him, and his first words to the others were: "We have to call this off. This is stupid. There's *got* to be another way."

Valance sized him up with a glance. "And here I thought you had ten-inch balls, Green. Turns out, you got none at all. We're moving ahead with or without you."

He turned to Brooks, who nodded. "It'll be fun, Green. Gotta die sometime."

"I'd prefer to wait until Kim can drive," he replied.

The women shared a worried glance, and Valance said, "I'll call for a supervisor."

Brooks stepped forward and put an arm around Green's shoulder. "Let's talk."

She led him away from the cars and into a dark spot between the coverage of street lights. The manor of Calliope Athanasiou peeked out above the trees at the top of the hill, bathed in moonlight.

"When I was in the war…" Brooks began.

"Oh God, not another war story."

"What do you mean, 'not another war story'? I never tell war stories."

"Valance does. And they're always batshit insane and leave me more confused than before."

"It's not fair that *I* don't get to tell you one just because she always does."

"Fine, fine. Go ahead."

Brooks crinkled her nose at him. "I don't know if I want to now. Kinda took the wind outta my sails."

"Sorry. I'm nervous."

"Right. That's what my story was about."

"Just tell it."

She nodded. "When I was in Ecuador, I wasn't some black-ops agent like Heather. I was just a soldier for most of it. I did eventually get on a smaller operations team, but we did basic things, the kind that are public record soon enough. But before that, when I was still just a soldier, I had to do whatever someone told me to do. Even if it was extremely stupid and practically guaranteed that I'd get shredded to bits by a tornado of vampire talons. I hated every second of it, not because I thought I was gonna die, but because I didn't have a *choice* in how I died. When I came home from the war, I was all kinds of fucked up. I'd seen things, sure, but it wasn't that. It was the being cut loose. It was having no decisions for so long that I forgot how to make them.

"I can't explain it exactly, but when I was just dropped back into civilian life, there was only one thing I cared to make a choice about, and it wasn't my life. It was my death. I was obsessed, Norman. All I could think about was how I wanted to die. Something in me craved that control. I dunno how else to explain it. I didn't care much how I lived, only how I died. But I never could settle on any one way. My inability to make a decision saved my damn life.

"Finally, I thought, well, hell, as long as I want to die anyway, I might as well do something in the meantime, so I applied to KPD. Then I got in. And for the first few years, every call I responded to had me asking myself, 'Is this how I want to die?' And if I said yes, then I got out of the car.

"I always got out of the car. Then, one day, I got out of the car responding to a domestic dispute, and I died."

Green took a hurried step back. "You're a zombie?"

"You idiot. Of course not. I died, and they brought me back. The natural way, not with any necromancy shit.

Gunshot, in case you're wondering. Yeah, that time with you was by no means my first encounter with a bullet. Anyway, when I came to in the hospital, and they told me I'd died, it was like a part of me *had* been put in the ground forever, the part that needed to have control. I'd chosen how I'd die, and it didn't do much for me. Now, I'm not gonna get all religious on you, but it felt like *something* had freed me. Like some higher power had said, 'Here you go, you control freak. You got your wish. Now can we get on with it and do something useful?'" She paused, putting her hands on her hips. "Way I see it, you got a choice, Norman. It's rare and conceited to think we get to choose how we die. But we do get to choose how we live."

"Right," he said, "but doesn't the way you live sort of, I dunno, determine how you might die?"

"Oh sure, maybe. But listen to this: my childhood friend dodged the draft. While I was down in Ecuador thinking my idiot commanders were gonna get me slashed up, that asshole stayed here and ended up devoured by some nasty thing that broke through an interdimensional portal in the middle of the road. I survived; he didn't. Who woulda thought? I may not have had a choice about what happened to me, but neither did Joe."

"Joe was the guy who—"

"Eaten by the portal monster in the middle of the road, yeah. The only difference is that he *thought* he had a choice. We're lucky bastards if we're ever given a choice in that. I lucked out once so I could get on with it. Or maybe it had nothing to do with that." She shrugged. "Who fucking knows, is what I'm saying. Now, are you going to head in there and try to get some kids back? You've done stupider things that haven't got you killed yet."

"Stupider than this?"

"Oh yeah. The warehouse thing was *very* stupid. It's kinda cute you don't realize quite how stupid." She pinched his cheek just as headlights caught his attention at the end of the road. She turned toward them. "Showtime."

Bannockburn had arrived.

"Look who I found," said the sergeant as he opened the back door of his SUV. B-Rat stepped out.

"Smells like piss back there," griped the possum.

"That's you," Valance replied.

"Nah." Bannockburn shook his head. "Not this time. It's fresh. Guy before him pissed himself on the way to jail. I washed it out, but I was in a hurry."

"Look at you," Valance said, "taking people to jail. You angling for Sergeant of the Year?"

Bannockburn motioned to the group they'd amassed to raid the home of a deadly immortal being. "Clearly not."

Valance chuckled darkly. "True. If your name ends up on a plaque anytime soon, it'll have 'in memoriam' above it." She inhaled the humid night air and straightened up cheerily. "Shall we?"

She led them to the back of her vehicle, where she opened the trunk. The moonlight glistened off the sea of ammunition inside.

"Sweet mother of God," Bannockburn whispered. "You buy out an entire gun store?"

"Please, Bruce," Valance said, "I'm not gonna shell out for this... Get it? *Shell?*"

"You telling us you stole this?" Bannockburn replied.

"I'm not a goddamn *criminal*, Sarge. This is surplus from my stockpile. I needed to make room for some new toys I have on order. Anyway, got some .45s for everyone—

stopping power is all we got with this bitch if she comes at us and refuses to die. The correct holsters for your belt are right over here. Leave that weak 9mm shit behind. No good…"

Green caught Brooks's eye and was relieved to find he wasn't the only one thrown off balance by this much ammunition in one place. What was it, five hundred rounds? Six hundred? A thousand? And the .45s weren't the only guns in there.

"Here." Valance held out a sawed-off shotgun and a bandolier full of slugs, nodding to Brooks. "You and I will each have one. I'd give you more, but the bulk might limit our stealth."

Brooks took the offering, slipped it easily over her shoulder, and nodded her approval.

"What about me?" came B-Rat's voice. Green had almost forgotten about him.

"I'm getting to it," Valance said. "Yours is at the bottom of the pile."

Bannockburn's eyes went wide. "You're giving him a gun?"

"I'd hardly call it that, and don't worry, I already filed the serial number off it. But we gotta keep him alive, don't we? He's our only shot at taking this bitch down for real if things go ass-up."

"And how am I supposed to take her down?" B-Rat asked.

"Claws. We talked about this. You slit her throat with your claws."

Green held his tongue, refraining from asking the obvious: What if the muse didn't have anything resembling a throat when that time came?

Brooks and Valance looked more like pack mules than police officers by the time they had their guns and ammunition in place. It left Green feeling unusually exposed, knowing all he could pack on his belt without drawing suspicion was a single handgun and two spare magazines of eleven rounds each.

Valance pulled one final object from the trunk before shutting it. "Here ya go, Boris." She held out the weapon.

He glared down at her open palm. "The fuck is this?"

"A pocket pistol. Aren't you a marsupial?"

"I ain't a fucking female!"

"Then find somewhere else to hide it. It won't do much, but if you get in a pinch, you can poke her in the eyes with it." She turned to the rest of the group. "If we end up using any of this, my guess is we'll have to use all of it. By my account, this will give us about a minute and a half of constant fire. Maybe two minutes if we can knock her on her ass enough times."

"That's it?" Green asked. "All that gives us two minutes?"

"That's what I just said. If you wanted a job that works at a leisurely pace, you should've been a firefighter. Plan for a minute and a half, and let's hope it doesn't fucking come to that." She nodded to the informant. "B-Rat, you're with Brooks and me. Everyone ready to get this party started and save some fucking children? Again?"

CHAPTER THIRTY-EIGHT

Bannockburn insisted on taking the SUV, and Green was pretty sure that was only because the sergeant wanted to drive. But the added security of the hulking vehicle was by no means a drawback as they pulled up to the gate and rang the buzzer to the intercom.

He knew they were on camera before he even spotted the small dome of the lens by the speaker.

"Sergeant Bruce Bannockburn. We got a report of a disturbance at this address."

A deep, feminine voice replied, "No disturbance here, but I understand you need to check anyway."

Then the gate pulled open in front of them. Bannockburn drove them through.

Green allowed his sergeant to do the knocking. It was just the two of them who arrived on the doorstep. Brooks, Valance, and B-Rat would be sneaking around the backside of the property at that moment, the women using their military training, and B-Rat using his incalculable years of living on the street to avoid detection.

Though Green had been here before, he hadn't glimpsed Calliope in the flesh. Not in the human flesh, at least. And a search for her name in the public records had failed to turn up a thing. Not even a driver's license photo. The cherub Marcos Ambrosia had described Calliope as an average-looking Greek woman, but since Green had never met one of those, the description hadn't been especially helpful in formulating a clear mental image.

The door opened just a crack before swinging open the rest of the way to reveal a major problem: the woman standing on the threshold was so beautiful that Green felt his eyes cross. He'd no sooner release a score of mongooses in an art museum as lay a finger on a woman like that. He snuck a peek at the sergeant, who looked equally as caught on his heels.

"Calliope Athanasiou?" Bannockburn said, struggling to get the name out, which Green guessed had less to do with the fact that it was a complicated name and more to do with an intense biological response to laying eyes on her.

"Yes." Her smooth voice, combined with the sight of her, made the words sound like a caramel-covered orgasm. The good sort of orgasm, too. The rare kind without any bitter shame immediately afterward.

"Just here to check for ourselves on the noise disturbance. Neighbor said they heard screaming. Everything okay?"

Her pillowy mauve lips formed a concerned O that made Green's mind race with indecent thoughts. "Yes, officers, everything's fine. I live alone, and I certainly wasn't screaming."

Bannockburn nodded and swallowed audibly. "Glad to hear it."

"Great. Good night. Be safe." And then she went to close the door.

Bannockburn slipped the toe of his boot in the jamb just in time for the door to bounce back. Calliope's eyes dropped to the obstruction immediately before returning to the sergeant's face.

"I hope you understand," he continued, not looking at her directly but rather gazing over her shoulder into the home, "that we need to just take a quick look around to verify."

"That's not necessary," she said. "I just told you that I live alone."

Green wanted to step in, to defend this woman's right to privacy. Maybe he'd write her an apology poem to smooth things out after Bannockburn's horribly rude behavior. Or he could take up the lute and write her a song...

He shut his eyes, and the moment she was out of his vision, his mind began to clear.

No, you will not become a minstrel. You're a cop. And you're here for a reason.

"I know you said that," Bannockburn continued. "And I'm inclined to believe you. But when you've seen as much stuff as I have in my years on the job, you know to ask just a few more questions always. Especially for a call like this. I just want to make absolutely sure you're safe."

She kept her emerald eyes on him for a moment longer, then said, "Okay, come on in." She stepped to the side and let them pass, and Green did his best not to gawk at her as he did.

They entered the large sitting room he'd previously glimpsed through the side window. Maybe a room like this was called a parlor. He didn't really know what a parlor was, but it seemed like it would be a lot like this. He saw the wing-back chair from before and the chandelier hanging above. But he lacked the vocabulary for almost everything else in the space. One of the pieces of furniture was probably a "credenza," but he didn't know which. Was it the one with the minibar on top or the glass case that displayed hand-painted plates and pitchers?

Calliope led them in, gesturing with a broad sweep of her arm. "Make yourselves at home. I think you'll find nothing appears to be out of place. I *was* listening to some music and dancing, up until about a half-hour ago. Perhaps that's what the neighbor heard and mistook for screaming."

"Possibly," Bannockburn replied, scanning. His eyes locked on to in the display case, and he sauntered over. "Say, that looks Grecian."

She followed him over, practically gliding. The long linen pants she wore flowed around her ankles like waves crashing suicidally upon a rocky shore. "It is. Family heirloom."

"I'm a bit of a nerd about this myself," Bannockburn said. "These brush strokes hint that it was made during the Minoan period. Wait, this isn't *satyr*-made, is it?"

Green desperately wanted to join them, maybe get another delicious sniff of Calliope. But then he remembered that this was part of the plan. Distraction. The display case was against the front wall of the house. Bannockburn was intentionally drawing her attention away from the rest of her home.

Green strolled around as if taking in the sights. He slowed by the doorway to the dining room. The pendant lights that ran the length of the table were all off, but the light in the space connecting to the far side of the dining room was on. He caught a glimpse of a modern dishwasher and marble countertops in the bright kitchen.

It was through a kitchen window that Kim had seen this woman dancing before. His mind inched toward something important, but before it could get there, a shadow passed across the lighted doorway. A lithe figure.

He recognized the movement instinctually. Brooks.

Green snuck a glance over his shoulder. How the fuck Bannockburn knew this much about Grecian collectibles, he had no idea, but it worked to keep the muse's attention away from the intruders.

It looked like Valance had successfully picked the lock, just as she'd insisted she could. He wasn't surprised. A lock wasn't that hard to pick, and security systems could be disabled. If the expertise for that sort of project existed between any two people, it was Valance and B-Rat.

Had Brooks been the first inside? Or was she the last? They would be spreading out now, searching for the children hidden away.

Meanwhile, his only job now was to help keep Calliope's attention for as long as he could, buy the others the time they'd need.

"Is that a Greek accent you have?" Bannockburn asked. Green turned to find the two of them seated on the armchairs beneath the glistening chandelier. It almost seemed as if Calliope was enjoying the attention, soaking it up. Or maybe she genuinely found Bruce Bannockburn, with his rugged masculine charm, attractive.

Jealousy surged inside Green, and he tamped it down. Then a visual of Bannockburn and the muse naked and entangled formed before Green's eyes, and something else surged inside him, a feeling he liked even less than the jealousy. He bit his lip hard to bring himself back to reality.

"It's from a lot of places," she said. "Originally, Greece, but I've been all over the world. And I'm afraid I pick up a little bit of wherever I go in my speech."

"How long have you been in Kilhaven?"

"Not long. I don't keep close track, but only a matter of years. Perhaps five or six?"

"And how are you liking—"

A crash from the back of the house cut off the sergeant's next question. The clatter was followed immediately by a hushed "Shit" that carried all the way through the adjoining dining room.

Calliope jumped to her feet and was rushing toward the source in a heartbeat.

"Wait!" Bannockburn ordered as he chased after her. "Let me go first."

Green had a head start of a few feet, already being so close to the doorway. He sprinted toward the kitchen, hoping he could do something, anything, to get the others out of sight before the muse discovered them.

He found B-Rat standing wide-eyed in the kitchen, caught in the headlights of Green's sudden appearance, but Brooks and Valance were nowhere to be seen. That was something. He could work with this.

"Freeze! Police!"

B-Rat's eyes were still wide as his hands shot up in the air. "What are you doin—"

Shots rang out from behind Green, and bullets tore through the possum-shifter's gut. The force of Bannockburn's .45 knocked B-Rat back into the cabinets by the sink. "You bastard," he said, groaning and clutching his middle.

Green didn't rush forward yet, worried the sergeant might need another clear shot. Instead, he gaped.

Go down. Go down and stay down, you idiot!

Bannockburn had done the only thing they *could* do, and now it was all up to B-Rat to pick up on the new strategy.

Play dead, you motherfucker. Play dead, and we might all live!

But the possum-shifter refused to do it, and Green doubted that any of them would live long enough to understand why.

"Hands up!" Bannockburn commanded. "On the ground *now!*"

Green had his gun out too, though he wasn't sure whom he would end up using it on first. "Hands up! On the ground!" he echoed.

B-Rat looked back and forth between them, clutching his middle and refusing to comply.

"Hands up!" Bannockburn yelled again.

B-Rat shook his head almost imperceptibly.

Lie down! Play dead, motherfucker!

Bannockburn moved in closer, gun drawn. "Hands! Up!"

And then, still on his feet, eyes wide, B-Rat complied. He let go of his middle, and Green realized in a sickening instant that it wasn't B-Rat who had made a terrible miscalculation.

The bullet holes in his middle had already healed. Blood stained his shirt around them, but the wounds had clearly closed, and no more blood gushed forth.

Oh. Fuck.

Calliope was on B-Rat in an instant, gripping his throat as she lifted him from the ground. "What are you doing in my house?" Her voice lacked the sweet richness of before, giving Green the distinct impression of a sacrificial blade veiled behind a satin cloth.

Bannockburn and Green shared a panicked look. The sergeant seemed as out of ideas as he was.

B-Rat couldn't answer the muse's question, as choked as he was. But his eyes darted past her to something on the wall opposite. It was only a split second, but it was enough for Green to pay attention. He followed B-Rat's gaze to discover an easily overlooked doorway. The door was wide open, but no light came from it. It might have been a pantry, but Green's instincts told him it was not. There was much more beyond that door.

"I said"—Calliope's voice rattled his bones now, and shimmery waves of cerulean energy began dancing around her—"what are you doing in my house, immortal?"

Green aimed his weapon at the woman and was relieved when Bannockburn pushed his arm away, redirecting the barrel of his gun. Shooting *this* immortal was a last-ditch move. It would start the clock ticking, and they couldn't do that yet. Not when they had no idea where Brooks and Valance were; not when they still had no solid leads on the missing teens.

"Let him go." Bannockburn rushed forward, but what he had in mind, Green didn't get a chance to find out.

Still holding B-Rat a few inches above the ground with one hand, Calliope lashed out. Her blow knocked Bannockburn off his feet, into the air, and face-first into the refrigerator. There was an involuntary grunt before the sergeant crumpled to the ground and didn't get up.

Green whirled back toward the immediate danger. B-

Rat's eyes darted to the open door again. This was his only lead, then. Green nodded. He understood.

A shadow eclipsed the shifter's face, a resigned stoicism. Green recognized it in an instant. It was what Brooks had told him about hardly fifteen minutes earlier.

B-Rat, an immortal in every way but one, had just decided how he was going to die.

His hands, which gripped Calliope's wrist, turned to possum claws, and he dug in. The sudden pain was enough to make her flinch, and he took that opportunity to kick her between the legs. She dropped him. He grabbed the pocket pistol and fired two rounds into her face. It was enough. "They're in the basement!" he hollered.

Calliope's change was immediate. One moment, she was a sexy Grecian bathed in a shimmery blue glow, the next, she was a jagged jet-black nightmare.

Green had no time to wrap his mind around the horror of what she'd become, all daggers and dread, her hair a cat-o'-nine-tails of fury. She shrieked, and it launched a shock wave that nearly swept his feet out from under him. He only managed to catch his balance as one of the terrifying blades that might have been her fingers slashed with frightening speed, catching B-Rat across the throat and spraying warm blood from his jugular in a deathly arc across the kitchen cabinets. Another merciless swipe and his entrails poured from him.

And that was when the firestorm began. He didn't know exactly when Valance and Brooks arrived in the kitchen, but he was glad they had. They blasted the thing that had been Calliope with silver rounds. The short shotgun barrels sent a spray of pellets into her each time. Fire. Knock her back. Wait till she was back up. Fire again.

The metal tearing through her body was enough to keep her at bay, for now.

But the countdown had begun. A minute and a half to go.

Green sprinted for the dark door. He clicked on his flashlight and confirmed his suspicions. It wasn't a pantry. It opened to a steep staircase down, down, down.

He hoped to God, or Dracula, or whoever the fuck might listen, that this wouldn't become his tomb, and then he clambered down the steps.

B-Rat had been their secret weapon, and he was gone. His entrails wouldn't spring back inside him this time. Their shot of each getting out of this alive was next to none now. The objective had narrowed to one thing: save the kids.

His knee hyperextended as he found the bottom of the stairs without expecting it, and he gritted his teeth against the sharp pain.

The smell hit him first, and he was certain he wouldn't like what he found down here. He raised the beam of his flashlight.

The place was a goddamn mess. Except that didn't begin to cover it.

What *did* cover it was the ruddy brown of dried blood, rotting flesh and fur and feathers, and a scattering of splintered bones.

The continued blast of gunfire echoed down the stairs. A minute fifteen? Then he saw it. On the far side of the gore, beyond the giant black cauldron in the middle of the basement, was a sliver of hope amid this colossal clusterfuck.

He dragged the beam of his flashlight across the steel bars of the makeshift jail cell, and no fewer than a dozen scared faces blinked back at him. He held a finger to his lips, though the odds were low that any speaking or even screaming would be heard above the ruckus taking place upstairs.

The cell had a giant built-in lock, of course, and as Green looked around for the keys, hoping to fucking everything holy that they were not currently on Calliope's person, one of the kids spoke up. "It's already unlocked." The one who'd spoken, a stout boy with a round face, stepped forward from the back of the enclosure and pushed open the door. "The smelly guy picked the lock and told us to stay put."

B-Rat. He'd made it all the way down and back before drawing Calliope's attention. Green rushed forward, pulled the door open further, and gestured for the teens to hurry up already and file out.

Only a few of them did. The majority remained in the illusion of protection afforded to them by the bars. "It's fine," Green assured them. "I'm here to rescue you."

A minute five?

"We don't want to be rescued." A taller boy stepped forward, and Green, who might have thought he was past the point of being shocked by anything else tonight, felt his mouth fall open.

"Jesse?"

"I don't know what Kim told you," said the shifter boy, "but we don't need to be rescued. We *want* to be here."

Green definitely didn't have time for this shit. The *thing* that had been Calliope was upstairs battling two totally outmatched officers with no chance of stopping her. It wasn't a matter of *if* that nightmare killed his friends, it was a matter of when.

And this little brainwashed twerp was ruining everything.

"Yes, you do want to be rescued. You'll end up in that cauldron if you don't come with me."

Jesse folded his arms across his chest. "That's the whole plan!"

"Your plan is shit, kid. We're going with my plan." Green motioned again. "Come on."

"No. We're not coming," Jesse insisted. "It's our responsibility to feed the Bride."

"*Bride?* For fuck's sake!" A frantic shriek from above sounded an awful lot like Brooks. "You don't have to die."

"If we don't, someone else will."

"If you don't *move your ass,*" Green said through gritted teeth, "we're *all* gonna die."

But still, Jesse Montegue refused.

If the department had ever covered a scenario like this in training, Green couldn't remember it.

Fuck it, then.

He pulled his gun on the boy. "Get out. We're going."

It had the intended effect.

From his experience, most people who planned on dying had a very specific scenario for it in their mind. It was like Brooks had said. People didn't want to die any old way. They wanted to die in a particular way, and if you offered up an alternative, they didn't tend to be too keen.

One by one, the children filed out of the cell. "If you're so hellbent on letting her eat you," he said as they shuffled past, "don't worry, it might still happen. Let's just get upstairs first."

He put a few of the taller and more willing escapees at

the back of the group to bring up the rear and then led the way up the stairs, gun drawn.

Forty-five seconds? Forty?

The confrontation had relocated in the moments he'd spent underground, though he could still hear the steady rhythm of gunfire somewhere downstairs as he crept into the sliver of light streaming in from the kitchen. He turned to the children, checked with his flashlight to make sure he had roughly the right number, and then stepped out into the open.

The plan for this part hadn't changed: lead any captives out the back door, then run like greased fucking lightning.

B-Rat's body was splayed out on the tile by the back door he'd snuck in through. He was a limb and a half lighter than before. Each of the kids would have to step over the corpse on their way out, but it seemed too late to worry about massive mental trauma now.

Green motioned for the first in line behind him and said, "Keep low. Run. Don't look back."

Something, or many things, about the scene that met them in the kitchen seemed to break through the spell that had taken hold. Even Jesse gaped in horror at B-Rat's mangled corpse. There was no resistance once the first teen took off toward the door. The rest followed in short order, stepping over the bloody, mangled corpse and sprinting off into the night air.

Green realized with a slow and incomplete recognition that Bannockburn was no longer on the ground by the fridge.

As the last captive disappeared, the gunfire came to an abrupt halt.

He tucked his flashlight away and freed up that hand for his backup rounds.

The deafening silence was shattered by the heavy, desperate drumming of boots as Brooks, Valance, and Bannockburn sprinted into the kitchen from the direction of the sitting room.

"You get the kids?" Valance shouted.

Green nodded.

"Then *get the fuck out!*"

"You go. I still got rounds. I'll cover till you're away."

That stopped her in her tracks. "You absolute idiot." But he didn't miss the suicidal grin that followed. She turned to the others. "Go after the children. Make sure they're okay."

Neither argued, just turned and left. Not as cowards, but as sane people doing their duty. Green wished he could live long enough to be like them.

He tossed a full magazine to Valance, who caught it just as Calliope charged through the dining room toward the kitchen.

The others had done a stellar job of blasting her ten ways from Sunday, but the damage only made her look even more terrifying, as bits of her mangled flesh dangled and fanned out, flapping as she charged straight for him, the angry ebony of her talons whipping around with each frenzied step.

He fired the first shot from his .45, and it hit her right in the face. What might have been considered her cheek exploded in a spray of crimson, and she stumbled back but kept her feet. He was buying time now, that was all. The final moments of his life were upon him, and he would fight for each one now, just for the hell of it. He fired again, hitting her shoulder and causing her to spin off course.

The creature flailed, and as she did, two of her taloned fingers disappeared. Valance whooped victoriously and fired again, hitting the nightmare's meaty middle and sending her another half-step back.

Valance moved to stand shoulder to shoulder with him. Their eyes met, and his racing heart skipped a beat.

She grinned. "Till death do us part, Mr. Heather Valance." Then she proceeded to unload the rest of her rounds into their target.

There was no point dying with a bullet left, so Green followed her lead, soaking up a grim satisfaction at tearing Calliope apart. Tiny crimson explosions announced each fresh hit, and he didn't miss. Not once.

He was so awash in the brutal ecstasy of it that it hardly registered when the ground began to shake below his feet.

Then the click of doom. He was out of ammunition. The ground shook more furiously.

"Green, get out of the way!"

Get out of the way? And go *where*? They were supposed to die here. They'd made their decision.

He was lunged at from two directions in the same instant. Valance got him first, knocking him to the ground beneath her so that Calliope's taloned death blow missed them both by inches.

He scrambled to get out from under Valance and put eyes on the muse once again.

But when he did, the thing wasn't looking at him at all. Something else had drawn her attention.

A trumpeting sound from just outside the back door announced the source of the growing earthquake. Before he could tear his eyes from the monster, the exterior wall exploded.

He grabbed Valance and rolled them both clear of the path of the charging elephant bull. Its entrance was preceded by a splintered plywood, drywall, bricks, and exposed wires that ignited a shower of sparks that the elephant didn't seem to notice. The great beast made for Calliope, lowered its head, and lanced her with its giant ivory tusk.

A sound like a car accident in reverse escaped the chasm of her mouth. First, the *pop-crash*, then the squealing.

She was hoisted off the ground like a rag doll, and her head smashed into what ceiling remained after the live wrecking ball had charged through a split second before.

As the last of the sparks and debris rained down, Green remembered to breathe. The elephant turned to look at him, the limp immortal terror still skewered on his tusk. Calliope didn't move. She was dead.

A busted pipe gushed its contents over the elephant's head and shoulders, and the sound of rushing water was all Green could make out now. It was the only movement in the entire place.

Then he felt Valance squirm underneath him, and he scrambled to his feet.

The elephant raised and lowered its head again, causing the dead passenger to flop about.

Green took the hint.

Officer Ivory Namises couldn't shift back while he still had this heinous bitch attached.

Green helped Valance to her feet as the elephant lay down and lowered his head. Green tried to find a less disgusting part of Calliope's flayed body to grab hold of, but unable to do so, he opted for her shoulders and pulled. She was lodged on there pretty good. Once Valance joined in, though, they managed, and the dead immortal crumpled into a messy heap in the rubble of the kitchen floor.

Valance unceremoniously ripped down one of the linen curtains from the dining room and held it out for Namises as he shifted to his human form.

He was no less drenched in blood or wet from the leaking pipe after changing, and he accepted the covering from Valance with a tired nod.

Nobody spoke right away.

Once Namises had dried off and wrapped the curtain around himself, he surveyed the total damage. "Not sure how we're going to explain this one."

Green was fresh out of ideas, too. He turned to Valance. "Any ideas, Mrs. Norman Green?"

Her gaze was full of fire and carnage. "Oh, I got a few."

CHAPTER THIRTY-NINE

The detective's exam felt like a footnote. Months and months of studying for it, hours and hours of frowning over the material while Kim patiently quizzed him, and it came down to this, four hours of pencil on paper.

It was only through the miracle of celebrity and public heroism that Green was allowed to take the test while on administrative leave following the rescue. He knew that. He also knew, now more than ever, just how important it was for him to get into the Organized Crime Division, where he could make an impact on these sorts of cases before some beat cop had to go in, guns blazing, just to keep children out of harm's way.

But it felt hollow and unimportant nonetheless, and his mind struggled to focus on the words on the page.

An hour in, he thought he got a whiff of the same stench of rotting flesh bits and dried blood that he'd experienced in the basement of the manor. When he only had thirty minutes to go, the image of B-Rat's entrails pouring out of him dropped by and lost Green a full two minutes as he stared absently out the window of the classroom.

He handed in his booklet and left the testing room in a mental haze. Somewhere in his brain, he was sure he knew the legal consequences for dairy farmers using shifter milk that resulted from the *Moulton vs. the City of Emerald Lea* verdict and what the exact charge would be for summoning la Llorona in a school zone, but he hadn't been able to conjure any of that learning to the forefront in the last four hours.

His mind was bisected, with half in the past, half in the future. He didn't remember the drive home. When he opened his front door, he found Kim snuggled with a bunched-up throw blanket on the couch, watching TV, her eyes visibly red and puffy.

She sniffled and looked up at him. "How'd it go?"

He emptied his pockets and tossed the contents into the bowl by the front door. "Fine."

It was a Saturday morning, but she wasn't watching cartoons. She had the news on. It was hard to resist in the days following the horror show.

"We'd better get ready," he said, feeling exhaustion creep in again, not at all identifying with the hero he would be expected to play in an hour.

"They were talking about you again," Kim said.

"Lucky me."

"They said you'd saved more kids in this city than anyone else. They interviewed a woman with your face on her shirt."

He groaned. Was it bad to show up to a memorial drunk? He could go for a beer.

"It wasn't a very good picture," Kim added. "But she did propose to you."

He poured himself a glass of orange juice and brought it over to the couch next to her. "You think I should accept?"

"No," Kim said seriously, "she seemed like kind of a mess."

Green chuckled.

"But maybe you should date *someone*, Nor."

He arched an eyebrow. "Got anyone in mind?"

Someone came to *his* mind. But it wasn't so much for the purpose of dating as for…

"I do. I think you should date Aliyah."

Hearing the name derailed him. But of course. Brooks. That was a much healthier idea. "I wouldn't know what to do with a woman that perfect," he said. Then he patted her knee again. "You'd better get ready."

She tossed the blanket off her and shuffled stiffly to her room. She must have been in the same spot on the couch all day.

He leaned back and let the local news wash over him. The elves had been beside themselves all week, making the Kilhaven Police Department look foolish. Yet again, they said, Officers Green and Valance had been forced to take matters into their own hands. It was always those two names: Green and Valance. Occasionally, a mention of Brooks and Bannockburn, or Namises, who reportedly arrived just after the action ended. Did Brooks and Bannockburn mind being left out of the spotlight? They shouldn't. Especially when one of their crew hadn't been mentioned a single time.

B-Rat. He'd found the children first. He'd picked the lock. Green wouldn't have been able to do a single goddamn thing with those captives if that hadn't happened. The shifter who had been there at the start of Green's career, playing possum on the sidewalk, at the end of a long, immortal road, had used his last few moments to be a hero, a real one. The drunk maniac's watch had ended.

Green sipped his OJ and thought about the last thing Boris Romanov had done before being murdered by that Greek nightmare: *"They're in the basement."*

B-Rat had helped them save fourteen teenagers in all. Green wished the smelly mongrel could have lived to see that, at least, to know he'd done something right. After so many years of living on the streets, leeching off others, and using informant protections to get away with so much crime, the shifter had redeemed himself. He'd decided how he was going to die.

The TV cut to the preliminary scenes of what would be a large outdoor memorial for the children who didn't make it out of the basement that night. Hundreds of names had surfaced already, missing over the span of five years. Many had been verified, but most had not. There wasn't enough time, and no harm seemed to come from adding a bit more grief to the ceremony. Loved ones were asked to bring photos of those they'd lost. There would be an altar for all the images, bright, hopeful faces of children who would never grow up.

It would be a goddamned mess. But sometimes, Green thought, finishing off his orange juice, it was best to let things fall apart completely before you tried to piece them back together.

CHAPTER FORTY

Green knew Jesse Montegue wouldn't be at the memorial, but Kim searched for him anyway as they arrived in Kilhaven Square ahead of the public service. She never said that was what she was doing, but he knew.

He hadn't told her that it was Jesse who had put up a fight, tried to defend his right to be eaten by "the Bride." He still wasn't sure what that title even meant, but it had Draculan nonsense written all over it.

Bob and Janice Montegue were in custody now, though, and where Jesse and his sisters, already orphaned once, had landed, Green didn't know. They were yet another casualty of this evil.

Kim spotted Aliyah Brooks in the crowd and hurried over, likely glad to see a familiar face among all the mourners.

Brooks pulled Kim into a tight hug, and the two of them stayed there for a while as Green gave them a bit of space.

"Hey," came a voice from beside him. Green almost fell over when he saw Heather Valance in a silk blouse. She had the jet fabric tucked into expensive charcoal slacks, and her mocha hair fell in soft waves down around her shoulders. There were flecks of gray in it that he'd never noticed, and when he saw his slack-jawed shock reflected back to him in the lenses of her sunglasses, he snapped his lolling mouth shut.

"Anyone recognize you yet?" she asked.

"We just got here. But yeah, pretty much immediately."

She nodded. "Don't worry, you have a forgettable face. This won't disqualify you from Vice."

"Pretty sure my test score will do that all on its own," he grumbled.

"Nah, those are just for show. OC pulls whoever they want, scores be damned." She turned toward the thick of the growing crowd. At the center was a small dais with a pulpit and microphone.

"Jesus," he said. "Please tell me we're not about to get served denial of responsibility from the Draculan Church today."

"I'm sure we are. This was an isolated incident, after all. That's the case they'll make, at least."

He thought again of "the Bride." An easy enough religious role to fill with whatever evil beast needed a sacrifice. The church probably had brides up in Pan City, too.

"I brought some pictures with me," she said. "Thought you might want to help me add them to the wall."

He nodded, and then she did a strange thing. She slipped an arm around his waist. And he did a strange thing, too. He put his arm around her shoulders.

As the two of them made their way to the center of the mourners, he blocked out the sounds of cameras flashing around them. Valance pulled out the photographs from her pocket and handed him one. The face of Anna Pfaff stared up at him from the glossy image. They'd had no concept of what they were dealing with back when the girl had gone missing, but they did now, and she deserved to be here, counted among the victims. She was among the first casualties of the muse, stolen for experimentation, never recovered.

He stuck her photo on the board next to the one Valance had just placed of Caitlin Holloway.

"Glad I wasn't the only one thinking along these lines," came a man's voice from Green's other side.

Detective Jason Felps stepped forward and pinned a photo of Melvin Brown beside Anna's. He kept his voice low as he leaned forward and said, "I might've been late to the party, but I see it all now. You saw it first, though. I won't forget that." He clapped Green on the back and then disappeared into the crowd.

Valance wasn't done yet. She continued to pin more and more photos to the board, and those closest in the crowd were starting to take notice. She paid them no mind, though, and one by one, the children who'd been lost to the wolfenvamp experiments began to populate the mosaic of loss. It was the first time Green knew of someone publicly tying the two atrocities together.

He made his choice in an instant and held out his hand. Valance slipped him a few of the remaining stack. Together, they paid tribute to the full breadth of this evil, laying bare the scope of the horrors they'd been fighting alongside each other for over four years.

As photo after photo was added, Green began to understand: she'd known the whole time. She'd seen the full picture from the start. Somehow, she'd known, and she hadn't stopped until it was done. But now it was.

Wasn't it?

When all the photos had been added, Valance stepped back to take it in. Green suspected that her sunglasses perhaps served the additional purpose of helping her remain incognito. Because she'd given that up the second they'd started adding the photographs.

She slipped her hands into the pockets of her slacks, and he did the only thing he knew how to do: he moved close and stood beside her.

"Officer Valance," came an unfamiliar voice from the crowd. "Can you explain the photographs you just added to the memorial?"

She turned slowly toward the eagerly awaiting elfin reporter. "I think it's pretty self-explanatory if you have half a brain. Oh, also, fuck you for being here. Let these people grieve in peace, you fucking scavenger."

Green pursued her as she took off into the thick of the crowd. "Hell of a sound bite," he said when he could lean close enough for her to hear.

"I hope they choke on it. How 'bout a drink?"

"You're not staying for the service?"

"I'd say we've done our part."

"Kim wants to stay."

"Have Aliyah bring her later, then. You and I don't owe anyone here a goddamn thing more."

Green had to admit, for the thousandth time, that Heather Valance had a point.

CHAPTER FORTY-ONE

As Green and Valance stepped into the cool air of Roman's Ramen and the rich, salty smells hit his nose, an unfamiliar sound greeted their arrival: a genuine welcome.

"Sit anywhere you like." Roman waved to them from across the restaurant. "Food and drinks on me."

The officers shared a quick look, and Valance almost cracked a smile.

They grabbed a round booth in the corner, which not only gave them plenty of space for when the rest arrived but also granted them a bit of privacy in the meantime. And once they had two cold beers in front of them, they clinked their pints in a silent toast. Green drank half of his down before setting the glass on the table again.

"I could tell from the start, you know," she said.

He arched his eyebrows at her. "Tell what?"

"That you were the one I needed for this shit."

"Wow, Valance, I've never felt so manipulated and flattered at the same time."

"I'll be honest, when Montoya said I'd been assigned a

human to train, I thought that was the end of my career with KPD. I thought you'd get yourself eaten in the first week for sure. Or you'd snap. Something obnoxious like that. But I don't think this would have worked if you were anything other than a human. People underestimate you."

"You did."

"I did. I don't anymore." She tilted her head slightly to the side, and the fluorescent lights reflecting off the sunglasses on her head created an astigmatic halo. "You think this is over? The kids going missing and all that?"

"Are you actually asking me, or is this another test?"

"I'm asking you. Because I don't know, and you're the only other person whose judgment I trust on this."

He tried to disguise his shock with another sip of his beer. "I think *this one* is over. But I imagine there are others."

She nodded. "Yeah, no happily ever after for us, Green. Not so long as we work this job."

He scoffed.

"What?"

"I don't believe for one second that you only do this because it's your job, like you'd give up and forget about it if you got fired."

Valance feigned offense. "Fired? Why would anyone fire me? I'm a hero, you know."

"Do you feel like a hero?"

She considered it silently, then said, "Well, I can't sleep due to chronic nightmares, I feel lonely and furious all the time, and people are buying me drinks." She held up her near-empty glass. "So, yeah, that checks all the boxes for feeling like a hero." She leaned her elbows on the table and flashed him that kamikaze grin.

Green leaned forward as well, cradling his pint glass

between his palms. "Is *that* what it is? Here I just thought I had PTSD and depression, and now you're telling me it's just a bad case of heroism?"

She nodded. "Yeah, Norman. I can see it in your eyes. You got it bad."

"Any hope of recovery?"

"No. But there are a variety of experimental treatments."

Her ankle brushed against his calf underneath the table. He swallowed but steadied himself. He knew better than to blink when she was looking at him like that. No signs of weakness. "Any side effects of the treatments?"

"It's nothing *but* side effects. The temporary relief makes it all worth it, though."

"Risk of death?"

"Only if you're lucky."

Someone cleared their throat nearby, and Green jerked around to find Ivory Namises standing next to the booth, holding a pint of dark amber. "I hope I'm not intruding."

Green blinked and opened his mouth to reply, but Valance beat him to it. "You're absolutely intruding, but you seem to have a knack for doing it at just the right time to save Green's ass from certain death, so I won't hold it against you." She scooted over to make room. "Slide on in. I'd like to have a word with you anyhow."

"Sounds like an interrogation." But he took a seat anyway.

Roman brought over two more drinks, drawing Green's attention to the fact that he'd only had one so far and couldn't blame whatever storm had been brewing moments before on the alcohol. Only once the owner had left did Valance dive in.

"How'd you know?" she said.

"How'd I know what?" said Namises, then took a dainty first sip off the top of his brew.

"How'd you know to show up when you did?"

"You live long enough, and you develop a pretty refined gut instinct. I thought I could be of service. He'd been asking around about immortals, and I figured he was after one. When I heard the heavy fire coming from the house as I pulled up, I knew you fools were toast. You can't shoot an immortal to death, you know."

"That wasn't the plan," Green added lamely. "We had one with us."

Namises appeared unimpressed. "Yeah? That work out for ya?"

"How'd you find out you couldn't die?" Valance asked.

Namises narrowed his eyes at her. "I think if we learned anything in that crazy woman's house, it's that I *can* die."

"You know what I mean."

He shrugged. "I learned the hard way. As far as I knew, I was just your average elephant-shifter. Came from a whole tribe of shifters. Thought I'd live about a hundred and twenty years and then die like the rest of them. Just didn't turn out that way. Kept getting myself stabbed. Even got crucified once. Never died. Sort of a bummer, really."

"So, you're not a lesser god?" Green asked.

Namises chuckled. "Who said I wasn't?"

Roman stopped by with two baskets full of hot, greasy wontons that none of them had ordered. Valance thanked him with a nod, waited until he was out of earshot, then asked, "The department knows about you now?"

"Eh," said Namises, "who knows? On the one hand, the fact that I was able to kill an immortal is sort of an elephant in the room, pun intended. But on the other hand, you know how well departments can ignore that elephant."

"Boy, do I." Valance helped herself to a wonton. "I talked to Detective Felps yesterday. He says he's reviewed the call history and listened to the audio leading up to the confrontation, and it checks out why the five of us all ended up at that scene."

Namises scoffed. "No, it doesn't."

"Well, no shit. I mean, hell, there's footage of B-Rat rallying with us, for fuck's sake. And why two officers, a Robbery detective, and a supervisor would respond to a single disturbance call is inexplicable. But Felps says he has a way of explaining it."

"Any clue what that is?"

"All I could get out of him was that the chief plans on taking full credit for the success."

Namises nodded. "Okay, I've seen this episode before."

"When you talked to IA that night," Green said, "you know, after the hospital and blood tests, did they tell you why you were being put on admin leave?"

"Aside from being on scene covered in blood and wrapped in nothing but a drapery?" Namises said.

"Right. But you didn't fire a weapon. Brooks, Valance, Bannockburn, and I all fired ours."

"I think it was the tusk," Namises replied, and Valance smirked. "Yeah, pretty sure it was that I'd run a woman through with my *tusk*." He sighed. "Didn't take investigators long to realize she should have been long dead from the bullet holes before I had to drop by and kabob her. They asked a hell of a lot of questions. I told them as little as I could, but I think they realized that immortals might not be as immortal as we let on."

"You think it'll get out?" Valance asked. "You know I'm not usually one for a cover-up, but this one might actually be for the best."

"Sheesh." Namises sipped his beer. "I hope they have the sense and skill to keep this one quiet. You know what would happen if the general population found out about my kind? Chaos. Panic. Probably even worse treatment of the homeless, once it gets out that we usually end up in the gutter. And if they found out there was a way to *kill* immortals?" He shook his head. "The magical tomfoolery would kill us all in a matter of days. Hags and evil spirits trying to control immortals to do their bidding; necromancers getting in on the action once any immortal dies. And the suspicion among neighbors when anyone could be an immortal—Jesus! I've seen civil wars started from less."

"We can worry about that when it comes," Valance said. "Looks like the rest of the party is here."

Brooks and Bannockburn had just entered the restaurant. Bruce received a friendly handshake from Roman before making for the corner booth.

"Dropped Kim off at your place," Brooks said, motioning for Green to make room for her on the cushioned seat. "Figured it was best for her emotional development if she didn't see us get absolutely smashed at a ramen joint in a strip mall."

"She doing okay?" Green asked.

"Are any of us? She'll survive until you catch a ride home, if that's what you're asking. She could probably use a good cry anyway. You missed a real tear-jerker of a memorial."

Valance said, "Doesn't look like it got to you."

Brooks shrugged. "Crying's not really my thing. I have other ways to cope. Speaking of which, who's buying?"

No sooner had she said it than Roman hurried over carrying two fresh pint glasses in one hand and two full pitchers in the other. And once they were all set, Valance cleared her throat and raised her glass. The others around the table fell silent. "Six of us went in, and only five made it out. Here's to one of the smelliest pieces of shit I've ever met. To B-Rat. To Boris Romanov. May he rest in oblivion."

And as they clinked glasses, Green suspected this marked the end to something he would miss before long.

"Wake up!"

Green did not want to.

"Wake *up*, Nor!"

He cracked open one eye and realized daylight was already creeping in through the blinds of his bedroom. The silhouette of Kim hovered over him.

"What is it?" he mumbled, his lips sticking together from the same slobber that left a large wet spot on his pillow.

"It's results day!"

Results?

Then it hit him. He sat up too quickly, causing edges of his vision to shimmer. "Oh shit. Grab my laptop." He scooted up to lean against the wall at the head of his bed, and Kim returned a second later with the computer, already typing in his password, which she should *not* have had.

He'd address that later.

She jumped onto the bed beside him and watched as he logged into the secure Kilhaven Police portal. A few more clicks, and then slowly, painfully slowly, the posted results began to load from the top of the page down.

There was a brief introduction at the top—all results public, high placement wasn't a guarantee of an offer, so on and so forth.

And then the header appeared. *Name, badge number, score* across the top of the columns.

He wasn't surprised by the first few names. They'd been the brainy ones in his graduating class, though they'd since proven they weren't especially talented at the nitty-gritty of the daily grind. He imagined them getting an offer from White Collar Crimes or IA and snickered to himself before remembering that he didn't even know if he would get any offer at all. At least not until the divisions had picked through all the names above his. That could be a year, two years, or he might be forced to test again, depending on how his score panned out.

He'd counted roughly sixty people testing alongside him that day. How many slots for promotion were there? Ten, tops?

The page continued to load lower and lower without revealing his name, and his stomach sank. His urge to slam the laptop shut so that he didn't have to share his humiliation with his sister was strong, especially once the top ten names were revealed and his wasn't among them. He fought against the urge.

Then he saw it.

"There you are!" Kim yelled, pointing. "Number twelve!" She held up her hand, and he realized she was waiting for a high five. Huh. Okay, then.

Twelfth wasn't *that* bad. Just about the top twenty

percent. As someone who'd graduated in the last quartile of his high school class, this was progress.

"Who do you think is going to recruit you?" she asked excitedly.

He laughed. "It doesn't work like that. It's a whole process. And the fact that I'm still on admin leave means I probably won't be hearing from anyone until I'm officially cleared by IA. That could be another few weeks, at least."

The corners of her mouth drooped like she'd tasted something bitter. "But still, as soon as you're cleared, who do you think will pick you?"

"No idea. Maybe Brooks will put a word in with Robbery."

"Vice? I thought they liked you."

"It's super competitive to get in with them. I don't think they've ever hired a human. We're not much use for operations." He shut the laptop and said, "I need some coffee."

"And waffles?"

"Isn't it Wednesday?" His question was genuine. He had no clue.

"It is, but we need to *celebrate*."

"You have school, Kim."

She groaned and flopped her way off the bed, stomping out of the room.

As he poured himself coffee minutes later, and as Kim wrangled her homework from the night before off the table and into her backpack, his phone rang. He pulled it out of the waistband of his boxers where he'd tucked it.

"This is Norman Green."

"Officer Green? This is Detective Sergeant Cassandra

Strauss. You rode out with one of my units not too long ago. They were impressed..."

By the time Green ended the call, Kim had already stepped outside to catch the bus.

He tossed the phone on the counter and ran after her.

"Kim!"

He caught her just as she made it to the bottom of the stairs, and she looked up at him, her brows pinched together.

"You're not going to school today."

"What? Oh God, Nor, you forgot pants."

He ignored her embarrassment, though the observation was accurate. "You're skipping school today and coming with me. We're getting waffles. All you can eat."

END OF BOOK 4

HEX TRAFFICKING

Two Kilhaven Police officers pulled over a commercial semi-truck traveling north on FM 293 at 1:30pm last Monday after it was seen careening between lanes. Officers suspected the driver, Margery Roan Huffman, human, 49, of distracted driving and pulled her over to issue her a verbal warning. However, during the verbal interaction, officers report that she began acting erratic and agitated, and they asked her to step out of the truck so the cargo could be searched. At first glance the enclose cargo space appeared empty, but upon closer examination, a false bottom was found. In it were 7,000 hex bags, some of which had broken open during transit.

Huffman was arrested and Stubborn Hauntings Unit agents were called to the scene immediately. Huffman claims she was herself under a hex that could only be lifted if she completed the shipment, but she refused to provide further information as to who might have hexed her or why. She faces up to twenty years in prison for hex trafficking and two counts of hexing a law enforcement officer. Both officers suffered severe boils and unwanted erections as a result of the broken hex bags and are still undergoing testing and treatment by licensed witchcraft professionals.

Want wild weekly dispatches from Kilhaven sent straight to your inbox? Get a year's subscription to hilarious highway pursuits and bonkers drugs busts when you subscribe to the Kilhaven Police Blotter.

Sign up:
www.ffs.media/kpb

UP NEXT_

The next phase of Norman Green's career has yet to be written.

Want to know when it's available?

Here are two easy ways to receive a notification:

1. Follow H. Claire Taylor on BookBub

You'll be notified anytime a new book is available to buy.

Go to: www.bookbub.com/authors/hclairetaylor

2. Sign up for Kilhaven Police Blotter

When a crackhead kangaroo-shifter boxes an officer in a supermarket parking lot, you'll be the first to know. Get weekly updates from Kilhaven along with notifications anytime Brock & Claire release cool shit.

Go to: www.ffs.media/kpb

The Jessica Christ series

What readers are saying about Jessica Christ:

"H. Claire Taylor offers gentle yet pungent humor and is a worthy successor to Garrison Keillor, Edward St Aubyn or Mark Twain."

"Sometimes random scenes pop into my head and I'll start hyperventilating from laughing so hard all over again."

"The humor in this series is somehow so dark and light-hearted at the same time. . . . H Claire's writing is amazing—the flow and tone keep you reading and wanting more, like a conversation with a dear and raunchy confidante."

Read the first book:

www.books2read.com/JC1

ABOUT THE AUTHORS_

BROCK BLOODWORTH is a private person. He wishes to remain "off the grid" as much as possible. You will not find him on social media, so don't waste your time. If you wish to reach him, consider contacting H. Claire Taylor instead. She's much friendlier.

H. CLAIRE TAYLOR is the author of the Jessica Christ series and deserves a morsel of credit for co-writing the Kilhaven Police series and putting up with Brock's shit. You can learn more about her and her comedy projects at www.hclairetaylor.com.

Find more by Brock and Claire:
www.ffs.media
contact@ffs.media

facebook.com/authorhclairetaylor
twitter.com/claireorwhatevs
bookbub.com/authors/hclairetaylor
goodreads.com/hclairetaylor
amazon.com/author/hclairetaylor